AWAKENING FIRE

V. A. Sanchez

This book is a work of fiction. All of the characters, organizations, and events portrayed in this novel are either products of the author's imagination or are used fictionally.

Copyright © V. A. Sanchez 2024

Book Cover Art by Ann Bugarin

All rights reserved. No part of this book may be reproduced or used in any manner without the prior written permission of the copyright owner, except for the use of brief quotations in a book review.

To request permissions, contact the author at authorvasanchez@gmail.com

Paperback ISBN: 979-8-9922985-1-2

Hardcover ISBN: 979-8-9922985-2-9

WORLD MAP

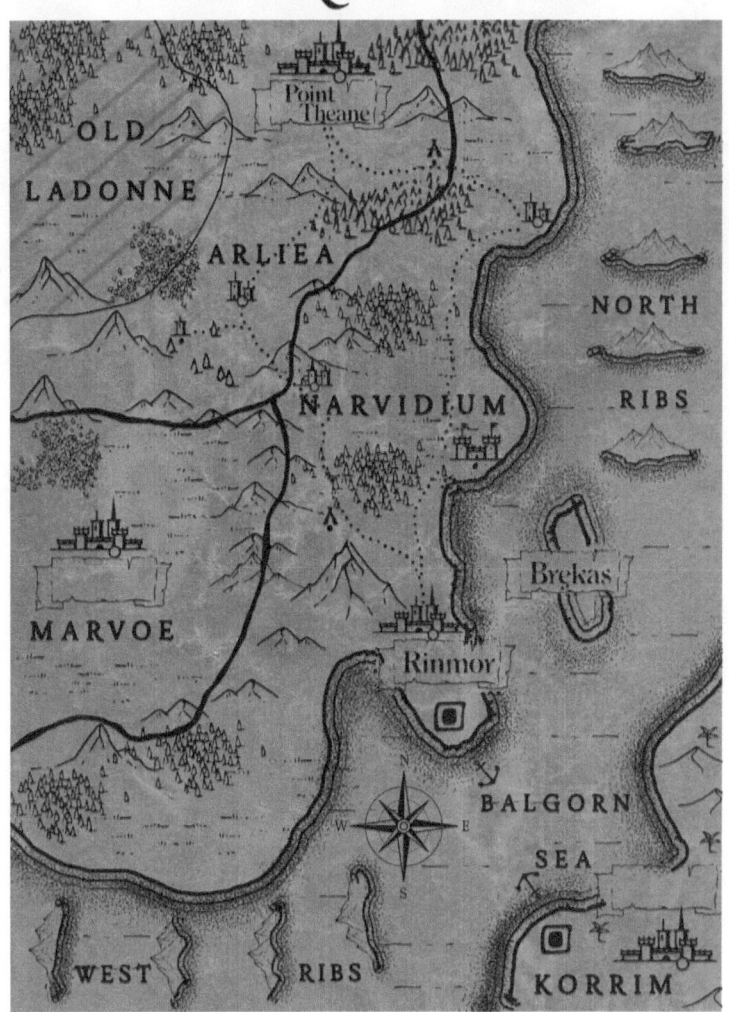

*To every orphan who has ever felt alone
and wanted to feel special to someone.*

Chapter 1
Lylah

"You have three days to find a new place to live." Ms. Gentrow's words cut through me like I'm made of mist, not flesh and bone. She doesn't turn to face me, which stings even more, but I don't let it show. The only way I've learned to survive this place is to pretend I don't care.

"Three days?"

She pivots to study me. "You're nearly eighteen. Certainly old enough to fend for yourself. You'll find a way to survive." The dark circles under her eyes are evident, and there's a stiffness to her shoulders.

Her calloused hands fold a blanket before moving to pick up another from the next cot. Today is laundry day for the second floor of the orphanage. All the bedding gets scrubbed by hand and dried on the lines outside before we put the sheets back on our beds with the fresh ocean scent. At least the musk from so many bodies being crammed into one room is gone for the day.

"I have nowhere else to go." The facade of not caring begins to crack. "You promised me a bed for another six months. You can't do this."

A small sigh escapes her cracked lips before tucking the blankets into a wooden cabinet. "As headmistress, I have a hundred children I'm responsible for. King's guards are bringing in new children every day. I don't care where you go, it just can't be here."

My heart pounds wildly in my chest knowing she won't change her mind. I try to look at anything but her, like the carvings of children's names on the walls of the long room. The lines of the cots with just enough walking space between them. The only shelf of rag dolls the little girls can play with for a bit before sharing with someone else.

Her faded blue wool dress shifts as she turns to leave before glancing back from the doorway.

"Your help with the chores and children will be missed." There's a pause. "I do wish you the best of luck." She vanishes around the corner before my thoughts reach my mouth.

I clench my stomach as the contents threaten to spill onto the dusty rug. Forcing the feeling down, I put back my facade piece by piece. My hand slips into my dress pocket and lingers on the curves of a compass. With each deep breath, the familiar surface soothes my racing heart. The rusting and broken compass is the only link I have to my birth parents. From what I was told, it was tucked in the basket along with me and left on the orphanage doorsteps.

I squeeze it. I can find a new place to live and work in three days. There must be a sewing shop or a laundry wash place that's hiring. Perhaps a boarding house has a room I can rent for a reasonable price. Endless lists of chores kept me from exploring much of the outside world. Despite having always dreamed of leaving this place, it's scarier than I ever imagined.

The shadowy walls in the golden afternoon light reflect my childhood memories. Spotting the board where a mean-spirited boy bumped me so hard my head dented the aged wood. My fists clench with each step as I descend the same stairs where a girl once stuck her foot out and I fell, tumbling to the bottom. Those weren't the only instances but I've learned to keep my head down and wait for each day to end with minimal injury.

Hope never grew beyond a single ember. Every day gave me a reason to doubt that life would ever get better. It shouldn't surprise me that they are kicking me out. The only thing I'll miss about this horrible place is the consistent meals and a falling-apart bed to call my own.

The sun beams down on me as soon as I step outside, and the air around me feels different. A new purpose fills my lungs. Three of the children run past me and one screams at the top of their lungs. Sounds like a normal day, but I don't let anything distract me.

I smooth out my skirt and adjust my scratchy collar. Everything has to be perfect. My fingers graze over the rip on the side, but perhaps if I put my hair down, it won't be visible. I do just that and let my wavy blonde locks bounce below my shoulders.

A bell rings in the distance and my feet carry me to where my heart wants to go. I have no plan, and no place to start looking, but right now I need a view of the ocean. It's the only anchor keeping me grounded when everything is falling apart. I need to see it, smell it, feel it wash away the panic in my chest like the receding tides.

The familiar smells of seaweed, saltwater, and gutted fish get stronger as the docks appear. Gusts of frigid wind pull at my hair with each wave that hits the harbor barrier. One of the merchant vessels in the harbor has vast cloth sails inflating with the wind and an anchor splashes into the blue ocean water. Sailors scurry around the deck, pulling ropes and tying them to the sides.

The city of Rinmor has the only port in our kingdom of Narvidium; on the whole continent actually. Our school teachers talked about how it boosts our kingdom's economy, but seeing the sailors' malnourished bodies makes me wonder who is truly profiting.

Along the dock, warehouses line the road, storing most of the supplies that come from Korrim, the only kingdom not on this continent. Fishermen haul caught fish out of their boats in crates.

Three scruffy sailors glance up at me. I clear my throat. "Hello, do you know of any available work around town?" The whistling wind engulfs my voice so it sounds like a whisper.

"Girl, ya gotta speak up. These old ears can't hear much."

I move forward. "Do you know of any available work?"

His bushy eyebrows scrunch as he looks behind me at the various buildings. "A lotta folks struggling right now. If ya're interested, I've got a fish-smoking shop on Liam Street and could use the help."

My nose wrinkles briefly before I mask it with a quick smile. "How much are you offering to pay?"

The man's forehead creases. "I suppose four dekari a week."

It doesn't sound like a lot, but perhaps that's a liveable wage. I should probably find out the cost of renting a room before I accept anything.

"Thank you for the offer," I say as I turn to leave. Smelling like fish and smoke every day also sounds like the worst kind of torture, but I may be desperate enough in three days. Mentally, I put it at the bottom of the list.

Wandering to the southern square just past the docks, I stop to admire the tremendous oak tree, its stretching limbs providing protection to the entire square. To Narvidium, this tree signifies that our ancestors settled on this peninsula, a claim to our future.

Five statues surround the trunk as my eyes roam over the moss that clings to the bark. Vines are creeping up the chiseled limestone and I venture close to inspect their faces. Their history is ancient. A pull deep inside draws me to the statue of Movak Torgan, a Fire Mage said to have lived two hundred years ago. The stories of their adventures and heroism are told to us as children. But Movak was from Arliea, an enemy kingdom to the north. His statue is cracked, as if someone tried to hit it with a hammer.

The other three statues I don't know much about, but next to Movak stands the proud statue of Bella, who was the only one of Movak's mages from Narvidium. The overgrown vegetation has been removed and fresh light blue flowers are laid at her feet. The masterfully carved stone depicts her strong jawline and beautiful flowing hair. A bow and arrow are drawn as if staring down her enemy.

The other older kids have snuck out at night many times to come to this tree. They talk about how breathtaking it is when the lamps are lit. The girls giggle at the stolen kisses. I don't have anyone to admire this ancient tree with. Vicious rumors that were started about me when I was little made sure of that. No one wanted to associate with me after I was labeled as possessed by dark spirits. Often I would hear them whispering lies about how I lit curtains on fire and nearly burned alive everyone inside or done other heinous things.

The variety of shops and buildings outlining the square piques my interest. A wooden sign for a laundry shop creaks in the slight breeze as I enter.

"Welcome to Birdie's Wash, how can I help ya?" a gruff voice says before I spot the speaker. A woman appears from between two patched curtains, steam following her into the room. Her disheveled hair is piled high on top of her head and she adjusts her stained apron.

"I'm looking for a job," I say as I fidget with my fingers.

The woman laughs and the wrinkles on her face become more pronounced. "Child, I can barely keep this place open. Barely takin' anything home for myself. If ya willin' to work for no dekari to help an old woman, I'll gladly take it."

I nod curtly and begin to sweat in the humidity. "Thank you for your time, ma'am."

She laughs again. "Ain't nobody call me ma'am before."

Cool air washes over me once I am back outside. Maybe the southern part of the city isn't the best place to look. Folks here are fishers, merchants, and small shop owners who, just like the fisherman said, can't afford extra help.

Heading north, I ask about work in every shop along the way, but all of their answers are the same. A colorful green sign for a bakery catches my eye just off the center square. This square and everything beyond are tailored for the wealthier citizens. Women pass by me in their expensive satin skirts and lace bodices, causing me to tug at my faded sleeves.

Tucking a strand of hair behind my ear, I open the heavy door. A fluffy gray cat jumps down from a nearby chair and strides over. I kneel to pet its soft ears and it rubs against my leg, purring for more.

"Ash, leave the customer alone." The woman's head bobs up from behind a few baskets filled with golden bread.

"What a beautiful cat," I say, standing.

"He definitely thinks so." She looks at me before continuing, "What can I get you? My loaves just came out of the oven so they are nice and hot."

Putting on my brightest smile, I shake my head. "That sounds delicious, but I'm here to ask about work. Are you looking to hire any help?"

Her rosy cheeks grow round as she smiles back. "As a matter of fact, I am. My last girl just gave birth and I don't think she'll be coming back anytime soon." She scans me from head to foot. "Do you bake?"

My hope dies. "Uh... I helped with some of the cooking back home."

"Define 'some'."

I swallow hard. "Well, I helped peel potatoes and chop beef for stews." Her lip twitches. "Among other things, of course. My mother was a stern woman and didn't let us in the kitchen much." I find the lie leaves my mouth as easily as exhaling a breath.

Her finger taps on the wooden countertop. "Unfortunately, I am looking for someone with more baking experience. Making bread is a temperamental thing and I can't afford to lose any batches."

Disappointment ripples through me, but it doesn't sting as much this time. I can tell she's a kind-hearted woman who simply couldn't afford to make mistakes.

I smile softly. "I understand. Thank you for your time."

The door jingles behind me as I leave.

Long shadows cast themselves on the cobbled street as I make my way south again. Tomorrow, I'll start fresh towards the western docks. More people are out than usual, our bodies moving around each other in a dance. I look down when an unexpected pain shoots up my arm as a towering figure slams into me.

"Oww," I groan out and rub my shoulder. "Watch where you're going!"

There's someone in a cloak walking in the opposite direction as a ray of sun catches his auburn hair. The man doesn't turn around or stop, apparently unfazed by what just happened. He disappears into the crowd and my voice dies in my throat.

Sighing, I reach into my pocket for my compass but it's not there. Frantically, I feel around the pocket. I know I put it in there. I quickly search the other. There's no hole and no way it could have fallen out.

It finally dawns on me.

I've been pickpocketed.

Chapter 2
Ellis

My quill scratches rapidly across the page of my leather-bound journal. Orange and red reflections of the early morning dance across my desk as I write. When I moved in, the first thing I bought was this small desk that could fit right up against the window. Now, I enjoy mornings like this and I'm convinced I have the best view of the Rinmor harbor. I inhale the fresh dewy breeze that floods the small room.

Some mornings I sketch the skyline while others I write down my thought, but not today. Today is business first.

Numbers flow as I take note of my current money inventory. I don't have urgent expenses besides the room I'm renting from a fisherman. In the last two years, he has only slightly increased my monthly payment.

I count the dekari gold coins again and rub my fingers into my hair. There should be enough here to get me by for a week or two but not enough to live on comfortably. My palms begin to sweat at the thought of taking another mercenary job.

Cold metal brushes against my fingertips as I pull it out from my cloak. The compass I lifted from that girl's pocket two days ago rests in my palm. The metal digs into my palm as I clench it, thinking of the moment I spotted her. It's a rusting old object that has seen better days but there are some shiny rounded spots as if held often.

Sadly, it won't fetch anything at the market and I don't have any use for a broken compass. Tucking it back in my cloak, I shake away the guilt that creeps in and focus on placing the gold dekari coins back into the pouch. Pickpocketing is something I despise and only resort to when absolutely necessary. This latest score barely made anything. I'll have to see the Shadow Dealer for a job. His payments are as unpredictable as the jobs themselves but it's better than nothing. That'll have to do for now.

I stand on my bed and gently lift free a board in the ceiling. Placing the pouch and my journal to the side, I secure the board back into place. Streams of dust float down as I step back onto the uneven floor.

Slipping on my cloak, I check that my stubbed throwing daggers are in their custom sewed holsters I made myself. Each one glimmers in the light before I close the flaps and venture out into the common area.

"Early morning, Ellis?" Carther sits by the blazing fire. His graying hair is brushed back as he holds a steaming mug between his hands.

"Yeah, I have some business to take care of."

Carther smiles at the dancing flames. "When are ya not runnin' off to take care of some business?"

I can't help smiling back. While I try to be discreet, he always seems to notice my movements. "Nothing gets past you does it, Carther?"

"I'm an ole man. Some things are startin' to slip my mind." He takes a sip and I don't believe a word. He's sharper than ever and old age is just a ruse to get pretty ladies to help him out when he pretends to be lost.

I adjust my collar. "I'll probably be out late tonight."

"That's alright, I'll be out on the boat for a few weeks so I won't see ya for a while. The king put out a request for lobsters."

I want to roll my eyes at the king's extravagant requests, but at least he offers a higher rate for whatever his cooks are seeking.

"Quite the request." Stuffing my hands in my pocket, I say, "But I believe my rent is paid for the next two months in case I don't see you." It's true, I usually don't see him for weeks, sometimes months. This morning is a rare occurrence.

Over the years, I've learned bits and pieces about Carther's life.

He was always a fisherman and even owned three boats that brought in quite a profit. When the Arliean war occurred almost twenty years ago, his entire crew volunteered to fight. His boats sat for years before he eventually had to sell two of them. He bought this building and renovated it to rent out for a steady profit. It was a smart move. Now, he fishes with his small crew on the remaining boat while enjoying an easier life.

His dark brown eyes hold mine. "Yeah, I have it noted in my book." He pauses, "Ya know that if ya ever want, I can always use another set of hands on the boat."

Amusement laces my voice as I reply, "You've been trying to get me to work for you for years."

"I can tell ya're a hard worker and strong." There is kindness in his voice. "Those crates are too heavy for an ole man like me."

I swallow hard. "Fishing isn't my thing but perhaps one day, I could change my mind." My father was a fisherman and that life will never be for me if I can help it. But I want to keep that door open in case things get dire.

"I understand. Offer is always there." He turns back to the fire and dips a cookie from his favorite bakery into his cup.

Once outside in the morning mist, I venture north a few streets on my new mission. It's still early with only a few hard-working ship crewmen starting their day preparing to depart. The incline with each step never gets old as my eyes settle on the palace at the top of the hill. It's an enormous stone structure carved out of the northern cliff that it's pressed up against. High walls with guard towers surround the king's palace with only authorized soldiers, councilmen, and staff allowed in. Based on whispers in the street, the king has only been outside of his fortress a handful of times. I honestly don't blame him, especially after the slaughter of his entire family by Arliean assassins. Even though he is rarely seen, King Addard demonstrates his power by hanging criminals from the palace walls.

The threat of death or the fact that his guards patrol the streets has never really deterred me from thieving and mercenary work. I'm trained to always think ahead and how not to draw attention.

I turn left down a familiar path. The entrance to the Shadow Dealer's warehouse is well concealed from prying eyes with crates and barrels blocking a very narrow alleyway. It's easy enough to find when sliding a barrel out of the way and sliding through a loose fence board. I knock on the door and a pair of blue eyes stare out from the little window.

"Business?" A gruff voice asks.

"Tell him it's Ellis," I say as my thumb grazes over the small handle of a throwing dagger secured inside my cloak. There's no telling what the Shadow Dealer will choose to do.

Minutes tick by before the wooden door creaks open. One of his guards leads me past stacked crates with the Shadow Dealer's symbol on them, two black feathers crossed in the middle. A feared symbol in the port city.

"I didn't think I would see ya so soon." Chills run down my spine at his low voice. The Shadow Dealer closes the lid to one of his crates before pivoting to face me.

"I didn't think I would need to but here we are." His blue eyes meet mine as I hold my breath. My eyes move further up his arms. The bulging muscle on them could easily knock a man out with a single blow. He picks up a long hunting knife from the top of the crate and twirls it as his forearm muscle dance. His shaved head displays healed scars that mark up his scalp. Each of them no doubt holding an intriguing story.

"Looking for a job?"

"Do you have any?" My palms sweat from being in his presence, but it's a small price of dealing with him. I straighten my back, refusing to break his gaze.

The Shadow Dealer is known for his cruel ways of dealing with business. That's why he solely dominates the city with his illegal trade and criminal network. I've taken a few jobs from him in the last year because why work for a foot soldier when you can get paid by the big man himself?

"As a matter of fact, I do have something." The knife stops moving as he grabs a roll of parchment lying on top of his desk and takes his time reading it. The only sound is the distant commotion of his men and the roaring fireplace to my left.

"Sir Horrick of Winhester is a wealthy spice merchant from Korrim who docked last night. He carries somethin' and I need ya to steal it." His head swivels to me. I shift on my feet.

"What's the object?"

"A gold pocket watch. I'm told he never goes anywhere without it so he'll have it on him tonight. He frequents the Golden Oak Tavern just off the southern square every night when he's in the city."

"Yeah, I know where that is." My brows scrunch. "That's all I have to do? Just steal the watch and bring it back to you?"

His eyes harden. "I expect it in my hand tomorrow mornin'." He rolls up the parchment and tucks in his vest. "I'll pay fifty dekari for it."

That's quite a sum for such an easy-sounding job. I desperately need the money but there must be something else to it.

"And that's all?" I ask slowly.

His jaw flexes and the scars on his scalp dance. "Yeah, and of course, the other thing too."

That's right. I have to bring back a secret or rumor I heard but I expected that. I don't linger further and show myself to the door. The guard latches the door behind me as I step out into slightly warmer air.

The Golden Oak Tavern is sizable but in a good location for the job. There are plenty of tables and it tends to get pretty rowdy at night. I'll be able to blend right in.

I smile to myself and feel hopeful for the first time today.

It'll be an easy score.

Chapter 3
Ellis

The rickety old fence post I'm crouching on groans in protest under my feet. It's the only vantage point hidden enough to see where my mark will be entering the Golden Oak Tavern below. It's a perfect place to watch for him under the cover of darkness.

The tavern window creates a warm glow in the wide alleyway, and joyous music spills into the street. A piano player strokes the keys between drunken sips of mead and townsfolk talk amongst themselves. Roaring laughter follows a jolly story that makes me wish I heard it too.

Rinmor is gloomier tonight. Thick dark clouds form overhead, threatening a storm at any moment. The crisp smell of freshly caught fish fills my lungs with a sense of familiarity. Regardless of where I was out there in the world, this place was always a beacon, like a lighthouse to a ship.

The stone wall at my back radiates the same chill that has turned the city from summer to fall. A wool tunic keeps me warm in the slight breeze. My freshly oiled leather cloak hangs loosely around me, the small throwing daggers ready to be in my hands at a moment's notice.

Rain begins drizzling down in almost a mist when a man passes the opening of the alleyway with two men at his side. The silver ornate embroidery of his cloak makes him stand out in the poor glow of the lanterns. A round belly leaves no room in the vest he wears, the fabric strands struggling to hold together.

His pointed shoes tap on the smoothed cobblestone road as the tavern door opens, and he steps inside. I recognize him the second he comes into the dim light through the window. Sir Horrick of Winhester, my target. With wide eyes, he stares only at the woman who sashays toward him seductively. Her hips sway with extra effort and her eyes solely on the small fortune he'll likely spend tonight.

But I'm focused only on the gold pocket watch he has barely tucked away in his vest centerfold. My concentration slowly drowns out all other city noise. There are several ways of going about this. Wait until the merchant and the guards are drunk enough to not notice or cause a tavern fight that would force his guards away from him.

A loud-pitched voice tenses my muscles and cuts through my thoughts.

The voice hints at an accent I recognize of a sailor who belongs to one of the ships in the harbor. Their words are half-spoken, drawn out with slang, and indicate minimal education. Ship hands are notorious for causing fights in taverns, pleasure houses, and alleyways such as this one. Their sense of freedom after long trips at sea makes them instinctively seek out trouble. Unexpected anger washes over my body and my fists clench.

"Where ya think ya runnin' off to, brat?" The man says with a mocking chuckle. The sound echoes off the cold plastered stones of the surrounding buildings. He reeks of confidence given to him from working under a sea captain.

A girl is pressed against the building on the other side of the alley. Her blonde hair is disheveled, and her dress torn up to her knee. The pale skin of her leg is exposed to the crisp air. She struggles to stretch out her hands between her and the man's chest, but he keeps pressing in closer.

Clenching my jaw at the sight, my stomach churns at the thought of walking away knowing what's in store for a young girl like her in a perverse world of men who take what they want.

I sink further into the shadows and wait.

"Get your hands off me, you pig!" Her voice cracks as she spits in the man's face.

In the blink of an eye, the back of his hand strikes across her cheek.

Time slows as the girl's head snaps to the left at the impact and a startled cry escapes her. A dagger appears in my hand as silence seems to echo.

As if turning into a wild animal, she lunges at him with both hands. Fingernails claw at him with every ounce of strength in her petite frame. He struggles for a second before pinning her to the wall with his body. One hand holds hers firmly above her head and the other clenches her jaw.

"Worthless girl. Ya ought to be grateful when a man calls ya over." His face is so close to hers that their lips nearly brush.

"You aren't even a man." Her voice is clear and firm as she twists beneath his pressing body.

Another companion appears as I closely survey the alley. He's taller with a cap that sits on his dark hair. A tall pint sloshes in his hand as he watches, clearly amused at the scene before him. He settles on the end of a wagon, the thick canopy of the wagon bed making a dark shelter.

"Ya be comin' with us." He moves to grip a fist full of her hair and drags her towards his companion. She lets out a deafening scream. He clasps his hand over her mouth as she struggles to pull away.

Hesitantly, I look at the merchant in the tavern window, the gold watch gleaming with temptation. Cursing under my breath, I jump down with the cloak surrounding me in a swift motion.

From the shadows of my hood, I state grimly, "I believe the lady said to get your hands off her."

The first sailor turns but holds her close to his chest. "Why don't ya mind yar business? The girl and I were just havin' a chat." He sniffs her hair as she struggles to turn her head against the pressure of his fingers.

Her eyes are wide with fear, her arm stretches out to me. My chest tightens at her helplessly grasping for aid.

The taller companion puts down his drink and retrieves a sword from the sheathe at his hip. My eyes flicker to the covered cargo they must be eager to protect. This is an unexpected turn of events. I may walk away with more than I planned.

I take a step closer, assessing my opponent in a matter of seconds. His stance is off center, which will make it easy to knock him off balance. The way he grips his sword shows the limited times he's had to use it. For me, every skill I've learned is accessible at my fingertips. My body vibrates with anticipation of the first move.

As expected, the companion runs towards me with the glistening metal raised high over his head. He stumbles slightly, clearly off balance from the mead he had just been gulping. Inexperience is also obvious as he swings at me with all of his might.

I dodge his attack with enough time to sidestep and give him a quick knee to the stomach. He doubles over in pain. His cap and sword fall at my feet with ease. I kick his sword off to the side.

The first man shoves the girl away roughly, and she stumbles into the wall. My eyes pivot quickly as he draws a long dagger from his belt. His face lifts in a smirk and a prematurely triumphant gleam flashes in his eyes.

My lips curl into a smile at the sweet defeat he's about to endure.

Dagger thrust in the air, the shipmate runs towards me. I glance at the girl, who stays frozen as she timidly watches me. Why doesn't she run? The strong whiff of body odor brings my attention back as the man approaches with significant speed.

The fighting skill of a sailor is enough to keep him alive onboard a vessel carrying high-priced goods and an occasional raid. They don't compare to my years of training and adapting to expertise in mercenary work. I sidestep his reaching blade as I had done with the other man. His dagger aims at my chest, but I dodge every attempt like a dance.

This dance feels like it could be a predator taunting its prey.

My heart beats steadily.

His boots slash the still water that collects between the cobbles as he calls behind him, "Taggard, ya okay?"

The taller man, Taggard, groans but shifts to venture onto his feet. I pivot on my heel, striking my leather boot into his face. The feeling of it connecting with bone vibrates throughout my body before he lets out a deep groan.

His body goes limp.

The handsy man takes the opportunity to lunge at me again with uncoordinated steps. I meet him quickly with a forward kick to his chest. He catches himself before almost falling backward.

Rain taps rapidly on the cured leather of my hood. He wipes the water out of his eyes and jolts up in irritation. I survey the weak points of his body: kneecaps, neck, ribs, and face. I don't want to kill him but hinder his recovery time.

With one swift movement, I use the nearby cobblestone wall as leverage to spin my body up and plant my heel directly on his jaw and nose. His eyes reflect pain briefly and roll to the back of his head in the time it takes me to land on the ground again. His limp body collapses at my feet and I can't help but smirk at the blood trailing down his wide nose.

I tilt my head to the girl. She's still pressing herself against the wall, almost into the shadows. I pick up the sword from the ground, wipe it off on my cloak, and secure it between my belt and pants.

Shadowy figures rush towards us from the far alley entrance. Their angry voices carry over the rain. By estimation, three of them.

"Hey, you. Stop!" A voice shouts as they approach. Perhaps they heard the fighting or the scream the girl let out earlier.

I grab the girl's hand. "We need to go."

She roughly jerks away from me. Her eyes dart to the two bodies in the mud before looking up at me again.

Grunting loudly, I retort, "You can either stay here and hope those men are nicer or come with me."

She frantically nods at me with wide eyes. The voices grow louder, calling after us. I grasp her hand again. Being touched by another person is the last thing she must want, but surviving the next few minutes is the only thing I care about.

Glancing at the wagon, I eliminate it as an immediate means of escape. It would take too much time to get up on the seat with the girl in tow while trying to find the reins to the horses in the dark.

The mud forming around the wagon wheels is another issue.

A sharp ache of frustration grips me. I don't get to complete my job or walk away with the cargo. At this moment, the girl beside me becomes more important than any of those things. An overwhelming feeling to get her to safety is new for me.

The second option it is. We start running towards the outskirts of town, which is the most familiar. We can make it to the rock caverns on the beach and head west for a while until we lose them.

I tug her arm to keep running. A wagon comes barreling down the street only inches away from the girl but I manage to pull her towards me at the last second. Her shoulder slams into my side and we stumble backward before I catch us.

Breathing heavily, her gaze is unfocused, as if disoriented by the commotion. I gesture for us to continue further down and a small nod is all she manages.

I decide to cut through another alleyway just around the corner. Right as we take a few steps into the alleyway, two men block our path and a third man stops behind us.

I motion the girl towards the wall and she listens, pressing herself into the shadows. The daggers at my hip and the stolen sword at my back are available to me.

One of the men shouts over the pouring rain, "Drop your weapons!"

They're mere shadows with a hint of blue around their torso. Analyzing their height and threat level is impossible from here.

My hands slowly wrap over the dagger handles as long seconds crawl by. Two daggers inch in between my fingers on the left and right hands. My heart beats wildly. Anticipation buzzes in the air.

All three men come towards me at once from different angles. I kick the first man to reach me in the chest and use the same motion to connect with another man's chin. A yelp escapes him and he grips his face while staggering back. Mud forms thickly now as my boots stick. The other two men wrap their arms around me and shove me to the ground. The third man throws his right foot to the back of my leg and my knee hits a small patch of stone under the mud with unexpected force.

The girl gasps loudly behind me, but doesn't move. I want to tell her to run for real this time. But my pride won't let me. I know I can turn this fight around. That I can win and get her to safety like I threw everything away to do.

From my kneeling position, I recover quickly by dodging an attempted punch to the face by swinging my other leg under him. The splashes of mud from his fall spray around us. The first man gets to his feet, wrapping his muscled arm around my neck. I choke briefly before shoving one of my short daggers into his side from my kneeling position and thrust another short dagger into the thigh of the one behind me.

A shout rings in my ear as the thick arm releases me. The other man hesitates as he gets up from the mud and takes a step back. I struggle to my feet and pain shoots up from my impacted knees.

The man in front of me staggers back, holding his side with my dagger still in him. Raindrops stream down his face as our eyes briefly connect.

"Watch out!" The girl's voice screams behind me, but I don't react in time. A glimmer of a shorter sword catches my eye to the left. The tip pierces through my tunic and into the lower left side of my abdomen.

My mind goes blank.

Time slows before shooting pain sears through every part of my body. My breathing hitches as my fingers feel the depth of the wound. Thankfully, it doesn't feel like it went too far. Grabbing the man's sword arm, I twist it away from me. With a crunch, his wrist gives way under my grip.

I focus on the enemy to my right, who moves closer. I don't think before I kick my foot into his hip to gain some distance. They encircle me as I grip my side. Hot liquid seeps against my hand and waves of hot pain crash into my mental clarity. My vision blurs for a split second before I attempt to retreat.

Something metal strikes the back of my head from the right. My eyes close as nausea overcomes my senses. I catch a glimpse of the girl pushing herself further into the wall. The chilling sound of her cries stays with me as darkness consumes everything.

Chapter 4
Lylah

The wind whistles through the iron bars on the small opening beyond my reach.

I grit my teeth in annoyance. The sound alone is enough to drive a person crazy in here. The following would be the size of this prison cell, just wide enough for two people to lie down on the jagged, uneven floor. Chilled morning temperatures don't promise comfort either, as I wrap my dress around my legs and shawl around my shoulders.

A bucket with a lid sits in the corner by the door, which I can only imagine is for bodily needs. I scrunch my nose at the thought and further curl up into a ball.

The morning glow gradually brightens the room I was thrown into yesterday by the same men we were running from. Spending the night in the dark was the hardest of all. The uncertainty knotted my stomach and nausea dwindled only a little while I slept.

I bite my lip and look over at the stranger lying limply on the floor just on the other side of the iron bars that separate our cells. Last night when he was trying to help me escape, he fought with skill and precision that only someone with extensive experience could have done. He moved like flowing water, dodging attacks and standing his ground against three men.

With the rising sun casting more light into the room, I can make out the shape of his body in his cell. I find myself moving closer to him. I had avoided looking at him since I settled into my chosen corner. It was furthest from the door and his dangerous tendencies.

Memories of that ill-mannered man in the alleyway touching me makes my skin crawl again. I shut my eyes quickly, wishing the memory away from my mind forever, but I doubt it will be that easy. Nothing in my life has ever been that easy.

The stranger is covered in mud, as thick as the bottom seams of my ripped dress. A hood conceals most of his face as I lean against the bars. Auburn hair in messy locks comes into view the more I examine his features. Dried streams of blood trail down to his rigid jawline from the hit that knocked him unconscious. His tanned complexion is glistens as if with sweat.

He sits up hurriedly and I jump away from the bars. The figure shifts to his side and grabs at his cloak before the most exquisite pair of greenish-blue eyes match my startled expression. Like the magnificent color of clear sea water with the reflection of a blue summer sky. I break his gaze, feeling flustered at the lack of judgment. Suddenly, I wish there was a solid wall between us so I could push myself into my corner and disappear.

His eyes soften. "Sorry. I didn't mean to startle you." The deep voice that escapes his lips is hoarse.

A simple nod is all I manage as I wrap my arms around my knees again. The crisp wind continues to howl through our cell windows but heat rushes to my cheeks this time. My pulsing embarrassment magnifies and I scold myself for thinking it was a good idea to come so close to an unpredictable stranger. My curiosity simply got the better of me.

He pushes himself up slowly with gritted teeth and looks around. "Where are we?" He asks roughly.

Avoiding his gaze, I shrug casually. "A prison I imagine. I've already checked the door but it's latched from the outside. No escaping that way."

He lets out a stifled groan as he struggles to his feet. "How long have we been here?"

"Since last night," I answer as I stare up at my small barred window, pretending to enjoy the view, but all I can see is a corner of a colorless sky.

"Ah." He grips his head as well as his left side. "My head."

I pretend to ignore him as he shuffles to the door and gives it a jiggle, a motion I have done a hundred times already on my own door. I sigh with slight irritation. "I told you already. It's locked from the outside."

He gives me a pained yet confused look, as if still orienting himself to our new surroundings. Determination quickly slides across his face, the firm lines of his brow drawn. I watch curiously as he circles his cell, touching every stone and small crack in the wall. His towering figure tries to reach the bars on his window, but it's just beyond his outstretched fingers.

Finally giving up, he takes a seat against the opposite wall of his cell. The mess of curls sway briefly as he holds his side. When he sweeps his cloak to the side, red liquid seeps through his tunic.

I gasp. The wound must be deep as blood is already spreading across a large portion of the cloth. This handsome stranger saved my life when I thought the worst would happen to me. It's only fair that I try to help him now.

But why am I so hesitant to help him? A voice in my head laughs at me for not being able to protect myself. He made me look weak when I thought I was strong and independent. He showed me that when it came down to it; I wasn't.

I approach the bars slowly, studying him as his head rests against the wall. His eyes are closed, his breathing shallow as I fixate on the seeping blood.

"Let me see your wound," I breathe out shakily, unsure of how I should offer to help when he's so far away.

His eyes open, those deep seafoam green eyes threaten to freeze every spinning thought. Something about the way he looks at me stops me mid-motion. Maybe he sees a victim who was there at the wrong time. Maybe he sees a helpless girl with no one to call a friend or family to go home to. This stranger risked his life to save me. The pain that decision caused him is evident.

"What?" I ask as his eyes continue to bore into me. My pulse quickens under the intensity of his gaze but I repeat, "Let me see your wound."

The stranger nods and moves his hand away, wiping the blood on his leather trousers. He lifts his shirt while I prepare myself for the raw exposed flesh underneath. He grimaces as I do my best to ignore the bile that threatens to rise.

He pauses as his fingers inspect the cloak. "They took my daggers."

I watch as he laughs with no humor in his voice.

"They took all of them," he says tiredly.

It was dark when the guards patted him down while he lay unconscious on the floor. They didn't seem to think I had any weapons on me because they didn't approach me at all.

"Yes, they did." I shift my eyes to the growing red stain. "Stop moving. You're causing the wound to open again."

I force myself to focus as he gently raises his tunic over his head, revealing rigid muscles underneath. His sweat covered torso flexes as he adjusts himself. A rush of heat rises to my cheeks unexpectedly. I've seen boys I grew up around with their shirts off but this feels different. More intimate somehow.

In the pouring rain last night, I warned him of the swinging sword, but didn't realize it ever connected with his body. Guilt eats away at me. I let a man bleed all night and barely looked in his direction.

Blood starts dripping out of the wound as he shifts again.

"We need to alert the guards." I stand frantically. "That needs serious medical attention and I can't do anything from here."

Pounding on the door, I yell as loud as I can manage. "Guard!"

My voice seems to echo in the hallway behind the thick door. "Guard! This man is wounded and needs a healer."

I pound and kick the door for several minutes but only silence replies.

Feeling helpless, I slide down until I'm on the stone floor. We sit in silence for a while, each of us occupied with our own thoughts. The birds begin chirping outside and thankfully, the wind has ceased. I fidget with the edges of my ripped skirt, trying hard not to think about the last few days, but unauthorized tears roll down my face. I went from one cage straight into another.

Wiping my tears away quickly with my sleeve, the stranger looks at me with a piercing gaze as if seeing right through me. I divert my eyes and resort to staring out of the window again.

"What's your name?" his strained voice whispers.

I try to swallow the lump in my throat. "Lylah."

He closes his eyes as if soaking in the name and repeats it quietly over his lips.

"What's yours?" I ask the question back to him, growing more curious about my prison mate.

"Ellis."

I test the name on my lips as well, wanting to always remember the man who saved me. Every time I glance at him, the closer he appears to my age. Maybe even only a few years older than me. I honestly can't remember the last time I celebrated a birthday, but I'm seventeen years old from what I've been told.

"Who were those men after you?" Ellis' eyes flicker closed.

I fidget with my dress more, unsure of how to answer. "They were pathetic men who cornered me in an alley."

I feel his eyes on me. "I'm sorry they thought they could do that to you."

A tired sigh escapes. "I should have known not to go out late at night by myself."

"Why did you?" His jaw flexes and his eyes trail my face, stopping briefly on my cheek where the sailor struck me. It must have left a mark.

"I was trying to find a job in the city and wanted to check in on a few more places." I shake my head at my careless thinking. "Stupidly thought I could do it after sunset."

He closes his eyes again. "Work is hard to find these days."

I nod, but the weight of his gaze earlier leaves me uncertain. Honestly, I hope to get out of this cell and never see him again. But something is pulling me to him. Maybe it's intrigue. Maybe it's the exhaustion from the night, but I feel an invisible string connecting me to him.

"What were you doing there last night?" I keep my voice light. "A fighter in a mysterious cloak coming to rescue ladies in distress?"

He grits his teeth. "Trust me, saving you was not the plan."

The words sting more than I expect as his eyes flutter closed again. He mumbles words barely audible, something about being safer here, but doesn't clarify.

Minutes crawl by in silence. I want my compass so badly, knowing it will help calm me. The only thing that soothes me in this depressing place is the steady breathing of Ellis as he falls asleep.

Chapter 5
Ellis

I'm shaken awake by rough hands pulling me to my feet. Two towering men hold me upright before I feel cold metal chains clasp tightly on my wrists. The chains swing as the guards move me toward the open cell door.

Looking over my shoulder, Lylah's eyes are round. As round as the night I first saw her grasping for me. Her arms are wrapped around her knees like a scared animal.

"Where are you taking me?" I struggle against their firm grip with the last bit of strength I have left. Surges of pain overtake my body and my knees nearly buckle as I get shoved through the narrow door.

We walk through several hallways before I hear strained voices coming from a corridor on the right with hands reaching out through the bars. The guards push me left, ignoring my question. My mind fixates on their recently shined metal armor which is fastened to their chests with various leather straps and buckles. I breathe through the pain and try to memorize every turn we take. There's a fogginess to my thoughts and pretty soon, I can't keep track like I normally can.

Several minutes later, I'm dragged into a sizable wide-open room with a vast number of shelves filled with bottles, branches, and plants hanging from wooden beams. A wide window channels light to stream onto several cots which line the edges of the room.

An older man in a dark gray floor-length tunic pounds something in a stone bowl on a long table, the movement causing it to squeak. His wrinkled forehead is scrunched before a small smile spreads over his face, not seeming to notice we are standing in the doorway.

"Put him over there." He gestures behind him without looking up and pours in a powder from a bottle he retrieved from a shelf.

I'm guided to a well-kept bed with a thin mattress on top before the guards force me to lie down. The man pivots slowly with the bowl in his hands and looks at me through a pair of eyeglasses. The rarity of eyeglasses rules him out from being someone insignificant in society.

The man's white beard sways as he turns to the two men and says, "Gentlemen, please leave us."

To my left, the short guard scratches his thinning hair. "But His Ma—"

"I don't care what he told you." He waves his hand at them dismissively. "Get out."

After reluctant steps towards the door with their swords clang against their armor, they station themselves outside.

The bearded man chuckles down at me. "They can be so stubborn sometimes."

Looking at him curiously, I ask, "Who are you?"

Long minutes pass in silence, his focus entirely on the bowl in his hands. "A healer." His eyes scan my blood-stained tunic. "I'm just going to look at that wound."

My chains clink as I move to give him more access to my side. White spots cloud my vision as I drift in and out of focus. I've never been to an official healer. The back alley remedies I'd purchased for my injuries were always a gamble. There was almost no way of telling if the medicine was genuine or a coin scheme.

"Ah, you are lucky, young man," he says as he moves my tunic up. "The lady made sure to alert the guards in time."

It's true, she had pounded on the door for a long time, shouting and kicking it to make as much noise as possible. How long was I asleep before the guards came?

"Where are we?"

My question hangs in the air. He doesn't answer again but instead moves his face closer to my wound. I try to focus on the wood beams above me, on the hanging dried herbs and flowers of various colors.

It doesn't take long for the metallic smell of blood to drift up to my nose. My face scrunches, but the healer doesn't seem bothered by the gruesome puncture. He hums a cheerful tune as he works, rubbing a wet salve from the bowl and patting it into my wound. Grunting slightly, I feel pressure before a numbing sensation unexpectedly spreads across that area.

"You're very lucky indeed. That gash barely missed your kidney." The healer glances at me over his long nose.

"I don't feel lucky."

He only shakes his head. A soft hum fills the room again as he spreads a different salve from another bowl on my skin. There's no sharp pain from his touch and I relax a bit.

"This is the most painful part," he says while pausing his melody. "I am going to sew the wound shut. I put a numbing herb to help a bit. I do have some strong wine if you want to take a swig for courage." He waits a few seconds but I shake my head. Alcohol would not only dull my nerves, but my senses too. I can't afford it in this time of uncertainty.

"Take deep breaths and try not to move too much."

I nod and take a few deep shaky breaths.

The numbing herb works fast as he sticks a needle and thread into my skin, the pain is subtle but still noticeable. With each stab of the needle, I clench my jaw and ball up my fists to keep from moving.

"All done. See... not too bad," the healer says as he smiles warmly. "Sit up please."

"Thank you," I reply with a smile and slowly sit up.

"Now, don't make sudden movements or you'll tear my stitching. Trust me, that will be way more painful." He continues working, wrapping clean cloth strips around my torso tightly to keep the stitching and herb paste in place.

The guards reappear when the healer wraps the last strip and ties it. Their grim faces keep a close watch with every slow passing moment as the healer lowers my shirt. I subtly look around the room for a possible weapon, but there's nothing within reach.

I should want to escape. My freedom so close I can practically taste the sea air but a surprising part of me pushes to stay. My mind flashes to Lylah, the way she was curled up against the wall in terror. She deserves her freedom too. I grunt at the inner turmoil, knowing full well what I've subconsciously chosen to do. What's wrong with me? I would've done anything to fight my way out of this place.

I let them take me from the bed without a fight. I have to work smarter, especially in my current condition. They lead me back to the cell, the wood and iron door about to secure my captivity again. Once they remove my chains, I'm pushed roughly inside. My bindings don't budge, thankfully, as I catch my footing.

The girl is standing when I stumble in. Her shawl wrapped tight around her shoulders as she watches me intensely. The hollowed cheeks of this malnourished girl paints a vivid enough picture of her upbringing. Slightly matted blonde clumps of hair hang around her face, but in the light, I spot a streak of ginger hair waterfall across her left eye. I've never seen hair like that before. I let my eyes wander for a little too long.

Grunting slightly, I lower myself against the wall and find a semi-comfortable spot between two flat stones on the floor. I feel the familiar smooth leather of my cloak exactly where I left it.

"What did they do to you?" Her voice is barely a whisper.

My hand stretches over my new bandages. "They took me to a healer who stitched me up and put some kind of herb paste on it."

"That's good." A few moments pass before she speaks again, "I couldn't get you to wake up. I tried shouting your name but nothing awoke you. I thought you died."

I laugh dryly. "I don't die easily."

She doesn't respond but stares up at the small window.

"Have you always had that?" I gesture to her hair.

Her eyes narrow before turning to me. "Yes, ever since I was little."

"I've never seen that on anyone before." I yawn, the exhaustion starting to creep in again.

I adjust myself against the wall again when something hard pokes into my leg. Feeling around my cloak, my hand landing on a round object.

The compass. Why didn't they take it with everything else? Perhaps the rusting edges didn't entice them.

I take it out and twirl it in my fingers.

"Where did you get that?" Lylah straightens as leans forward.

"It was my father's," I lie.

Her eyes go wide. "No, that's mine."

My mouth goes dry.

"Someone stole it out of my pocket three days ago in the square." The edges of her bright blue eyes crease. "Someone with auburn hair like yours."

It continues to rotate in my hand as I stay silent. I thought she looked vaguely familiar. I had spotted her that day in the central square coming out of a shop and nervously patting her pocket. Only guessing she had dekaris in there, I pickpocketed her.

"You can have it back." Holding it out to her, she hastily reaches through the bars, takes it and grasps it close to her chest.

I huff out a laugh and lean back against the cold stones. "It has only ever brought me bad luck anyway."

The conversation dies as fast as it started, and silence falls like a heavy blanket. Her blue eyes close and a single tear rolls down her cheek.

Chapter 6
Lylah

Sections of light move along the tiny crack under our door. I sit up as anticipation courses through my veins with searing speed. The keys jingle past the cell door but it's just a guard on his patrol. My shoulders sag as we're surrounded by darkness again.

Two guards come by a few hours later to give us each a small loaf of bread and two smoked fish. We drink from a ladle of crisp water before they leave just as abruptly. The lock sliding back into place with a loud thud.

Like starved animals having a taste of something delicious, we barely chew the bread as we devour every piece. Though the bread is mediocre at best, it's enough to fill our stomachs. The dried fish slides down my throat with some difficulty, and I wish the guard had left us some water.

Ellis coughs up a piece of crust and spits it out onto the ground. "This bread is barely edible."

I have to agree, but I say, "It's better than nothing."

He grunts and eats the rest quietly.

Eight guards appear later that night after we attempt to make ourselves comfortable for another night on the rough floor. The rattling of chains and shifting plates of armor wakes us from a restless sleep, the sound echoing eerily. Their torches illuminate every shadow in the both rooms as I shield my eyes.

Earlier, Ellis lied about stealing my compass and I spent most of my efforts after that keeping him as far away from me as the tiny cell would allow. Now, oddly enough, his presence is the only thing that keeps me calm. I follow his lead as he lets the guards bind his wrists.

After the chains are secure, four guards position themselves on each side of us. They lead the way into the hallway, where the passing torch light brightens the crevices of the stone walls. We ascend a curved staircase as the guards push us up each step until we reach the top of a vast space that nearly takes my breath away.

"Keep moving," a guard grumbles as he pushes me forward.

Our steps echo in the intriguing and beautiful corridor, each wall adorned to the ceiling with paintings and sculptures on either side. Exquisite art framed in gold gleams as we pass. Somber and regal portraits with piercing eyes that seem to stare right at me are oddly fascinating in this shadowy place.

"Where are you taking us?" I ask, my mouth dry at the possibilities. It must be the middle of the night and the little sleep I had forces every muscle in my body to tense painfully.

"Stop talking," are the only words I get.

Gloved hands push me roughly to the left. We stop in front of an immense set of wooden doors reaching up into the surrounding darkness and secured to the stone walls by forged iron. In the slabs of oak are masterful carvings of tall ocean waves crashing down onto a shoreline. I let my eyes trace every curve and intricate detail.

Guards with deep blue uniforms and swords at their waist secure the entrance to whatever is waiting on the other side. My chest tightens with anticipation. I glance at Ellis, but I can't see him clearly with all of the guards between us.

Two guards nod to those securing the entrance. Before long, a creaking sound vibrates from the grand doors as they are pushed open. Inside, it's a room made entirely of marble, with higher ceilings and pillars on either side of a blue carpet spread out to the back of the room. Torches secured on every pillar cast long shadows on the great hall.

A marble throne is centered on an extended dais. As we approach, a man becomes visible, sitting on it with his hands on the armrests. A glimmer from a crown on his black hair catches my attention, and stubble accentuates his face as we abruptly stop below his throne.

I swallow hard as realization hits me. Everyone has heard of the man looking down at us but only a few people have ever seen him in person. My mind whirls at how this situation keeps getting worse and worse.

The guards fall on one knee with a loud thud and raise a hand to their chests. "Your Majesty."

One soldier pushes me down before I have a chance to register what's happening. Chains rattle as my knees hit the hard floor. I bite back a yelp and peer sideways at Ellis, who is kneeling as well.

King Addard nods at our bow, acknowledging the gestures from his high place.

He isn't what I pictured him to be. Rumors have always been that he's an unsightly man and that's why he hides in his palace. But the man before me is quite the opposite. His chiseled cheekbones and eyes, hidden in shadow, make it seem like he isn't afraid of anything. A loose blouse, dyed a deep blue with gold patterns embroidered with thread from the finest merchants, rests on his broad shoulders. A common fashion style among the wealthy families in our kingdom of Narvidium.

A new wave of fear ripples through me as my fate now hangs in the balance of the king.

Our king.

I'm not sure why I'm imprisoned when I did nothing wrong. The only reason that makes sense is I got grouped with Ellis for the damage he caused. I should've run when I had the chance.

We stand as Ellis looks straight ahead with eyes solely on the king before us. There's nowhere to go now. I turn back to the throne and prepare myself for a harsh punishment like flogging or death, regardless of my innocence.

A guard's voice radiates from my right. "Your Majesty, we brought you the two prisoners who attacked the king's guards as requested."

The king leans forward, his eyes moving along the blood stain that has now dried on Ellis's shirt. He nods to a guard who lifts it up. Fingers adorned with gold rings tap against the ivory hue of the throne.

"Is this Finnon's work?" The king's voice is commanding with each word.

Ellis's eyes are steady as his gaze matches the king's. His jaw clenches and unclenches as if chewing on this recent development. There's something behind those ocean-colored eyes as he looks up at him. Calculating and perhaps daring.

The guard nods in response, but the king's attention has already begun traveling to me.

Feeling the full weight of his analytical stare, I shift uncomfortably. It takes him long seconds to observe my mud-crusted skirt and the tear along my knee where a part of my leg is exposed. He stands suddenly and descends the stairs, a fur-collared robe trailing behind him.

The guards shift as their hands snap to rest on the hilts of their weapons. I straighten too, but my lower back screams in pain from the jagged floors we've been forced to sit and sleep on.

My mouth goes dry again as he approaches me. The reality of the situation sinking deeper. Questions swirl at dizzying speeds, but I try to ignore my racing heart the most.

I wish I could feel the comforting surface of my compass. I keep it tucked away within the safety of my dress pocket.

He stops in front of me. The gold crown is more visible now, with the embedded blue gemstones catching small rays of light while the red ones seem to glow.

"What is your name?" His tone is surprisingly soft.

I try to catch any emotion on his face, but there is none. Cold eyes blink back at me. I can only imagine what I look like, but I haven't had a chance to fix my appearance for a king I didn't know I would be meeting. I must look unsightly to him. My knotted blonde hair clumps around my face. Scratches along my jaw from the rough takedown in the street. Dirt clinging to my fingernails, which I try to hide in the folds of my dress.

"Lylah," I manage to breathe out and attempt to curtsy as I've seen in tattered picture books. The motion feels unnatural and my sore knees protest. "Your Majesty," I add quickly.

I shift my eyes down to the floor only briefly. He has been known to be cruel. The bodies of criminals hanging from the palace walls point to that conclusion. My life hangs in the balance.

Golden eyes tower over my short figure as he seems to take his time with his thoughts. "How old are you?"

It takes a moment to remember. "Seventeen," I reply.

"Causing harm to my soldiers is grounds for serious punishment."

I try to swallow the lump in my throat. "Your Majesty, if I could explain..." The words fly from my mouth, but I pause before he nods. "I was being attacked in the streets by sailors when Ellis came to fend them off. We heard the men coming and thought it was more of their buddies. The pouring rain made it difficult to see past only a few steps. The attack on your soldiers was only meant in self-defense."

The king ponders this as he strolls leisurely to Ellis next, his face more rigid as he takes in his appearance as well. "You must be Ellis." He pauses. "The soldiers that brought you in had the most intriguing story to tell. A mysterious figure fighting ever so hard to protect a girl."

Ellis doesn't say anything and only looks straight ahead.

King Addard inspects him with narrowed eyes. "How old are you?"

"Nineteen," Ellis's jaw flexes as he answers. At least I was close when guessing his age.

King Addard's face turns serious again. "Attacking my soldiers is against the law in this kingdom and punishable by death."

My palms sweat. Will he be executed?

The pause creates a palpable tension in the hall as King Addard circles Ellis with his hands behind his back. The guards move out of the way but hold steady hands on their swords.

Ellis speaks for the first time. "I'm aware of your laws. Visibility was low that night and your soldiers did not announce themselves, nor were they wearing any identifying uniforms."

"A crime was still committed. I must punish accordingly, or everyone will use excuses to get away with them. Good news for you," King Addard pursed his lips. "I do not like to kill unnecessarily. You will serve me until I find that you have completed your sentence."

Ellis clenches his jaw. "How long will that be?"

"Only you can be the judge of that depending on how hard you work. It could be months or even years but that's the fun of it. Only I can declare your sentence complete."

Ellis opens his mouth before closing it. The chains rattle as he shifts on his feet and a few of the guards move closer.

My stomach churns. I can't fathom someone thinking this is fun. Ellis's face remains void of expression as the king continues to move around him.

He continues. "The soldier you stabbed barely made it through the night and looks like you were just as lucky." A brief second passes. "Your wounds have been mended enough to heal in due time. Finnon's work is the best in the kingdom, so be sure to say grateful prayers tonight."

Ellis' face is neutral, as if absorbing every word but fighting to hold back his true thoughts.

The king stops in front of him again, their eyes connecting with calculating stares. "You will serve me in the kitchens. I believe there is much work to be done as one of the servants injured himself, causing the kitchen to be a man short. Maggis will train you, as he is head of my household staff. If you try to steal or escape, I will find you and the punishment will be a spot on my wall."

The king turns his attention to the guards. "Take him down below to the servant quarters. He will begin his sentence tomorrow."

Guards escort Ellis towards the door we came in but not before he looks back at me with an unreadable look. We connect in a splinter of stilled time before he's shoved into the darkness of the corridor.

The king's voice draws me back to face him. "What were you doing in that alley so late at night?"

The shackles jingle loudly. "I was hoping to speak to the tavern owner about a job. I was in desperate need of one."

His face remains unchanged. "A girl like yourself would take work in a rowdy tavern? With men who would do more to you than what those sailors tried to?"

I understand what he's implying. "If it meant that I could support myself, I'd take almost any job, regardless of the dangers."

"Almost any job?" His head tilts slightly.

"I want a better life than ending up in the pleasure houses. Or working with fish. So yes, almost any job." Many girls that I grew up with had the life trajectory of pleasure work. I refuse to have the same fate. After their first year, they looked like they aged ten years. Like walking corpses, they carried a sadness that could not be described.

His voice turns soft again. "Understandable on your part. If it is a job that you seek, my household is always in need of maids. There is always work to be done in that regard, and you will be compensated better than in any tavern."

Perhaps he pities me for throwing me in a cell when I'm innocent. Maybe he sees a girl with nowhere else to go. I feel in my heart that's the closest to the truth. I have no money, no clothes, no belongings. Just the will to survive and leave the past behind me.

Accepting his offer, I state my thanks, but he has already turned to leave. As the guards guide me out the same way as Ellis, I cast a last glimpse toward the king before the doors shut. His robe drapes behind him as he enters a small door to the left of his throne, the crown no longer on his head but in his hand.

Chapter 7
Ellis

A few weeks have passed since my encounter with the elusive King Addard. He isn't what I thought he would be. The rising tension with our neighboring northern kingdom seems to have his mind occupied. Perhaps I caught him in a good mood, but I doubt that's the reason I'm still alive.

The punishment of servitude has been more merciful than what he has done to those who have attacked his soldiers before. Attacking them was the last thing I ever wanted to do, but between the pouring rain and pumping adrenaline, I acted out of pure instinct. Now, I have to pay the price.

A battlefield of inner turmoil claws at me daily since being imprisoned in this insufferable place. I should've not interfered, but my morals had to win for the first time in my life. I can't blame Lylah entirely, even though I want to target all of my anger to her. I'm the one who chose to jump in to save her. I'm the one who drove the knife that almost killed a king's guard.

The Shadow Dealer must think I've run off with the pocket watch by now since I failed to bring it to him by his deadline. I hope, with every fiber of my being, that he believes me when I get the chance to explain. That the relationship I spent years building helps him believe this wild tale.

It would be easy to escape this place. The cracks in the security are so evident I almost laugh. But the inevitable torture I would endure if the Shadow Dealer doesn't believe my story also keep me in these dark walls. King Addard believes in swift death, the victims feeling pain for only a few seconds. The Shadow Dealer is quite the opposite, the torture long and precise.

The head chef, Jorge, was hesitant to have me in his kitchens when Maggis first brought me down into the belly of the palace. After a few hours of waiting for Jorge to acknowledge me, he finally showed me my tasks which turned out to be mostly washing dishes using buckets of warm and cold water to scrub pans clean. The other kitchen staff hurried around the kitchen, plucking feathers off of chicken carcasses and making dishes for the various meals throughout the day. Jorge barked orders as they moved from one task to the next like an organized swarm of bees. I stayed out of the way in my corner of the kitchen, away from the wrath of Jorge and the constant movement of people. My hands became red and tender by the end of the first day.

That night, I took the bunk furthest away from the stable hands without looking for anyone's permission. A pungent smell of horse manure overpowers the small room which had only two windows.

Someone flipped open the wooden shutters as if it was routine for them.

"Take a bath, man!" Another man scoffed gruffly from the bottom bunk opposite of me. The room erupted in a commotion of laughter and chatter.

A scrawny boy whose bunk I took looked up at me and decided it was not worth arguing. The small bunk could barely be classified as a bed and swayed under my weight. A mattress sewn together with thick squares of wool and stuffed with straw was as uncomfortable as it sounded. Two blankets were provided and I overlapped them to make sure I had enough to cover my body.

I was told that the room house male servants in the palace who owed the king a debt. Each of us at the king's mercy provided us unspoken common ground. Since my arrival and to my surprise, no one has bothered me much. A few of them intentionally bump into me and look me up and down but I don't react. However, the thoughts in my head tell a different story. Playing out scenarios where I drive each one of their heads into the stone wall if pushed too far.

Now, during the few spare minutes I have before we're forced to our bunks in the evenings, I walk whatever hallways I have access to, mapping every square inch in my mind. It's easier when I'm not half asleep and under the delirium of a bleeding wound.

I see Lylah in the servant's dining quarters the next morning at lunch. Her blonde hair is combed and braided, trailing down her back over a simple light gray cotton dress that hangs on her slim figure. She looks around nervously while holding her bowl of stew and bread. It almost feels like eternity before her eyes land on mine and she makes her way towards me with a wide smile. The first smile I've ever seen on her.

"Lylah." Her name feels oddly soothing on my tongue. "What are you doing here?" I ask as I feel my face form a smile back. The gesture feels unusual. I let it fall as quickly as it appears.

She sits on the bench opposite me. "After the guards took you away, the king offered me a job as a maid. I figured that working here would get me higher wages than in a town with at least a bed to sleep in."

I stir my stew with a wooden spoon. "At least you're paid to be here."

Lylah's bright smile fades and an awkward silence envelopes us. I do my best to ignore the sudden uncomfortability and eat my meal. I shouldn't have said anything to make her feel guilty for my situation but my stirring bitterness won't let me.

The chatter of the other servants in the dining quarters finally fills the void between us. We were never friends, but somehow, we probably know only each other here beyond first names and quick hellos. Her shoulders sag in a way that wasn't there before as she takes a small bite of her stew.

I clear my throat and break the silence first. "How have you been?"

She doesn't take her eyes off her food. "I've been better."

Taking another bite of my stew, I nod as well. I've certainly been better too.

Someone behind me laughs at something that was whispered. Her eyes snap up before nervously taking a nibble of her bread. Another person whispers and several people laugh louder.

Putting my spoon down, I rotate slowly in my seat to look at them as soon as I hear Lylah's name is mentioned. Three girls laugh again before pausing at my sudden interest.

"What was that?" I ask, clenching my hands on the edge of the table. My bottled-up anger threatens to spill over at any moment.

Lylah grabs my hand, holding me against the table. "Ellis... don't. They're just stupid girls with nothing else to do."

I struggle to contain my anger. My fists clench tightly in her grip but I choose to take a deep breath. What's wrong with me that I would almost let my emotions take over like that?

One of the girls conceals her giggle. Her eyes daring me to step off the bench and make a scene. Another one bites her lip and rests her head on her hand with batting eyelashes. She mouths something but I don't bother to pay attention.

Lylah tugs again. "Please don't."

Reluctantly, I rotate back. "How long have they been bothering you?"

"Not very long." Her voice is small as she sinks back to the bench. "I can handle it."

It doesn't look like she's handling it. The dark circles lingering around her eyes become more pronounced. As if every ounce of happiness has been sucked from her life. I doubt happiness exists in this place, but there are still small joys like the delicious meals and warm fresh bread.

I hesitantly let the topic go. "So, what do they have you doing as a maid?" I can't say I care about the tasks of a maid but taking her mind off of the snickering will help. My bitterness slips just a little bit.

She sighs. "Lots of scrubbing, sweeping, mopping, cleaning and mending." Dipping her bread in the soup, she asks, "What about you? How does the kitchen work go?"

"I wash dishes mostly but I'm learning about cooking too."

Lylah offers me a small smile before bringing the last spoonful of soup to her lips. I hold up my blistered hands and a slice of empathy crosses her face.

Holding her hands up as well, she chuckles. "Looks like we're matching."

A small smile passes on my lips, wishing for a brief second I can take the blisters away just to see true happiness in those blue eyes.

Maybe saving her wasn't the worst decision I ever made.

"How's the wound healing?"

I instinctively put my hand on my torso. "It's healing. Finnon, the court healer, checks on it every other day. The stitching should be ready to come out in a few days."

Her body seems to relax as I finish my soup. There's nothing I want to do more than sit here a few moments longer but I have a mission to do. Work hard, keep my head down, and do what I'm told. The king said that the length of the sentence depends entirely on my ability to do all of those things.

I stand with my dish in hand. "I better get back to the kitchens soon, lots of scrubbing to catch up on."

Lylah quickly stands too. "I should get going as well."

We walk between the rows of other servants talking amongst themselves as I observe other maids snickering in Lylah's direction. My eyebrows scrunch but I choose not to say anything as we make our way out of the dining hall.

"Will you be here for dinner?" She looks up at me with a scrunched brow.

I nod with a small grin, hoping it will help ease her. "Yes. If you get here before me, just save me a seat, okay?"

A sigh escapes between her full lips and she nods before disappearing down the stone corridor and around the corner.

Once in the kitchens, Jorge sets dirty pots and pans in my workstation, the last bits of stew already crusty on the edges. Sighing quietly so Jorge doesn't hear, I roll up my sleeves and get to work.

Jorge whistles as he throws pieces of chopped potatoes into a pot of boiling water. His muscular build doesn't match the appearance of a normal cook. The cooks I've seen are stout in size but Jorge is quite the opposite. A scar runs across his left forearm along with dark marks that peek out from his rolled-up sleeves tell a different story. My guess is he hasn't been doing this work his whole life.

I clear my throat. "How did you come to be in the king's service?"

At first, Jorge grumbles loudly but he answers after stretched out minutes. "I was a captain of one of the merchant ships." The knife dances in his hand as he chops. "Got caught makin' a bad trade and the king's guard arrested me at the port. I was given the option to swin' by my neck or to work for the king." He looks up. "Choice was easy."

"How long have you been here?" I can't help but be curious about his answer.

His dark brown eyes narrow. "Comin' up on ten years. My sentence ended last year but I chose to stay."

"Were you a captain during the Arliean War?" I ask hesitantly. The sensitive topic of the war usually stirs a wide range of emotions among older citizens.

He lifts his head but doesn't respond immediately. "No, I was only a shipmate at the start of the war. It was a brutal time when the Arlieans invaded us. They burned our northern cities and villages first as thousands of their soldiers marched south towards Rinmor."

I rinse another pot and frown. "Why did they invade us anyway? It makes no sense to me." Everyone I would ask, they each said a different answer.

Jorge exhales loudly like I've annoyed him. "They wanted our port, of course."

"Couldn't they have just struck a deal with King Medrin for the use of our port?" King Medrin was King Addard's late father and a stubborn man who rarely negotiated but demanded. At least those are the whispers.

"Greed is a powerful disease. It spreads until it's all-consumin'." He takes a deep breath. "If ya look at a map of the continent," he waves his knife as if drawing in the air. "Narvidium is on the southern portion of the continent and Rinmor, our capital, is at the tip down here. Now, there are long stretches of ragged rocks on the sides of the continent we call the Ribs. There's no other stretch of seacoast that would be able to have a port without the high risk of ships wreckin' into the Ribs. No one knows how deep it's between them. No one that has tried ever came back."

"Rinmor has the only port access to the Balgorn Sea," I say, finally understanding the motive. The Balgorn Sea is the only gateway to trade with the continent and kingdom to our east. Korrim is rich in luxury resources the wealthy need like spices and silk. When I worked on the ships, no one ever connected the two. They simply didn't talk about the war, avoiding the subject like it would curse them.

"Now ya're gettin' it, kid." He resumes chopping but I'm left with so many questions.

I turn to lean back against the sink as he continues. "Most of the trade stopped towards the end due to sailors joinin' the king's army in droves. Me bein' among them."

With the conversation turning over in my head, I decide to ask, "What made you want to join the fighting instead of waiting it out?"

Jorge slams his knife down on the table. "Because the royal family was slaughtered in their sleep, that's why. No warnin', no nothin'."

"Wasn't it King Addard's father who had the Arliean baby prince kidnapped and threatened to kill him to demand a stop to the invasion?" I ask and watch as his nostrils flare. "When the Arliean king refused peace, didn't they kill the baby?"

"Oh, so ya know that but not why they invaded us in the first place? Who even raised ya?" He looks away, annoyance clear on his face now.

I didn't realize I struck a nerve. Resuming my work with the next stack of dishes, I let my mind absorb the new bits of information.

His voice bellows behind me. "We may have killed the babe but they're the ones who refused to surrender, to stop the endless killin' of our people. We were peaceful when they decided to invade, burnin' homes and killin' women and children." He pauses before inhaling a deep breath. "Ultimately, they did the unthinkable thing. Killin' almost our entire royal family. The crown prince and the innocent twin princesses along with the king and queen. The Arliean King Founar let only four-year-old Addard live."

I don't say anything as the soap foams around my rag. There's nothing I can really say in this somber moment. I remember the tavern songs, how they depict a beautiful tale of the whole kingdom going into deep mourning. When Arliea came to try to take the port again after that, farmers and merchants banded together to drive them back. It's common knowledge that a treaty was signed after more months of brutal killing.

The agreement is approaching its twentieth year and according to the whispers in the streets, old wounds and hurt pride refuse to heal. Now, the appearance of peace between the kingdoms allows for trading across borders to be profitable for all but it hangs by a thread.

Hopefully, I'll be away from this city when the thread finally snaps.

Chapter 8
Lylah

I hate it here. I don't want to admit it but I do.

It's been over a month and I've barely adjusted to my new environment. Most of the other maids are mean and the living arrangement is only a step above what I had in the orphanage. Ten dekari a week with a place to sleep and three meals a day are the only things making me grit my teeth and bear it.

When I first met Eliera, head of the maids, she reminded me of Ms. Gentrow. Her harsh features were as rigid as her personality, with a defined jawline and upturned nose. A dark gray cotton dress adorned with a ring of keys at her hip signaled her presence.

She showed me the tasks I would be doing each day, and it wasn't much different from what I expected. A few of the other maids said quick hellos, but none of them were eager to get to know me. It only took me a week to realize why. They envy my freedom. I'm among four other maids who are here by choice. The rest are paying a debt for various crimes and were offered the same deal that Ellis got.

It didn't take long for them to start whispering behind my back. I ignored it the best I could. Their laughter and hateful words chipped away at my calm exterior each day. Now, I just channel the same tactic I did in the orphanage, removing myself from their attention the best I can.

The worst of them all is a maid named Jesimie. She snickers at me from across the room and has two other friends with her who are always where I happen to be. Commenting about me as if I was unsightly or deformed, but at least I am free. She's indebted to the king for some kind of crime and will likely be chained to this damp, cold place for a long time. At least that's the hope and it soothes me.

Ellis didn't hear what those girls said at lunch that day, but I think he knows I'm getting bullied. A small part of me is relieved he doesn't know where I come from. A child rejected by her parents and left on the orphanage steps. He risked his life to save someone who wasn't worth saving.

Today, Ellis waits at the entrance to the dining quarters like he promised and just gives me an acknowledging nod. The dining room is quite sizable to fit ten tables and benches all facing the same direction with large windows streaming in glowing light through dusty windows. A rancid mixture of sweat, dirt, and manure smells hit my nose as soon as we step in line for our meal. After a month, I still haven't gotten used to it.

We take bowls of steaming fish and potato stew and cups of water before walking to an empty table in silence. I don't mind the silence though. I'm just relieved I have someone to eat with me without feeling all alone in a room of strangers.

Ellis is lost in thought as he takes his first few bites but catches me staring a few times, to which I look away quickly. From the next table, Jesimie gives me an unreadable smirk, takes her dark brown hair out of a twisted bun, and adjusts it around her shoulders. She stands from the bench and walks towards us with oozing confidence. My gut squeezes as she takes a seat next to Ellis and puts her hand on his defined upper arm.

"You must be Lylah's special friend," she says as she looks up at him through full lashes.

I take in her perfectly slender nose and lush lips, wishing I could be gifted with such qualities. Her skin is the shade of fallen pine cones on a forest floor, indicating to me that she's not from Nardivium at all but from Korrim. It would be easy to use that against her but I know what it's like to be different from everyone else.

Ellis looks at her hand and shrugs it off. It falls to the table in a satisfying thud. I smirk into my spoon. The broth tastes sweeter from her obvious rejection.

Disappointment crosses her face briefly, but she tries again. "I'm

Jesimie." Her finger slides along his arm this time. "I hope you don't mind me introducing myself."

Her flowing black hair is displayed delicately around the outline of her breasts as she moves closer. My hand curls around my dress skirt as I watch her manipulations try to get in the middle of our meal. She clearly wants to claim the only person that matters to me here.

She leans in, causing her lips to brush his ear, as she whispers something to him. His expression doesn't change before giving a small smile as he sips his drink. I clench my skirt harder and breathe slowly through threatening tears. Ellis sets the cup on the table after she giggles at whatever she says.

His voice is quiet but clear when he finally speaks. "If you ever come over here or touch me again, you'll regret it. I would never be interested in you." His cold eyes are inches from hers. "I suggest you leave Lylah and me alone."

Jesimie's face turns from smugness to genuine hurt as the words sink in. Tears pool in her dark eyes before storming back to her table. Her friends comfort her instantly and whisper amongst each other while staring threats in our direction.

My face cracks the widest smile for the first time since being here. I would pay every dekari I've earned this week just to see her witness her rejection again.

Ellis stares up at me and I return his glance. "Thank you," I whisper. "But I have to know. What did she say to you?"

His expression turns contemplative before finally answering me.

"She told me to meet her somewhere so she can show me a good time. As tempting as it was, I could tell she had hurt you in some way so it was an immediate no."

Even though Ellis and I are the best each other has in this place, he has every right to be with whomever he wants to.

After we finish our meal, I nearly skip to my afternoon duties.

I've been slowly adjusting to this new lifestyle with each passing day. Comfort in the routine gives me solace. I tuck away every dekari into a slit in my mattress. Hopefully, I'll have enough to move far away from this place. Rinmor has been nothing but heartache. I want a new start and even explore the other kingdoms.

When I was little, I imagined myself getting on a ship and sailing away. In the orphanage, I was fortunate enough to sleep by a window facing the ocean. When the caregivers finally fell asleep down the hall, I would sneak out of my bed and look out across to the harbor. Street lanterns dusted the darkness and moonlight shone off the surface of the water, allowing my mind to wander. What if my parents found me and claimed me as their own? What if they never intended to give me up? They could be explorers of far-off lands and come back to whisk me away on their next adventure.

But it was all childish dreams. They never came, and I was still an orphan.

Now, I have a new dream.

After lunch the next day, I head to the library for my afternoon task of dusting the books in the king's grand library. I pass two female guards who merely glance at my light gray dress, a color which indicates that I'm a lower-class staff member, not an indebted servant who wears light blue.

King Addard doesn't use the library often from what I've been told, and the last scholar who kept the books died many years ago. The sheer size of it is too much to take in at once. Intricately carved wood shelves stretch up towards the high ceilings in a breathtaking way. Small square windows embedded on the right wall permit the afternoon sun to bask the room in a golden glow.

I trace my finger across the spines of rare leather-bound books tucked away in their places, categorized in order of title and name of scribe. I've never been one to love reading, but this place gives me a sense of peace I've never felt in my life. The dusty books won't judge me here. They only tell stories of history and people long forgotten.

Voices echo in the vast library and I retract my fingers. With the cleaning cloth in my hand, I begin my work dusting as I should have been in case Eliera comes to check on me.

A female voice sounds to the left. "We know you're here."

The tone is taunting, sending uneasiness through me. My chest tightens at the words.

Another girl's voice comes from the right. "Come out from wherever you are." A brief silence. "We just want to talk."

My breath quickens at the comment. My senses are on high alert.

I have to get out of here. Tucking my cleaning cloth in my apron, I walk briskly to the only doors leading out of the library. Every nerve in my body is telling me I'm in for another ridicule session that I don't have the strength to take today.

"Going somewhere?"

I gasp as Jesimie intercepts me.

"Yes." I swallow hard. "Eliera. She asked me to meet her when I finished." The lie is easy, but I don't think it'll save me.

She smirks. "You can see her in a bit."

Glancing over my shoulder, I spot two more girls standing a short distance behind me. A wave of fear thunders through my veins as I realize Jesimie has an unsettling coldness to her round eyes.

I assess my surroundings for a weapon in case things escalate. They are too close to me to push my way through, and the only possible weapon within reach is a brass candlestick that sits on a side table nearby. To get it, I'll have to run several feet and lunge. Either way, it will have to be my last resort.

Jesimie steps closer and laughs dryly. "Oh, you like to play games. I love a challenge." I try to move back but the other two are standing so close that I step into them.

"Ellis is quite the catch. Not sure how you managed to land him, but he's the most attractive guy in this depressing place." She circles me like a hungry lion and I'm her next meal. A shiver escapes down my back but I force my face to be void of all emotion like I've learned to do.

"I don't know what you're talking about," I reply. Jesimie has the wrong impression about us. He only hangs around me at mealtimes because he feels sorry for me.

"The muscles on that man could do impressive things." She stops in front of me and closes her eyes as if imagining him. "He's certainly delicious with those piercing eyes and chiseled jaw."

When I don't say anything, she clenches her jaw. "All wasted on a sewer rat like you." Her face contorts as she grabs my chin in her rough hands.

"I know what he said yesterday was..." She chews on her lip, "Hurtful, but it was only because you have him under some kind of spell. Why else would a gorgeous man like that look at you the way he does?"

She forces me to meet her eyes again, but I have no idea what she's talking about. Ellis doesn't look at me in any special way, only how he usually looks at me... with indifference.

"What if we carve up your face a bit? Then he won't find it so captivating." Jesimie pulls out a knife from her apron and presses it into my cheek in one sharp motion. Hands clench my arms to my body from behind with bruising strength.

"Are you crazy!" I exclaim as I struggle against their firm grip. "I have no clue what you are talking about. Ellis and I aren't together. We're barely even friends."

"I think I'll save the best for last." Jesimie moves the knife, the cool metal trailing down my right bicep instead. "How about just a little cut to start us off?"

She drags the sharp knife into my skin and down my arm. I

scream as the pain is instant and all-consuming. A hand clasps over my mouth and I cry underneath it. Hot tears stream down my face uncontrollably. Time slows as metal slices flesh with each passing second.

Searing pain racks my body. My mind fills with chaos.

"Stop!" I scream, but my cry is muffled. Her eyes are inhumanly lifeless. How can someone be this cruel?

"You want me to stop? Tell Ellis to meet me here tonight after dinner and make sure you convince him this time."

She moves the knife back to my cheek, blood dripping off of it onto the front of my dress.

I manage to free one of my arms and push the knife away from me. Panic ripples through me like it has never flooded my body before. Unexpected heat starts at my shoulders and shoots down to my fingertips. I cry out again and manage to free the other arm. Jesimie wrestles her knife further towards me despite my efforts.

A scream deafens my ears as Jesimie falls to the side. The knife drops with a clang on the stone floor. The other two girls release my arms in seconds, scattering away as I collapse.

Desperately, I crawl away from the sight before me. Jesimie's clothes are on fire. Flames burning brighter as the screams grow louder, the sound sickening. My ears ring. She screams more as she claws at herself.

Suppressing a sob, I keep crawling towards the door. My mind rages in every direction. Every feeling flashes through me as my hands go numb. Energy drains out of my body with each breath.

The other two girls run through the doors as I struggle to focus on it. Darkness creeps in. My body goes limp against the hard, cold floor.

Warmth hums in my chest as I feel another tear roll down my face and my eyes flicker closed.

Chapter 9
Lylah

My head is pounding when sleep tingles from my body. I grunt as I attempt to open my eyes but they feel heavier than normal.

The room I find myself in is dimly lit by a stream of light coming through a crack in drawn curtains to my left. A plush blanket engulfs me on all sides, softer than the smoothest leather. Every muscle screams in agony as I attempt to swing my legs from under the covers. Nausea rolls over me and I groan. A fur rug meets my toes and I frown at the unfamiliar feeling.

A glass of water glistens on a dark wooden bedside table as I glance over sleepily. I gulp it down quickly to satisfy my scratchy throat. My eyes wander curiously over the rim.

An older man sits at the table in the corner of the vast room with glass jars of dried leaves and flowers set in disarray before him. He holds one up in the small stream of light and shakes it before catching my gaze. His gray beard ripples down his chest as he gives me a kind smile with blue eyes full warm and full of compassion.

"Who are you?" I whisper hoarsely as I grip my covers closer to my chest.

My memory is still blurry, but bits and pieces of what happened in the library come flooding in. Memories of the knife slicing into my arm play over and over in my head. Moments that will be burned into my mind for as long as I live along with others I keep buried deep inside. I close my eyes in hopes of stopping my spinning head.

He remains seated where he is with the jar still up in the air. "I'm Finnon, the palace healer."

My fear slowly dwindles. I recognize the name as the healer who worked on Ellis a few weeks ago. Sinking back against the softest pillows I've ever felt, I reassure myself I'm safe for now.

Uneasiness still lingers in my belly. I've grown accustomed to it lately, more than before.

Finnon hums a tune while he pours dried plants from his jars into a stone bowl, using a rounded rock to crush them. Feeling small in this grand room, it's oddly comforting having someone else here. A stream of light pushes dances on the forest green and gold wallpaper. Vases of flowers sit on the fireplace mantle, bringing color to this darkened room.

The stones pound together when I ask, "What are you making?"

"Narvidium grows a rare flower called poifoss that holds a healing property only when crushed. I'm making you tea that will ease the headache you feel while releasing tension in your muscles. The king enjoys a brew of this tea on occasion, so nothing to fear, I assure you."

Finnon scoops a small amount of the mixture from the bowl into a steaming cup of water with a delicate metal spoon and stirs gently. He sets the tea on the bedside table before heading back to his seat across the room.

He nods towards the tea. "You can drink the leaves but be careful, it is hot." While gathering his jars into a basket, he turns to me. "How are you feeling?"

My fingers graze over a cloth bandage on my arm. A small throb radiates from under the barely noticeable bandage. I touch my face at the memory of my other wound. A thick cream covers my cheek, so I don't touch it for too long.

He straightens. "Would you mind if I inspect them? I want to make sure there is no infection."

The mention of infection sends a fresh wave of alarm through me. But if Finnon healed Ellis' wound, I conclude that I'm in the most knowledgeable hands.

I nod. He gingerly unwraps the bandage on my arm first and inspects the wound with skilled eyes, pressing on the surrounding skin. I avoid looking, knowing it will remind me of those horrible moments. My attention is fixated instead on a painting that depicts a beautiful grassy landscape. Two figures are running hand in hand. The brush strokes and use of yellow paint makes me feel like I can step into the painting and touch the tall grass between my fingers too.

Finnon scratches his beard and moves my arm back and forth.

"How odd," he finally concludes.

I peer at him. "What's odd?"

"The cuts," he pauses, "They seemed to have mostly healed."

"What?" I sit up and inspect the wound for myself. He's right. The gash has shrunk to a barely visible line.

I frown, touching the thin scab. "How long has it been? How long have I been asleep?"

Finnon answers slowly, "Only two days."

"I've been asleep for two days?" The answer is obvious but I feel like I'm dreaming. The throb forming behind my eyes makes it hard to think.

"When the knife..." I let the words die on my tongue. "The bleeding was significant. It went so deep it felt like it cut through more than just skin. How could it have healed this fast?"

I instinctively touch my face again. Beneath the cream, it's almost completely smooth underneath. It doesn't feel tender like I expect it to.

"Very odd indeed." He doesn't elaborate more but proceeds to push back the thick curtains to reveal a set of doors leading outside.

The doors push open and a chilly breeze blows in.

The fast transformation of light in the room forces me to shield my eyes. Shadows of trees swaying cast themselves onto the floor. While the change to the room is welcome, questions invade my mind as I analyze my arm under the brighter light.

Finnon finds his way back to where he was before with a dark gray floor length tunic wrapped loosely around him. A ring of various sized metal keys sit on the table before he hangs them on his belt. They clink together in a disjointed melody as he adjusts himself in the plush leather chair.

My compass. Where is my compass? I frantically feel around the folds of the bed covers.

Finnon's alerted voice cuts through my thoughts. "What are you looking for?"

"I had a compass with me." I look around. "I can't find it."

My heart is nearly pounding out of my chest. I can't lose my only link to my parents.

"Oh," Finnon fumbles around in his pocket before pulling out the one thing I possess in this entire world.

He brings it over to me and lays it gently in my hand. "I was keeping it safe for you."

I press the compass to my chest. Relief washes over me, like everything will be okay for the first time.

Settling back down against my pillows, I ask, "How did I get here, by the way? Where am I?"

I don't recognize this room. Not even from my time cleaning the many rooms in this palace. I reach for the cup of tea he left and take a long sip, awaiting his answer.

The silence engulfs us before he speaks. "You are in the king's wing of the palace. Another servant found you in the library and alerted the guards, who then alerted the king. His Majesty ordered you to be brought here to rest and for me to attend to your wounds."

I wrap an arm around myself as I process his words. Why would the king bring me, a lowly maid, to his guest rooms?

As if to sense my thoughts, he adds, "That is all I know."

All he knows? I don't believe for a second that's all he knows, but I press my lips together, anyway. Silence lingers once more like the dust flecks that dance in a downward spiral.

After nearly five minutes, Finnon looks around and smiles. "It has been so long since these rooms have been used. It feels good to see life in them again."

This room is shrouded in sorrow the more I look at it. I wonder whose room this is or was. The tragic story of the king's family lodges a lump in my throat and I feel closer to their memory here.

Just as I'm about to ask another question, the door swings open and the king walks in. Finnon stands slowly with a slight limp, but bows expertly. The king is only looking at me with an intense gaze that I can't begin to interpret. Do I need to stand as well? I tried that earlier, and it didn't go well.

"Finnon, leave us," the king orders.

My body tenses at the thought of being alone with him, a male stranger no matter his status. Finnon bows his head but whispers something in the king's ear before leaving. King Addard's eyes go wide briefly. Finnon's keys jingle as he heads out of the door with one of his baskets.

King Addard brings a chair closer to the bed and takes a seat cautiously. We hold a gaze for several seconds as I lift the bed covers up to my chin when I realize I'm only wearing a sleeping gown.

"Your name is Lylah?" The king speaks softly, and I nod. "We had quite a unique introduction, so I remember you." He presses his lips together before continuing. "I know you may not be the most comfortable right now. I want to ask if there is someone you would like to be here with you. Perhaps a maid you have befriended during your time here?"

My mind immediately goes to the only person I want with me. "Ellis. If you remember me then you must remember him." He's an unconventional choice, but I want him to know I'm okay.

The king raises an eyebrow but calls for his guard, who appears in just seconds. The guard nods at the order and disappears.

Minutes trickle by slowly and I nervously sip my tea again, finally noticing the taste. It has an herbal flavor with notes of sweet honey and citrus. I try to avoid looking at the king but catch myself glancing in his direction, anyway. When I do, he is looking out of the open doors towards the trees. Birds chirp in the fall air, but his forehead is scrunched in deep thought. I wonder what he's thinking about so intensely.

I examine him more closely in the light. The crown isn't on his head as it was the night I met him. Golden brown eyes accent his creamy olive skin. A thin nose and high cheekbones are framed by loose black curls that stop just above the nape of his neck. He doesn't look like a king but a young man, not much older than me, with the weight of the kingdom on his shoulders.

Ellis opens the door and his face twists when he sees me, almost as if concerned. To see such a distinct emotion on his face is unusual. His eyes shift to the king before his jaw clenches and gives a quick bow before turning his gaze back to me.

"How are you feeling?" He scans my face before settling at my glistening cheek and unwrapped arm.

I smile through the discomfort. "I'm okay. I've been better though." The familiar words we've exchanged several times lighten the mood. He clenches his fists before tucking them in his trouser pockets and stands near the farthest corner of the canopied bed. Somehow, it doesn't feel like he's in the same room but miles away.

King Addard observes our interaction before speaking again. "I just want to begin by apologizing for what has happened to you. The guards strictly enforce the rules here. I have no idea why those maids felt so bold to use such violence in my palace." He pauses and folds his hands. "Rest assured that she has been punished severely with a decade added to her sentence and strict guard supervision."

I nod at his apology and take another sip of the tea. It slides down my throat and settles warmly in my stomach. I'm glad Jesimie was punished for her crimes, but there's nothing else to say.

"Oddly enough, Ellis is the one that found you in the library. He told the guards that when you didn't meet him for dinner, he knew something was wrong and went looking for you. Good thing he found you in time. You had been badly injured, unconscious and bleeding all over the floor." He fidgets with his edge of his robe.

Ellis shifts his feet and I can't imagine what I must've looked like in the library when he found me. Unknown thoughts blaze in his eyes before looking away quickly.

The king clears his throat before continuing, "Lylah, I understand that you lived here in Rinmor when Ellis rescued you from those sailors. I don't know the backgrounds of my servants when I employ them, but I would like to learn your story if you are comfortable telling it."

I gather my thoughts; the truth will have to come out. I don't think I can tell a convincing lie at the moment. "Yes. I was born here, in the city... I believe." I hold the edge of the sheets. "I was dropped off at the city orphanage when I was a baby, so I don't know my parents. I was released from the orphanage the day we were captured. I was attempting to find work that day, as I told you."

Ellis straightens in my peripheral vision. The king rubs his stubbled chin and looks out of the door at the garden again.

King Addard finally adjusts himself in the chair, causing his robe's graceful folds to shift. "Jesimie was found badly burned in the library. Finnon has been treating her wounds, but he is not sure she will make it through another day."

I inhale sharply at the mention of the library and what had happened with her. Everything floods back in waves. Nausea twists in my stomach like a hurricane. Jesimie's mocking face swimming in my vision and her lifeless eyes fueling my need to run away.

Ellis murmurs something to the effect of, "What she deserves."

The king continues slowly, "We seem to think that you may have used the candle from the table close by to light her on fire, but the wax wasn't melted when I inspected it. It was a brand new candlestick placed there only that morning."

My brows furrow, but thinking back, I'm not sure how she got set on fire. None of it makes sense. My mind was consumed only with escaping in those last moments. The candle was my only option for a weapon, but it was nearly impossible to get to.

King Addard leans closer and rubs his face thoughtfully. "Do you remember feeling anything before she caught on fire? A pain in your chest or perhaps a burning sensation in your arms or hands?"

I look down at my hands as the sensations rush back at me. "Yes, I felt a burning sensation in my shoulders and arms."

King Addard exhales loudly and stands abruptly, pacing back and forth across the finely woven blue rug. Fiercely focused, he whispers to himself like a beggar gone mad.

Ellis moves closer to me without hesitation..

"What does that mean?" I sit up straighter. The tea almost spills out of the delicate teacup in my hands.

King Addard stops pacing with wide eyes. He mumbles to himself, "I can't believe this... it can't be true."

"What can't be true? What does this mean?" I raise my voice in a plea. Even Ellis stands a little straighter, seeming to assess the room.

The king sits back down, a hand over his mouth in what looks to be disbelief. He's staring at me with new intensity. My eyes scan his as I await an answer.

"I didn't think it could be true, but the sensation you felt has been described in history books as a sign of someone very powerful." The silence is deafening. "Do you remember the stories of the Five Mages of Old?"

"Yes." Everyone knows the stories, even the orphans. Two hundred years ago, there were five mages that fought to bring balance between the kingdoms. But they vanished after the last War of the Kings. No one really knows what happened and some speculate they simply retired and died of old age. Some say they died in battle and some believe they still walk among us.

"The legend states that Five Mages will rise again to bring balance to the kingdoms in times of war. Once a mage is awakened, the other four will gain their powers soon after." He pauses as he looks at me with wonder. "There was only one most powerful, the Fire Mage."

My brows burrow. Why is he trying to tell me a history lesson?

"Lylah, you are a Fire Mage." His eyes widen as if in awe. As if he is staring at something impossible.

My heart pounds uncontrollably.

My reality collapses with those six words.

Chapter 10
Ellis

"What do you mean she's a Fire Mage?" I interject him. "They haven't been around for two hundred years. They all supposedly died in the last Great War of the Kings. Most people don't even believe they were real." The words bubble out of my mouth before I remember I'm speaking to our king.

King Addard shakes his head. "Since last night, I believed that as well. When I inspected the library where Lylah was found, the fire started at Jesimie's face. The other maids confirmed it after we found them. They said flames came out of Lylah's hand when she was trying to push Jesimie away."

Lylah looks at the king like he just spoke a foreign language. Her mind appears to race behind those blue eyes and I feel mine doing the same.

He continues quickly, "The last two days, I pulled everything I could find on the mages' lives, every history book from that time, and even a personal journal from King Lenthor."

King Addard stands while chewing on his lower lip. "If you remember your history lessons, he was the king of Narvidium at the time of the last mages. His accounts confirmed my suspicions. So did you when you remembered that burning sensation. From what I found, an emotional event awakens the power of the most powerful mage of the five. Just like the one you had several days ago."

Lylah focuses at me, as if to gauge my belief in the king's wild tales. Her face reflects a mixture of confusion and disbelief, which isn't too far from what I'm feeling. I narrow my eyes at the king as he exudes a new energy. Like he has found a lost treasure and intends to never let it go.

"What if I'm not the Fire Mage?" Her voice is barely audible, and she pushes her blonde waves out of her face. "What if this is all a misunderstanding and I'm not who you say I am?"

King Addard shakes his head as he sits back down on the edge of the chair.

"There is no mistake. There is no other explanation for the fire in the library." His excited voice continues, "You are what we have been waiting for. Your birth and manifestation has been predicted in ink for the past two hundred years."

She puts down the teacup she has been clenching and rubs her temples. It's unbelievable, ludicrous even.

"I need fresh air... I can't breathe in here right now." Lylah pushes back her bed covers and stands up on wobbly legs. She grips the nightstand beside her and it takes everything in me not to run to her side.

King Addard reaches out to help her. She shakes her head. "No, I'm okay, thank you."

He lets her pass but keeps his eyes averted. Only my eyes follow her every movement. The thin fabric of her nightgown is evident in the light as she folds her hands over her chest once outside. Strands of hair sway with the wind in the privacy of the walled garden. Her shoulders rise and fall with each deep breath. I pry my eyes away.

"What will happen to her?" I ask with clenched fists still in my pockets.

A sense of protectiveness surges through me as I stand here watching her. The loose gown engulfs her small body, improper for her to wear in the company of two men alone in this bedroom.

All that aside, I can't begin to imagine what's going through her head at this moment. To be told she's a Fire Mage and the power of her fire almost killed a girl yesterday. Taking a life is something you never forget. I know that from experience.

King Addard turns to me. "I will provide her a luxurious life in my court. The world will want to see when they hear of her. They will come from every kingdom to witness this miraculous event. She will be well looked after under my protection."

"And after that?" I say quietly so only he can hear.

"According to King Lenthor's journal, she will learn to control her powers and lead the others when the time is right. Afterwards, they will go to the Tower of Mages in the Balgorn Sea with the other awakened mages. " He pauses. "War and mass casualties must be imminent if a Fire Mage is awakened."

My chest tightens as I say, "But the Tower of Mages has never been found since the last mages. Many merchants and pirates have tried to find it to plunder its rumored riches, but they never returned."

"It is true. It hasn't been found yet, but it was always written that the mages will know where to find it when it's time." The king shifts in his chair as if lacking confidence in his own words. It takes a lot of blind faith to believe in something that hasn't been found in two hundred years.

I pity Lylah as I glance at her again. The responsibility that will fall on her shoulders is immense. Almost crushing, even for someone experienced in pressure like this. I hope she will be strong enough to bear the expectations that will be placed on her.

Flower petals from the nearest cherry blossom tree drop with a new gush of wind.

Turning sharply to me, he speaks quietly but steadily. "You are the only other person that knows about this. Do not repeat this to anyone or there will be consequences for your loose tongue."

I swallow hard, not doubting a word of his threats. "You have my word of silence, Your Majesty."

"Good. Just because she trusts you does not mean I do. I have heard of your reputation in my city and knew who you were the moment we met." He smirks softly. "I did think the Shadow Dealer would be older."

Everything in my mind lurches to a halt. It's amusing he thinks I'm the Shadow Dealer but I can use that to my advantage. The threat is evident but subtle enough that I keep myself from correcting him. I already have a hard time sleeping in the crowded room with the other servants. I don't need to be afraid of the king's men slitting my throat in the middle of the night as well.

King Addard walks towards the main doors. "You get to keep your life, don't worry. Lylah will be well taken care of in my court and protected at my side." He smiles, but it doesn't reach his eyes. "I wouldn't count on seeing her any time soon."

My hands clenched at my sides, I exit without a way of saying goodbye.

Chapter 11
Lylah

The room is thick with tension, like a tangible layer has settled on every surface.

Maids come to dress me in my evening attire. Their eyes avoid mine. It's funny to think that only a week ago they turned up their noses at me and now they have to serve my every need. I smile at the irony and can't help but revel in their discomfort.

Eliera enters and ushers the maids out of the new rooms the king has been kind to assign to me. A strained smile spreads across her thin lips.

I refuse to let anything bother me because today is the king's birthday. To celebrate, he's planning to host a dinner with his advisors and councilmen. I never imagined I would be invited to join him at his side. With expectations set high for tonight, I have to be perfect in every way. I inspect my dress in the large mirror embossed in polished gold. The girl staring back at me looks like me, but I don't recognize her at all. Like an impostor playing dress up.

The dress I'm in is exquisite, with its deep blue silk fabric and detailed gold beading resembling flames sewn across the skirt. A bodice secures my waist with cloth outlining my chest and wrapping loosely around my arms to my wrists. The sleeves with its ivory carved buttons flow gracefully with any slight movement. My hair is curled and pinned elegantly at the nape of my neck with a few strands framing my face. The red streak in my hair is tucked back so as to not draw attention.

I inspect my face closer. Smudges of pink accentuate my cheekbones while a red liquid is painted across my lips. The cut on my cheek is barely visible now. The one on my arm has also healed, invisible to everyone but those who know what happened.

Eliera clears her throat and bends down to adjust the folds of my skirt.

Her voice is firm when she speaks. "My girls spent three days making this dress for you by the king's orders. It's odd to me that the king would request flames when you nearly killed Jesimie with that candle."

A tiny sting of hurt flashes across my chest. I was never considered one of her girls and made to work harder than the rest.

I push the feeling aside.

New found strength floods my veins when I meet her challenging gaze. She doesn't know who they think I am or why the king believes I'm important. She believes I harmed a fellow maid, but that's not the whole narrative. Eliera wasn't there when Jesimie gripped my jaw or sliced her knife deep into my arm. A part of me itches to tell her. What Jesimie really did to me. I want her face to turn to fear and awe. For the smug expression on her face to be wiped away, but my secret is not mine anymore. I'm at the mercy of the king and I quite like it here in my current arrangement, regardless of what I want.

"You may go. A guard will escort me to dinner."

She rolls her eyes slightly but proceeds to leave, nevertheless.

The room is quiet and still again. I smooth the folds of my dress, knowing full well they are perfect already.

Tonight is a big deal to the king. He has expressed the importance of using his birthday as the only opportunity to introduce me to his political partners. I've been trying to educate myself on royal etiquette while asking Finnon questions. In the last week, he came to my rooms to inspect my wounds and pretend to replace my bandages to not raise suspicion. After I asked the first time, he brought a few books on proper etiquette the next time he visited. I flipped through them, but they were just words on a page. Studying them tirelessly, I used my sitting room to practice as I muttered the descriptions to myself.

Self-doubt creeps in like an old friend the longer I stare at myself in the enormous mirror. What if I mess up somehow and make a fool of myself? I fidget with the cuff of my sleeve, feeling the smoothness of the ivory button.

A knock vibrates from the door, and I straighten.

"Come in."

The uncertainty of the night has my stomach in knots. Every inch of my body is rippling with excitement and nervousness, like ocean waves crashing against a steady shore.

King Addard enters and his eyes immediately scan the length of my attire with a polite smile. "The dress is exquisite on you. The flames truly mark who you are."

I give him a smile back and curtsy as low as my dress will allow. Having practiced curtsying in front of the mirror all day, I hope it's enough to convince people I belong here.

"Tonight, you will be introduced to my noblemen and advisors. I will not be disclosing to them who you are." His eyes turn serious. "Letting them know too early will have unknown consequences. I take your safety in the highest regard."

He stretches out his gloved hand which I take delicately. A black robe trails behind him as we walk through the unfamiliar hallways. He wears a dark blue vest with gold chains clasped to hold his robe in place with a collared black shirt peeking out. Blue jewels in his crown are perfectly shaped to reflect every light source we pass and the pointed pillars on the top rise resemble tiny knives stretching toward the stone ceiling. His display of royalty is complete with golden eyes that are overshadowed by distracting thoughts.

I chew my lip at the words he spoke earlier. I understand why he can't tell them, but my presence there is bound to make things awkward.

The king's dining hall is prepared with a long table fully set with a red silk table runner and gold plates expertly placed. Platters of different meats and magnificent smelling side dishes of vegetables and fruits enhance the middle of a long, oiled oak table. Freshly polished candlesticks with bright flames shine onto food befitting the king and his honored guests. A chandelier holding countless candles illuminates the room with a warm and radiant glow. Gleaming metal chalices sit waiting along with napkin cloths and silverware.

We stop at to the dining hall entrance as the king adjusts his attire, checking to make sure everything is perfect like I had done. He clenches his jaw and spins a ring set with red and blue stones as the minutes tick by.

It's clear he's nervous and unsettled about something. Somehow, at this moment, he feels more like a normal person and less like a king who hides behind a mask of power.

A group of men appear through the door and immediately bow to their king. Formal greetings are uttered on their lips before each of them give me confused looks and proceed past me to the table.

They turn to glance at each other and exchange whispers. Having prepared myself for sideways glances, I can see them wondering what a woman they've never met is doing on the arm of the king. I try to ignore the growing spikes of anxiety curling around my heart.

I stand by King Addard in an awkward silence that can easily suffocate me. From the jewels around my neck to the hems of my handcrafted gown, I feel more like a stranger in my own body. This show of grandeur is foreign to me, but this is how it must be now. The riches and customs are ones I've stopped myself dreaming of and all I had to do was almost kill a girl to get it. Maybe this is a dream and I'll awaken any minute to the four walls of the orphanage.

The king believes I'm the Fire Mage but I'm not so easily convinced.

A deep breath steadies my wandering thoughts. King Addard gives a reassuring smile before leading me to the plush black leather chair to his right at the table. Every pair of eyes are focused on me as I sit, placing the napkin delicately on my lap as I've seen several of them do moments before.

The king stands with the wine cup raised high. "Welcome, my nobles and advisors. This feast before you is in honor of Narvidium. Tonight, we celebrate the great accomplishments we have made as a kingdom. I know we have an even brighter future."

The guests erupt into applause. Wishes of 'happy birthday' and 'to a wonderful next year' rumbles around the table like a song.

He turns to me when the cheering has quieted. "This is Lylah Farrion, someone who is very special to our kingdom. I have invited her as a guest to this dinner."

There are a few head bows again before servants come with the main courses on silver platters. It's hard to believe that the food already on the table isn't the main course, but I watch spoonfuls from their platters appear on our plates.

I utter a thank you to each of them, and a man with a curled mustache across from me raises an eyebrow. Thanking the servants must not be the proper thing to do here. I squeeze my lips together and pick up a utensil farthest from my plate as the books instructed me to do.

Everyone waits until the king picks up his fork and takes the first bite before movement erupts around the table. Taking my first bite as well, my eyes almost flutter closed. The explosion of flavors is unlike anything I've ever tasted. The beef cooked in spices is tender, paired with simmered carrots in a honey gravy sauce.

"Are you enjoying your meal?" The king's voice is low as he watches me take another bite.

I place my fork down on my plate, wondering if I'm embarrassing him with my eating. I've been conscious of keeping my mouth closed while chewing, making minimal noise, and trying to appear graceful. The books also spoke of how ladies are to be seen and not heard when in the present of a king. I disagree with most of the rules. They seem harsh and unrealistic, but rules of the royal court are expected to be strictly followed.

"Yes, very much so. I've never had meat so delicious." I dab my face with the napkin and take a sip from my chalice. The deep red liquid is sweet with a bitter note when it meets my tongue. I try to keep my face neutral but nearly spit it out.

"Very good," he replies before turning to talk to the person on his left, which is the mustache man. He has observed our conversation closely, even if he tries to hide it between bites.

The rest of the meal is mostly silent except for the occasional conversation about politics or the latest news of tensions with the Arliean kingdom to the north. I've heard rumors of tension between the two neighboring nations, but listening to the discussion opens my eyes to the viable threat they pose to us.

A man three seats down begins telling the group about merchant wagons carrying supplies from Marvoe, the kingdom to our west, being attacked and set ablaze with much needed supplies of wheat and wool. Every head shakes in disgust, making me take another sip of the wine which doesn't taste as horrible this time. My senses tingle, but my body relaxes for the first time since Eliera left my rooms earlier today.

The mustache man gestures to me with his cup. "Your Majesty, are you truly not going to tell us anything about this magnificent lady sitting beside you? We are all so curious as to how she came to be your guest tonight."

The king takes a long sip of his wine. "Sir Yorshie, I will not disclose anything else at this time. You can try all you want or even send your spies to find out information, but you will find none."

The noble stiffens at the mention of spies but nods before popping a few grapes into his mouth. "Oh, how mysterious. Let us guess." He sits up and examines my face, "Is this a young lady you are hoping to make your companion or perhaps a prospective bride from an allying kingdom?"

My stomach drops at the mention of a companion. I know what they're implying, and my body flushes as all eyes stare at me again.

I look up at the king, despite every nerve in my body telling me to continue to stare at my plate.

He smiles slightly between more sips of wine. "She is neither."

"How unusual you have her at this table if she is neither." Sir Yorshie tightens his lip in almost a challenge.

King Addard puts his chalice down with a firm thud. "Who I invite to my birthday dinner is none of your concern. She is a lady of this court and you will treat her with the same respect you hold for me."

Several people shift as the noble averts his eyes quickly. Tension settles on the shoulders of the men at the table. Unspoken words clearly communicated as they give each other targeted looks.

"So there is hope for our daughters, after all!" another nobleman exclaims, holding his wine high towards the king.

Laughter echoes around me and the king chuckles as well. "Yes, perhaps."

Another noble raises his chalice. "May my daughter catch your eye at the Solstice Ball, Your Majesty."

"I have to admit that with everything going on, I've had little time to think about the ball this year."

A voice speaks up from the end of the table, past my line of sight. "You must have one this year, Your Majesty. It is tradition."

"Perhaps your charitable wife can assist in this year's planning, Sir Barhom," the king states in what appears to be a lighthearted tone. His brow still seems tense despite a smile that doesn't reflect in his eyes.

"Your Majesty, the honor would be hers to assist in whatever you need." Sir Barhom's cheerful tone eases some of the tension and I fidget with the edge of my napkin.

"It is settled then."

Chapter 12
Lylah

Talk of the Solstice Ball quickly dissipates and they move on to a new topic. The citizens of Rinmor know this ball well though. Every winter season, the city prepares for the influx of rich merchants, nobles, and town lords who descend to attend the ball with their families. The northern square of Rinmor is designated solely to lodge these individuals, but the pleasure houses and taverns down south are where the men are rumored to always end up.

Dessert arrives shortly after. A light blue pudding in a glass bowl with berries and fluffed cream. A bite of it is unlike anything sweet

I've tasted. The sour juice from the berries combined with the subtle sweetness of the pudding is masterful.

Looking at the intricate work of the dessert makes me think of Ellis. This dessert is the only link I have to him in the last week. I tried finding him after he left so abruptly that day, but I quickly discovered the bottom floor was off-limits and guards would stop me when I tried exploring a few times.

Pain tugs at my chest thinking of him. I wish I could talk to him about what has happened. Our meal routine was a treasured time to connect with someone, even if we didn't talk much. The familiarity of it in an uncertain place made it feel safe and comfortable.

Sir Barhom speaks again through the noise of clicking metal spoons against glass bowls. "My province towns are against the northern border with Arliea." He pauses. "Are there plans to send troops to the border to help secure it?"

The clacking ceases briefly.

I try to appear as if I'm interested in the conversation topic, but frankly, a lot of the discussion has only been rumors among the kingdom, whispers on the streets. Hearing it come from the mouths of those who can engage our kingdom in war is a surreal experience. It has been nearly two decades since the last war with Arliea. No one wants history to repeat itself. The fabric of our kingdom cannot suffer any more loss.

"Troops are assembling as we speak. They will escort you home before marching further north to set up a post along the border."

Sir Barhom nods as I spot him between parted heads. "That is very generous of you, Your Majesty. How many are expected at the post?"

The king narrows his eyes. "Three hundred for now. I hope the shop owners and taverns are well stocked for the coming winter. With how cold it is already, we are in for quite a freeze."

Sir Barhom licks his spoon. "The town is prepared for now but will the troops come with their own provisions?"

"Of course, but there is only so much we can send that won't spoil. The men are trained to hunt, but I'm talking more about entertainment."

It's widely known that soldiers also cause trouble when bored. The noble will need to be prepared for all possible situations, as Rinmor has learned to do. From the sailors to the soldiers, the nights are not safe. As I've had to learn the hard way.

"I suppose I will need to buy some extra entertainment when I leave."

Sir Yorshie strokes his mustache. "Wise choice, Barhom."

I know the entertainment they'll buy. Girls from the pleasure houses. Some of them will likely be girls I grew up with. How can they talk about buying human beings like they are animals? The thought makes me sick but I bite my tongue hard to keep from letting my true thoughts show on my face.

The room slowly fills with tobacco smoke swirling from pipes as King Addard stands. I follow his lead. The nobles venture to their feet as well and the misty layers curl around them as they bid us polite farewells.

After every last one of them leaves, King Addard extends his arm. "How about a walk in the garden?"

His warm eyes make it easy to accept his outstretched arm. From what I have read, the gardens surround the front portion of the palace to create a safe barrier between the outer walls of the city and the palace. A cliff side extends skyward directly flush with the back of the palace. The palace being carved into the mountain was a deliberate design to guard from invasions on most sides.

The moon is high in a star-filled sky as I take a deep breath of fresh air, relieved to be away from the palace luxuries for a moment and below an open sky. The stars have always given me a sense of peace and it's no different tonight. Torches light our way as we walk along the path of fallen leaves and flower petals being occasionally blown across by the evening wind.

"How are you enjoying your accommodations?" He asks as turns us down another path. "I apologize. We haven't had any time to see each other in the last week."

"The accommodations are very generous, Your Majesty. More luxurious than any I've ever dreamed of. You've been very gracious towards me," I say as I admire the stars beyond the treetops.

King Addard nods his head, expertly keeping his crown from shifting on his black hair. "I'm glad they are to your liking."

Several moments go by before he continues, "I feel as if you have something else to say." He pats my hand. "Please feel as if you can say anything to me."

The observation surprises me, and I hesitate to say what's truly on my mind. I take a few more breaths of the crisp air before proceeding with caution. "People see me as a companion at your side since they don't know why I'm here. I saw it in those men's eyes tonight. They looked at me like I was one."

A gust of wind blows across the garden again, the cool air refreshing across my skin. King Addard doesn't respond at first, but stares over the trees as well.

"You are a lady of my court. I would never take advantage of you in that way or any other way." He stops and turns to me. "I hope you truly understand that. You are under my protection. Everyone will think what they want, but unfortunately to keep you safe, we have to keep your abilities a secret for now. If the Arliean king were to find out, we would have daily assassination attempts on your life and I will not put your life at risk."

"I understand," I whisper.

"Attempts on my life are made quite often so I must also be careful. My food has to be tasted, my bedroom inspected for hidden assailants, and I have to be accompanied everywhere." As he says this, a sword clinks behind us and I turn to spot two guards following close behind.

I can see the difficult position he's in for the first time. I'm right in thinking my secret is no longer my own. It only puts my life and those around me at risk. Including him. Including Ellis.

"I can see now why we must be discrete," I say as my voice crack slightly and my throat tightens. I can't help but feel tears threatening to cloud my vision. I heard their whispers when they thought I couldn't hear. That I must have done something to pleasure the king so much he made me a lady in his court. I tried to escape that life, only to feel like I'm living it anyway.

A shadow by the archway leading to the southern garden square catches my eye. I look at King Addard, but he's lost in thought, not paying attention enough to spot the figure as I had.

Slowed moments pass before the shadow pushes off the wall. Auburn hair catches a ray of moonlight as the figure walks away without looking back.

Chapter 13
Lylah

King Addard dedicates the palace's second library to be my new study area. My heart soars in the vast space. Every towering bookshelf is filled with just as many books and scrolls as the other one. Intricately carved tables to study at and plenty of sunlight is all I need to get motivated to begin my reading.

There aren't any librarians or scholars here to help with uncovering whatever it is that I must learn. When I asked why, Finnon said that King Addard never replaced the last royal scholar who died. According to him, the king doesn't trust anyone else to fill that position and there hasn't been a need until now. The old scrolls and books have been simply dusted and maintained by maids like I had done.

Studying about my powers and the history of the mages here will allow my mind to absorb the information without feeling like I need to look over my shoulder every few minutes. Finnon assured me that no servants were allowed in this part of the palace without permission.

Flipping through the first few scrolls has already proved to be a daunting task. Curved writing flows across the pages in patterns I've never seen before and several words I don't even know.

On the first day, Finnon accompanies a maid carrying a tray of food when it becomes midday. He glances down at the chaotic scene around me with his spectacles resting on the bridge of his long nose. The king let him into the circle of people who know who I am and instructed him to keep an eye on me.

A delicious smell captures my attention. A sausage sandwich sits on a plate with layers of thinly sliced cooked beets and pickled onions. With a small smile, I graciously accept the tray but she avoids meeting my gaze. The sprinkle of freckles across her face and her rich earth colored hair indicates she's from the northern part of Narvidium. I've seen her in the dining hall, but we've never worked together.

I don't move until Finnon escorts her through the grand open doors and around the corner. He limps back after a few minutes and sits across from me.

"Quite the stack you have there," he says as his wrinkled hand pats the stack of books the king had brought.

King Addard said he studied them after my incident and instructed me to start with those. I search through the titles and oddly enough can't find King Lenthor's journal like the one the king mentioned. I was looking forward to starting with that one. When I see him next, I'll be sure to ask him about it.

Instead, I decide to start small with the thin scrolls first. But it quickly proves to be more difficult than I thought. At least the stack before me is a less intimidating place to start than the thousands of books surrounding me.

I slouch back roughly against the chair cushion. "How am I going to read through everything?"

Finnon flips a few pages of his own book, but his eyes are steady on the unbound scrolls in front of me. "Is there something specific you are having trouble with?"

"My education was..." I search for the right word, "spotty."

His bushy brows lift. "Do you know how to read?"

I refrain from rolling my eyes. "I know how to read, but this curved writing was never taught to us. I have no clue what some of the words even mean."

Blowing a loose strand of hair out of the way, the frustration is hard to contain. A part of me wants to give up, while another part of me craves for the truth. A way to prove to myself that I'm the Fire Mage for certain. I haven't been able to wield fire like apparently I did during the attack. What if I never will again? What if it was just a one time thing?

"How about you eat your lunch, and afterward, we can read the scrolls together?" Finnon pushes the sandwich towards me with the accompanying glass of milk.

I nod, feeling a pounding in my head taking root. After I eat every crumb off the plate, he stays with me for hours as we tackle every difficult text I had piled up. Stories of the mages and writing of the scholars during that time didn't reveal any new information, as a lot of their lives were known as children's stories.

But according to the scrolls, they were loved by the people and almost seen as physical gods. Movak Torgin, the Fire Mage from Arliea, the first and only other one before me, was said to be charming and generous, always stopping to help someone. There was Bella, the mage from Narvidium, who could move objects without touching them. Caetar, from Marvoe, could generate protective barriers. I couldn't find anything about Ladonne or Korrim's mages.

Flipping through a leather journal, I scan the contents for something useful but it describes tactics of war more than things that could be useful to me now. I scribble down notes on parchment paper with my quill nonetheless as I devour every page of a second hand account on the final Battle of the Kings. It could come in handy in the future, so I create a new pile.

The first interesting thing I come across is Movak's origin story. I shift the parchment paper more towards the light as the words feel like the only tangible link I have to him. He was born into a wealthy political family in Arliea and had close relations with the Arliean king and queen.

I chew on my lip.

Just those few sentences about his upbringing feel isolating. The polar opposite of the life I grew up in. With every resource and luxury at his disposal while I had to push into the shadows just to survive.

The paper is soft in my hands as I read further. It describes how Movak was attempted to be kidnapped at the age of twelve that activated his fire wielding powers. When the men dragged him from his home and shoved him into a wagon, he started a fire by simply gripping the wooden door. Soon after that, he became well known for his unbelievable abilities and under the protection of the king and queen, a prominent adviser during the Arliean war against the neighboring nation of Ladonne. The bloody war resulted in Ladonne crumpling as a kingdom and merging its borders with Arliea. The continental map changed forever.

I sit back, the words flowing through my mind like a wild river against jagged stones. History has told us these stories already. A question lingers after I set the papers down. If mages are known to be protectors of peace, why did they side with Arliea during the war? The songs describe them fighting on the front lines, defending the Arliean soldiers from harm and eventually securing Arliean victory. To me, peace would need to be unbiased.

Something doesn't sit right about the accounts. Pieces of the timeline seem to almost skirt around what actually happened. For ancient books that are supposed to accurately depict events from two hundred years ago, important information is definitely missing.

But the biggest question of all, why do none of the texts talk about what happened to the mages after the wars?

Days fly by as I immerse myself deeper into my studies. The sun sets as I read by candlelight most nights. I need to find the truth. I need to know what happened to them.

Stacks of fresh parchment are waiting for me daily, new gold pots of ink and quills are scattered across various tables that have now been moved together to create more surface area. A world map takes up at least one table with beautifully outlined continents and kingdom borders in gold ink. Drawings of mountain ranges, cliffs and oceans entice me to brush my fingers over the delicate artwork.

A cup of tea appears beside me and I nearly jump out of my seat, not having heard anyone walk in.

"Sorry, I didn't mean to startle you." Finnon's voice is soft as he lowers himself in the chair across from me.

He has been stopping by the library more frequently since he first taught me how to read old texts. From time to time, he even brings me a plate of food from the kitchens or a cup of tea to encourages me to take a break. Some days I'm overwhelmed with the volume of duplicate information, while other days, I'm excited when I discover something new. No matter how small of a detail.

"How is it coming along?" His brows crease in the middle. The parchments around me create tall barriers and I feel like the answer is quite obvious.

I take the tea in my hands, letting the heat soothe my aching fingers. "Better and better each day. Your help the other day was the motivation I needed." I point to the scattered mess. "My current frustration is that the accounts aren't in order and dated sporadically. The task right now is to just put a timeline together that makes sense."

Finnon sets down his own stack of parchments he had tucked under his arm. "I have no doubt you will figure it all out soon enough. You have proved to be very determined and bright."

I smile at the compliment as I grab another page. It appears old, with several stains from water or other liquid with a date in the right corner barely visible. But the contents are useless, so I toss it aside.

We sit in silence as we each turn parchment pages back and forth in our separate work. This routine has become comforting to me, enjoying the companionship in this solemn place.

Hours go by when I stumble across a page that I haven't seen before. It appears to be a letter written from a mother to a daughter with the words jumping off the page as I scan over them.

Dearest Viana,

I miss you, my sweet daughter. Please come home and find it in your heart to forgive me. I'm scared I'll never see you again and I need to tell you something that has been burdening my

> heart for many years.
>
> Our history is what will ground you in this world as it did me. My mother and her mother spoke of secrets long forgotten. They whispered tales of mages and powers no ordinary person could possess unless gifted to them. Their stories were not new to me as a little girl, but they spoke as if our family knew them during their time on this earth. They talked of how the mages fought for kings and defended those who were too weak to fight for themselves. When their purpose was complete and the balance of power equal, they vanished. Most believe they were only works of imagination. But our family knew the truth, passed down through storytelling from generation to generation.
>
> The stories always skipped over parts I urged my mother to tell me. Her face would sadden when her story got to the end. She spent most of her life telling me that something dark had happened but the day she died, she finally whispered the secrets to me.

Fearing the delicate handwriting might disappear, I hold the page tighter. These words have given me more hope than anything I've encountered so far. The emotion in them tugging at my motherless heart.

The letter continues:

> On the day she died, she whispered their secrets to me. I

hope to pass those words on to you when you return home. I know you're angry with me, but I want the chan to mend things between us.

My bones are getting old. I'm not sure how much time I have left. There's a shift in the air, like the one my mother spoke about. A shift she described was like the sky had split open and flowers bloomed brighter. She said I had the gift of seeing things that were not there, balances of energy that have only our family could sense. I thought she was speaking nonsense in her old age, but now, I think she was right. There's a tug from the depth of my chest towards the south, a whisper barely audible telling me to go. Your eyes were so full of curiosity as you observed everything around you. My darling girl, I wonder if you have this gift as well.

With each day that passes, the energy keeps me up at night and haunts my dreams. I need to see you. I need to know you're safe. You know where to find me when you're ready to forgive me.

A huff escapes as I collapse back into my chair.

Finnon raises an eyebrow.

"Did you find something?" he asks while sipping another cup of tea. I don't remember him getting up at all.

I read him the document and anxiously shift in my seat before I get to the last sentence. His face scrunches as if pondering the words.

"Is there anything else on the page?" He strokes his gray beard.

Eagerly, I look it over and spot a signature at the very bottom right.

"Yes, it says 'Maureen Loumon', dated eighteen years ago."

"Loumon..." Testing the word in his mouth, he repeats the last name over and over. "I knew a Maureen Loumon many years ago before the war."

My back straightens. "You did?"

"Yes." He chuckles softly. "A fiery woman running a little shop in Point Theane in Arliea. When she spoke, her eyes could just captivate you for hours." His gaze softens as if his mind drifts towards old memories.

"What if the woman you're referring to is the same Maureen that wrote this?" I ask excitedly as I pull him from his stroll down memory lane.

"I guess it could be the same person, yes."

Every page I've gone through has only revealed the same information over and over. But Maureen writes as if her family were guardians of the secrets that are not in any book and scroll. If her family had passed them down for generations through storytelling, this letter can't be all of it. What if she knows how to help me with my powers?

"Finnon, I have to go find her." I've never felt more certain of something in my life.

Finnon leans forward. "What do you mean, go find her? If she is truly in Arliea, there is no way the king will let you go into the enemy kingdom when soldiers from both sides line up at the border."

Hope flickers briefly as ideas swirl at dizzying speeds about how to convince the king to let me go to Arliea.

Lifting the paper up to him, I shake my head. "Something about this text feels like I need to find her. She writes like her family was there with the mages two hundred years ago!" I can't help but exclaim, my excited voice echoing in the stone floored library.

Finnon shushes me. "Keep your voice down."

"Sorry." I shrink back down into my chair but continue, "I'll just have to convince the king."

That task will be the hardest one yet.

Chapter 14
Ellis

Maggis finds me in the kitchens after lunch. His long black hair is pulled back in a ponytail that trails down past his shoulder blades. The man's squinty eyes have always unsettled me, but more so today. He starts a painfully awkward conversation before finally asking about my time as the king's servant under his supervision.

I shrug as I rinse a pan I've been scrubbing. "Fine as far as servitude goes," I chuckle. "Not like I have anything else to compare it to."

An uncertain smile creeps across his lips. "The king wants to see you in his study."

The king wants to talk to me? His threats flash through my mind, but I know I haven't talked about anything with anyone. No one has bothered to say hello much less discuss the rumors about Lylah with me.

"Thanks, I'll head there when I'm finished," I reply over my shoulder. I want my hard work to be seen so I can get out of this hell. The blisters on my hands ought to show that, right? If I do make it out of here, I'm certain I have a strategy that will keep me alive and with all of my ligaments.

"No, you'll finish now." His hand clenches around my shoulder. "The king doesn't wait."

I drop the pan in the soapy water. "Don't touch me," I say hoarsely, every muscle in my body tightening.

His hand retracts at lightning speed with widened eyes.

A guard accompanies us up to the second floor, but Maggis dismisses him when we reach a much smaller door similar to the one that opens to the throne room. Maggis knocks on it gently before we are instructed to enter.

The curtains are drawn back from the windows, allowing light to stream across the luxuriously weaved rugs. A desk stands along the back wall with the Narvidium crest sewn on a flag high above it: a ship anchor with a sword through it. To my right, a large portrait painting of a family hangs. The king's family who were killed that fateful night.

A lump forms in my throat. King Addard's father and mother wear the sternest of expressions in the portrait. My eyes wander to the oldest prince who clasps his hand on the shoulder of a younger boy I can only assume is the king. Their eyes seem to gleam with mischief and innocence. Next to them, two younger twin sisters smile widely, unlike the other expressions of the family. But it's the air of sadness preserved in this room that grips me the most as I glance between them all, my first time seeing their faces after a lifetime of stories.

I bow my head for a brief moment before clearing my throat. King Addard sits rigidly in a blue velvet and leather chair behind his desk. With his eyebrows scrunched together in deep thought, he glances down at a parchment on his desk. Lylah stands next to him, wearing a blue gown as dark as a midnight storm. I set my eyes firmly ahead to avoid her flushed cheeks and glistening hair.

I can't get distracted, I remind myself. No matter how different Lylah looks. Show him how hard you've been working.

The king nods past me. "Maggis, you may go."

Maggis gives me a sideways glance, bows and exits with quickened steps. I catch Lylah's grin when our eyes briefly meet.

"Lylah has been studying old texts about the mages these last weeks," the king starts. "She says she found something peculiar. It appears to be a letter from a woman to her daughter talking about their family's history with the mages. She claims to have a unique ability to sense energies."

He rotates a ring on his finger. "I'm not one for putting all of my beliefs in someone who states they can sense energies, but Lylah does have a point about the history part. No one has ever come forward stating they know secrets about the mages before, only written rumors at the time. My guess is that a lot of the personal accounts are in King Founar's library, not mine."

My mind processes the information, analyzing every word. I didn't know much about the mages but stories exaggerated for excitement and mystery. I will admit I've been trying to scour my mind for those tales now that Lylah is... one of them.

"What do you need from me?" I ask quickly before mentally kicking myself. "Your Majesty."

"Lylah has convinced me that we have to find the writer of this letter and gather all the information we can from her. Finnon thinks it is someone he knew in Point Theane when he studied at their school of herbology and arts of healing more than twenty years ago."

"Point Theane... as in the Arliean capital?" I know the answer but the question leaves my tongue before thinking. Again.

The king raises his eyebrow. "Yes, the very city."

My chest tightens. "Aren't we technically enemies with them? I highly doubt they'll let anyone in freely just to talk to some woman."

"That's why we are going to sneak in." The king challenges me with a direct glare while fidgeting with a gold quill.

"Sneak in?" I ask, considering the possibilities. I've snuck into hard places so it can be done if given the right guidance. The only time I've gone to Arliea, the tensions were minimal so travelers could venture easily across the border.

The quill bobs up and down in his fingers as he replies, "Yes, and you are going to do it."

"Me?" I shift my weight, glancing at Lylah who nods slightly, her eyes almost seem to be pleading with me. My eyes narrow. "Surely your soldiers or guards can do the task."

"This type of task needs to be done by someone with a specific set of skills."

"What do I get in return?" I grit my teeth. "Your Majesty."

"I will grant you your freedom."

The words almost stop time.

"If I go to Arliea to find this woman, dead or alive, you'll grant me my freedom?"

"Yes, that is what I said." He rotates his quill in his hand. "It should only be a short trip, a week or two."

My heart is racing. Yes, my freedom would be great, but the stakes are high. Too high.

Sweat beads on my palms. "If I'm caught within Arliean borders, I can only imagine the punishment for trespassers. I'll be labeled a spy and probably sent back here in pieces."

The king stares out of the open windows, down on Rinmor below. The bustling streets filled with vendors can be seen from this point of the palace. It's the first time in weeks I've seen the city streets and oddly enough, I miss it.

"I know the risks. The question is, how far are you willing to go for your freedom?"

How far am I willing to go? Silence creeps in as I consider this new development. My options are pretty much non-existent in this situation.

"I'll do it." The words cut through me with a confidence I don't feel. I don't want to do it but if it means getting out of this dreary and depressing place, I'll risk almost anything.

"Good to hear. This letter," he holds up the letter in question, "gives me hope they know more than is implied here. You will need to find out every piece of information you can before you return."

I nod at the order.

"I'm going with him," Lylah states in a clear voice.

The king turns abruptly towards her.

"Absolutely not," we both say in unison.

She glances at him with unreadable emotion in her eyes. "I need to be there in person. Secrets like that aren't something they'll tell just any random person." She pauses. "Maybe she'll know how to activate my powers again."

Lylah's voice is unwavering when questioning his decision. It catches me by surprise.

"Ellis is a trained fighter. I've seen him take down multiple men twice his size. He's more than capable of protecting me. Plus, no one knows who I am yet."

Dread pools in my stomach at the thought of holding Lylah's safety in my hands. Yes, I'm a trained fighter, but not a travel guide through enemy territory.

"I trust him with my life," she adds as she meets my gaze with a nod. The ginger strand of her hair falls around her face and at this moment, I wish she didn't trust me at all.

"No," I say flatly. Disappointment spreads across her features. Her confidence disintegrates.

The king doesn't react but turns to her instead. "Lylah, you would be safest here behind walls that can protect you. Out there, there will be limited protection. Two people is all I can risk sending. Adding a guard would draw too much attention."

I agree. She's the safest here behind these walls. With him.

Lylah chews her bottom lip slightly. "A guard is not necessary, and I understand it's dangerous. I know with all my being that the woman in the letter is who I need to talk to. Flipping through pages and books won't educate me on what I need to learn anymore. I've been trying for weeks, but they all say the same thing just in different ways. This is the best path forward."

Her body appears more relaxed as she speaks. Her tone is direct, as if they are friends and not a subject to a king. My chest tightens briefly but I can't seem to avert my eyes.

"You think I'm the Fire Mage, but I need to find the answers out for myself." She clasps her hands in front of her, "And I can't do it here."

King Addard interlocks his fingers, the wheels of his mind seeming to turn like pieces of a clock. He looks over the document again, as if to make sure the words convince him as they have Lylah.

"Yes, you may go if you wish." He sighs, agreeing almost too easily. "You are not a prisoner here. I will arrange for the supplies you will need to be gathered immediately. You leave early tomorrow morning, before dawn to not to raise any suspicion."

The king turns to me. "You will stay in a guest bedroom until your departure tomorrow. Your things will be moved as well. Dinner is always served at six so please do come dressed appropriately."

Lylah's face lights up with excitement at the king's approval and I make a silent vow to never save another girl again.

A servant comes in an hour before six and sets a stack of clothes down on the bed. He offers to help me dress, but I immediately decline before he can even finish the sentence.

I recognize him from the dining hall and our sleeping quarters, but we don't acknowledge it out loud. He's a quiet man, but always seems to enjoy a hearty laugh. I have no doubt this is as awkward for him as it is for me. A dozen questions must be running through his mind as to why I'm suddenly here and why he has to serve me. None of which I can answer without giving away valuable secrets.

There are only a few extra pairs of pants and shirts that he brought up from my bunk that I've accumulated during my time here. They won't work for this dinner though and out there, they'll not be warm enough.

I pick up the stack of folded clothes. "Here." I push them into his arms.

His brows shoot up towards his hairline. "Are you sure?"

"Yeah, I won't need them here," I say with a shrug.

He smiles shyly as he takes them and walks out of the room.

As soon as I'm alone again, I observe my surroundings with growing curiosity. The room is more magnificent than any I've ever been in. A wardrobe crafted of various slabs of walnut wood sits in one corner, followed by a velvet covered armchair big enough to seat two people. A washroom the size of my childhood home is off to the left with a deep bathtub elevated on bear-like gold feet.

Oddly enough, I think of the Shadow Dealer and how he would hire someone like me to steal those bathtub legs if he knew they were here.

The stack of clothes is a perfect fit but the feel of the fabric makes my skin itch with unfamiliarity. Black pants woven of silk are as soft as a deer hide. The blue collared shirt hangs around my frame in a fashion similar to the wealthy men of Rinmor. I secure the ornate embroidered belt around my waist over the top of the shirt.

I sigh at my reflection in the long mirror on a gold stand.

"I look like an idiot," I murmur to myself. It's not far from the truth.

A guard gives me directions to the dining hall and I follow them step by step. He doesn't follow me when I walk away, which surprises me for only a moment. The promise of freedom must be enough for the king to trust me not to escape.

Talking slowly grows as I pass the corner to open double doors leading to a vast dining hall. A table stretches out in the middle of the room with every delectable dish imaginable. My eyes gravitate to

Lylah listening intently to the king, who's telling an old children's tale about a bear and a wolf. It's really a ridiculous children's bedtime story, but Lylah is enamored with every word, like she's present when the bear and the wolf put their differences aside and become friends.

Finnon sits next to the king, listening intently too while sipping from a gold goblet.

"Good evening," I interrupt the story briefly and all eyes follow me into the room.

Lylah gives a fake pleasant nod with a coldness I didn't expect. My jaw clenches and the shirt suddenly feels a little bit too soft again.

The king gestures for me to sit next to Finnon. "It is informal tonight, so please serve yourself. I wanted us to have privacy without any disruptions of staff going back and forth."

I don't hesitate and start loading my plate with roasted duck topped with a mint berry sauce, creamy potatoes with carrots, and rolls that smell fresh from the oven. Jorge prepared this feast with the same skilled artistry as every dish I'd seen leaving the kitchen to feed the king. My mind flickers briefly to my time in the kitchens, always smelling the delicious food but never getting to taste the meals made for royalty.

The king did say the dinner was informal. Spoonful after spoonful, I devour every bit of food on my plate while Lylah and the king discuss various topics that I don't really bother to understand. Only nodding when there's a pause, I mostly focus on the food I have yet to sample. Finnon wipes his gray beard with a cloth napkin between bites of food and offers a few comments.

The king turns to me when we start on the dessert course. "There are two horses in the stalls groomed and ready for your departure in the morning. They will be in the front stalls by the double doors. Packs of food, clothing, bedrolls, and weapons are in a small crate to the left. I hope you don't need to use your weapons, but you may have to hunt for game if provisions run low."

I have to keep myself from rolling my eyes. Surviving in the wilderness is not foreign to me. For the king to sit in his high place and tell me how to survive at all is idiotic.

Small nods and thoughtful questions come from Lylah as if she's mentally taking notes. A flicker of irritation clouds my face, but I let it go quickly. Tomorrow morning, I will be on a horse with the smell of pine trees breezing past me.

"Did you include a map?" I ask between bites of baked apple pie with a sweet cream sauce drizzled on top.

"Saddle pocket on the black mare."

"May I ask a question?" Lylah asks with furrowed brows.

King Addard leans forward. "You never need my permission to ask a question."

"The journal from King Lenthor you spoke of when you told me I was the Fire Mage." She licks her lips gently. "I didn't see it in the stack of books you gave me to read. Is there a way I might be able to get it?"

For a split second, the king's eyes flash something unreadable.

"How forgetful of me not to include them. You are welcome to it when you come back. I hope you understand that if caught across enemy lines, those journals will be your death sentence." It's true. We can't carry anything that could identify who we are and where we come from.

We all take a bite before another request crosses my mind. "The daggers you took from me, I would like them back."

An amused laugh escapes him. "I figured you would ask for those eventually. They are among the weapons in your packs."

I nod approvingly, impressed that almost every detail has been executed. "We'll need Arliean coins. They won't exactly ignore it if we show up with Narvidium dekari." Lylah nods in my peripheral vision.

Several large bags of coins fall on the table with a thump. My eyes widen at the sheer size of the leather pouches, almost as round as a small pumpkin each.

"The red pouch," the king points to the one on the left, "was taken off of true spies years ago and collected dust in the vault. The other is Narvidium dekari."

I take the pouches in both hands and feel their weight. It will get us by comfortably if everything goes according to plan.

The rest of the evening continues without much more discussion of the looming trip ahead. Lylah states she's tired and wants to get to bed early for our dawn departure. I offer to walk her to her room, which she barely acknowledges.

We walk in silence through the many halls and corridors, but she expertly weaves through them. Not surprising at all since she's been navigating life upstairs longer.

She stops at a door and turns to me. Her violet dress swishing with her sudden motion. "I appreciate you taking me with you on this mission. You have no idea how important this is me."

I stuff my hands in my pockets. "The offer was too good to pass up. I would be a fool not to take it." Her expressions hide behind a carefully constructed mask that wasn't there before.

"You think that I'll do well out there?" In this glimmering light, her blue eyes don't leave mine.

It's not a question, but finally what's been upsetting her. "You've never been in a situation like this before. Hiding, stealing, watching. It's different from the dresses and having your pillow fluffed every night."

"I know about surviving. More than you'll ever know." The words cut deep and I close my eyes. I forgot she was an orphan and now, I'm a jerk.

"Lylah, I didn't–" I start to say.

"Your room is further down the hall and to the right. I believe it's the second door." She motions with her hand.

My head dips and I wish I can reach out to apologize, but I keep my hands tucked in my pockets. I turn to leave before a hand grips my arm.

"Ellis." Her voice is small, as if in hesitation.

"Yes," I say as I look back.

"I'm glad the king could see that you're the only one who can do this task." She pauses. "See it as my way of repaying you for saving my life."

She quickly closes the door behind her and I'm left wandering back to my room with a head full of new spiraling thoughts.

Chapter 15
Lylah

Ellis knocks on my door when it's still dark outside. He wordlessly gestures to follow him before guiding us through unknown hallways like he has walked this route multiple times already. The eerie stillness of the palace all the way down to the stables sets my nerves even more on edge.

Last night, I couldn't sleep comfortably, tossing and turning in my bed. Anxiety around the trip rotated over and over in my mind; uncertainty clawed at my heart. Around four in the morning, I decided to get dressed without the maids and wait for Ellis to come get me when it was time to leave.

The travel packs and horses are exactly where the king said they would be. Ellis takes no time to find his cloak, the metal of the small throwing daggers glistening in their holsters as he puts each arm through it. Next, he gathers the horses and starts securing our packs with expert hands. I offer to help but he ignores me so I resort to just watching him instead.

Patchy layers of fog float on the cold morning air. A yawn escapes and I clench my fur collared cloak around myself as Ellis ties a strap on one of the saddles tightly before meticulously going over everything.

Between moments of when he's turned to me, he looks as tired as I feel. His hair is more tousled than normal, and there's puffiness under his eyes. I wonder if he tossed and turned like I did.

"Come here," he orders in a slightly hoarse but firm voice.

I walk around the front of the massive horse nervously. The beast is magnificent with the light brown spots spattered on dark fur. Its enormous eyes follow me before dipping its head.

"Give me your foot." He interlocks his fingers and kneels with one knee on the ground. "I'll give you a boost up."

I grip my skirts with one hand and place my booted foot in his hands. A squeal escapes me as he lifts me up to the saddle while I attempt to swing my leg over the broad animal's back. I yank my skirts up but the only way to sit comfortably is for them to rest at my knees.

Ellis pauses as he takes in my boots and thicker stockings that extend towards my knee and tied with a simple blue ribbon. A jaw muscle twitches before he adjusts my cloak to cover me roughly, tucking it in around my legs.

"Do you know how to ride?" He doesn't meet my gaze but pushes my feet into the metal footholds.

"No." I chew on my lip. I don't want to worsen his mood.

He places the leather reins in my gloved hands while adjusting my fingers.

"These are your reins," he glances up at me briefly. "Use them to tug in the direction you want the horse to go and the metal piece in his mouth will pull him in that direction." I nod before he continues softly. "She's a very well-tempered horse from what I can see so I don't think she'll give you any trouble."

Ellis turns to his own horse. "You can command the horse to quicken their pace by tapping your heels against their chest. I'll lead so just do your best to stay close behind."

Once he makes it onto his mare, we move quietly out of the stable and palace gates without detection. A small smile creeps on my face, knowing the king had something to do with the guard tower being empty at this hour as well as the palace halls. I hope my plan is worth it and we find everything in Arliea.

Ellis' demeanor changes as soon as our horses trots out of the city gate. His body relaxes and the sternness in his face floats away in the wind. I feel my own anxiety melt away with the sun that peeks over the horizon, reflecting the glowing reds and oranges of a beautiful sunrise.

Pivoting us north, Ellis sets a steady pace which teeters on the edge of comfort and pain, but I grit my teeth and push on. We ride for several hours before the insides of my legs begin throbbing. He slows down just a bit, perhaps sensing my growing discomfort. Warm rays radiate now from the east as we climb the steep road toward the Volsan Mountain pass.

Only a few travelers pass us on the road, most of them probably heading south toward Rinmor. We dip our heads in polite greetings but their attention doesn't linger, which is a relief.

I lose track of time when Ellis gestures for our first stop by a creek only a short distance from the main road. We let the horses get water and graze while I survey the food supply in our packs. Dried berries in cloth bags, strips of cured spiced meats, fresh apples and oranges, nuts of various kinds, and leather skins filled with water are what we have for provisions.

Ellis pats his horse's neck when I say, "These are more like snack options than full meals. I think we'll have to stop at taverns on the way for some actual food."

"I can hunt for our dinner," he says without looking at me.

The horse nudges Ellis' arm and he scratches her nose. I smile at the scene, enjoying this new side of him.

"If that's what you think is best." I groan internally at the thought of sleeping out in the open.

He finally turns to me. "No, I think a proper bed tonight would do you some good. You've never ridden on a horse and we still have a long way to go."

I agree, but try to hide my excitement behind pressed lips. The mountain air is drier than I'm used to but I take deep relieved breaths. If I had to ride all day and sleep on the ground too, I think I would hate this trip way more and regret coming.

He retrieves something from his pack. "According to the map, there's a small village less than half a day's ride ahead. Travelers journey this road often, so I know there will be a place where we can get a decent meal and something that resembles beds."

A gust of wind brushes my hair sideways as I nibble on a small handful of nuts. The crunchy almond tastes glorious after the hard morning and I have no doubt I could easily eat half of our food supply right now.

"Do you want something from the pack?"

Ellis glances at the food I've pulled out. "I'll take an apple."

Tossing it towards him, the apple lands perfectly in his grip. He tucks the map back in his pack before chewing his apple in big bites and motioning for us to continue.

The rest of the afternoon is even worse. My thighs, back, and everything in between pulsate in raw pain, my vision focusing in and out. Elston, a small Narvidium mountain village, known for raising all the kingdom's beef supply, appears over the horizon. It's nestled in a grassy valley surrounded by patches of birch trees. Lanterns have already been lit when we trot through the dirt streets. A dog barks in the distance as we approach what I assume is a tavern. Several other travelers move around us to find space to leave their wagons for the night. Lively music and laughter pour out from the building as we tie our horses to the posts outside.

Ellis appears at my side and helps me down from my horse. I allow myself a brief moment to enjoy his hands on my waist before agony floods in. Turning back to his pack, he secures the bags of coins on his belt and covers them with his cloak. I recover quickly so he doesn't notice the level of pain I'm in. I want him to think I'm strong enough to complete this trip.

Once inside, Ellis effortlessly finds us a semi-clean table. With a simple nod, the tavern owner brings over steaming bowls of potato and carrot soup as well as wooden mugs of a strong-smelling liquid.

"What is it?" I sniff my mug.

Ellis takes a big gulp. "It's blueberry mead which is made from fermented honey." He smiles and takes another sip. "I've missed it."

Following his example, I take a gulp as well, but gag at the pungent taste. It burns down my throat and I quickly wipe at my mouth with the back of my sleeve.

"You don't have to drink it if you don't want it," Ellis says as he lets out a soft laugh.

I push the mug to him, and he takes it gladly.

Exhaustion creeps in on both of our faces as we slide the bowls closer. Every bite of soup is delectable and satisfying. Not in the same way as palace food, but more like a meal cooked with modest hands. It's similar to the food I grew up eating, bringing me back to oddly comforting flavors. The other patrons in the tavern devour every spoonful as I am before chasing it down with their own mugs of mead.

"I'll be right back," Ellis grunts out as he stands and walks over to the bar. After several exchanges of words, Ellis drops a few coins on the counter towards the tavern keeper. My body relaxes when he sits back down, sipping his mead again as he glances around.

It doesn't take long before singing ripples through the crowd, a common way to display love for our country and connect in a deeper way. They sing old songs of wars and kings loved by the people. One of them depicts King Medron and the story we all know by heart. The former king of Narvidium who fought bravely before the Arlieans slaughtered the whole family, including beautiful twin girls who slept in their beds.

In pools of red, their bodies lay,
Black curls are like a halo they say,
Facing death with tender hand,
Dancing now in eternity's land,

Some wipe away tears as they join in, the melody turning slow and mournful. The palpable emotion around us tightens my throat.

Ellis interrupts my thoughts. "I spoke with the tavern keeper about a place to stay. After a few extra coins, he said we can stay in an empty room upstairs. I could only get one room since the rest have been filled." He clears his throat. "So we'll have to share."

I only nod, too tired to feel anything about sharing a room with him. Nothing will be more embarrassing than seeing each other use buckets for our bodily needs through prison bars.

We board our horses in the small stable attached to the tavern and bring our packs to the room. A couple more coins in the tavern keeper's direction assure us the horses will be watered, fed, and taken care of for the night.

My back and thighs ache as I climb the stairs to the second level, only to find our room even further down the hall.

"I'll take the floor," Ellis utters as he tosses the spare blanket and extra pillow from the bed onto the cracked wood floor.

With a single candle being the only light in the room, I wait until he's settled on the floor before moving to get ready for sleep. I take off my corset and place it on the small stool by the bed. Chewing my lip, I think about how hard the floor must be and almost offer for him to sleep in the bed with me.

My cheeks warm and quickly dismiss the idea. I try to tame my tangled hair into a braid as I lay down on the stiff mattress and small pillow. The wool blanket is scratchy and thin as I pull it over me. An unexpected thought of missing the plushness of my room in the palace flashes in my mind.

I blow out the candle and darkness engulfs the room. Ellis shifts and a loud creak follows.

"How is it?" I ask the darkness.

Another shuffle before he answers, "I've slept in worst places."

"If it's any comfort, the bed isn't much better." I let out a tired laugh and hear him huff out a laugh as well. It's the first moment today he has truly let his guard down.

Minutes tick by but my eyes refuse to close. Small patches of light from the room next to us start to come through as my eyes adjust. Music and singing continues downstairs, only muffled slightly by the layers of wood boards.

A question burns in my mind. "You still awake?"

"Yes," he replies from the shadows.

"Can I ask you something?" Tiredness making me braver than I've been all day today.

"What?"

I pause for a moment and wrap the blanket closer. "The night we met, what were you doing in that alleyway?"

Seconds stretch between us before he answers. "I was doing a job."

"What kind of job?" I whisper back.

"I was hired to steal a pocket watch from a spice merchant."

I mull over this new information. "Was that how you made your living?"

He remains silent but answers yes after the long pause.

"Do you have a family?" The question seems odd to ask, but he hasn't said much about himself or his past. I sometimes feel like I don't know anything about him. We were only a mutual familiarity in an uncertain place who ate meals together. Both lonely and unsure of the future.

"No," he answers with veiled pain. "Not any family I talk to."

"Any girl waiting for you back home?" A lump lodges itself in my throat, but I await the answer. He pushed Jesimie away, but he must have someone back home worrying about him. Someone he hasn't been able to send letters to.

The floor groans. "No, not anymore."

Not any more? I want him to elaborate, but I can tell he doesn't want to talk about it. I want to know more about this mystery girl who once had his attention. I bite my lip to keep myself from prying any more. He's the only one that can get me to the answers I need. I don't want to sour our trip with tension.

"Can I ask you a question?" He suddenly whispers back.

"What would you like to know?" I reply, my mind spinning with the possibilities.

I sense him hesitating as well. "Have you been able to summon fire since that day in the library?"

I swallow hard at the question and fidget with the end of my braid.

"No. I've tried many times, but nothing happened. Even Finnon tried to help me with meditations and focus exercises, but it didn't work."

Ellis sighs sleepily. "The first time was an emotional response, so maybe something is stopping you from doing it again because of your emotions."

I recognize the observation as one I've had many times. "Yes, I came to that conclusion after weeks of trying. I don't know what it could be though."

"I'm sure you'll figure it out. You seem pretty determined to figure it out."

I smile as I settle into the only position that doesn't make my back cramp and fall asleep thinking about my first compliment from Ellis.

Chapter 16
Ellis

The tavern keeper kept his word and our horses were taken care of with plenty of hay and water from the well outside.

Lylah yawns and uses a nearby stump to hoist herself onto her mare before I have a chance to offer to help. After a few tries and quite vocal grunts later, she finally gains enough momentum to slide her leg over.

I bite back the urge to laugh. She ignores me while stroking the dark fur of the horse's neck. Pink flushed cheeks contrast against her black fur collared cloak as she straightens in the saddle.

"You ready?" I say as I use the stirrup to hoist myself up onto my own mare. She nods as curls of fog escape her full lips. We trot out of the village before the sun has a chance to lighten the sky.

The riding hasn't been the most challenging part of this journey. Making sure to do everything I can to keep Lylah comfortable has been. My left hip still aches from the stiff floor boards I slept on last night.

She hasn't complained about anything so far this trip which has been a relief, but her safety weighs heavy on my shoulders. With each traveler we pass, the men dip their heads in greeting. My fingers graze the daggers in my cloak but no threat rationalizes me to use them... yet.

When the sun beams down over us, we stop briefly for a lunch break consisting of a few strips of dried fish and oranges before continuing to push north toward the border.

The sound of the wind whishing past my ears becomes a peaceful constant and the cadence of the horses turns serene again. My mind wanders to various thoughts, worries long forgotten having a chance to resurface. I think about my small apartment, wondering if it's still as I'd left it. I think about the Shadow Dealer and how they may come after me when I'm free. The job left unfinished definitely soured any future dealings.

But how do I explain what happened to me while keeping Lylah's secret? In Rinmor, he has eyes everywhere so it won't take him long to find me. Maybe if I complete the job when the spice merchant is in the city next, the Shadow Deal may choose to forgive me.

A roaming thought jumps briefly to my mother. Her scared face when she looked at me the night I ran away at the age of twelve. Abruptly stuffing that memory deep inside, I shake my head. Thinking about her right now would only bring up old regrets and poisonous questions of what if.

Lylah pulls me out of my spiraling mind as she trots up beside me. "It's getting dark pretty fast, and I don't think we're near a town. Looks like we'll have to camp tonight."

No one is out on the road when we turn west into the thickest part of the forest. We find a small hill with a cluster of large boulders and a patch of grass in the center, perfectly hidden from the road. With the saddles removed and the horses tied to a nearby tree, they graze on the tall green grass. Lylah lays out bedrolls while I gather fallen branches and twigs for a small fire.

I turn to her, feeling slightly embarrassed. "Could I possibly have a small strip of cloth from the bottom of your skirt?"

She rips a piece without a question and hands it to me. Moving a few steps closer, she watches me curiously. I use the hard edge of a throwing dagger and strike it against a flint stone from the pack. I wrap the cloth on the edge of the stone and a spark lights it with a tiny flame.

I move the cloth quickly under the pile of wood. Clawing red flames ignite when I blow lightly on it.

Lylah claps her hands. "That's incredible."

It was easy but I savor her fascination with the simple trick.

"I'm going to hunt down a small animal or two for dinner. I'll be back in a little bit."

She only nods.

I grip a blade by its tip and walk out into the darkness. The glow of the fire brightens behind me as I listen for any scuffle of leaves or branches. To my left, I hear something that's undeniably a critter and I toss my dagger soundlessly. Sure enough, my dagger pins a rabbit in place when I retrieve it. I listen again before my dagger lodges into another.

Light humming comes from the camp when I make my way back. The soft singing stops me in my tracks, the sweet notes washing over me. I revel in it until my stomach clenches with hunger.

"I found some rabbits that should cook up nicely." The heavenly sound dies and my shoulders sink just a little bit.

It doesn't take me long to skin the animals and cut out their insides. Lylah refuses to watch and hides her face in her cloak hood.

"You'll have to get used to this eventually," I state as I toss the guts into the fire. Better to burn them than have any bears or mountain lions sniffing around.

Lylah's hood shakes. "No, that's disgusting."

"How do you think the meat you eat comes to your plate? Someone had to kill and gut it." I hold back a laugh at her dramatic response. This is the only way to survive out here.

Her head raises a little bit, "I mean, I've plucked feathers off of chickens but never watched someone cut out their insides."

"It's not that bad," I say as I use my dagger to shave a stick that's somewhat straight, and I spear it through both carcasses. Forcing the stick into the ground, I tilt the meat perfectly over the reaching flames.

Lylah tosses me several apples and strips of dried fish while we wait. We sit in silence, taking bites of our food and watching the flames dance between us. With my back against a boulder, I close my eyes. The gentle sound of rustling leaves and the aroma of roasting meat makes my mouth salivate but my mind silent.

"How far do you think we are from the border?" She asks softly.

My eyes flicker open and my breath catches. The orange firelight gleams across her face, highlighting flushed cheeks and bright blue eyes that pin me in place. She adjusts her cloak around her and uses her skirt to hold strips of fish she's snacking on.

I clear my throat. "About half a day's ride, maybe more. By midday tomorrow, we should be able to cross."

She begins untangling her hair out of the braid and combing her slim fingers through it. My eyes trace the lines of her jaw, the way her lashes flutter when she's thinking, and the curve of her slightly upturned nose. A feeling I can't explain tightens my chest.

I turn to look intensely at the fire instead. A drop of grease falls on the flames and it sizzles. I rotate the stick and make sure it's secure. Anything to keep my focus busy.

Lylah breathes out a sigh. "The palace seems so far away now." Her luxurious life these past two weeks has been nothing compared to what this trip offers. I wonder if she regrets ever wanting to come along.

I look at the stars above. "It does." The palace is far but its invisible chains tying me to it are not. I never thought I would be in servitude to the king. Having to earn my freedom seems unnatural.

"I've always longed for adventure. I guess I got my wish."

Silence slips back into place. I guess she's just as much in his service as I am, only in a different way. Questions swirl about her past. I've been able to piece together bits of what she has told me over various conversations, but not enough to form a full story.

"I'm really sorry for what happened to you."

I mean what happened to her in the library, the cruelty still making my blood boil. Lylah scans the fire with a frown but looks up with eyes that seem to look right through me.

"All the hurt I've suffered led me here, to this moment. I'm fed, clothed, respected and cared for. That's more than I could've ever hoped for. I discovered my purpose and what I need to do." Wisps of her hair float in the slight breeze. "Not many people can say that."

I can say I have similar goals for myself. I've spent these last months pondering ways to make my life mean something. When I regain my freedom, what do I want to focus my life on? What purpose should I chase after?

"I'm sorry for what happened to you too."

Her words settle uncomfortably in my gut. I only nod, but shift my gaze on the dancing hues of the flames. Admiring the way blue ribbons of light flick on the crackling branches, I try my best to avoid her observant gaze. The same one she had in the prison cell when looking at my wound with analytical eyes.

After a few more bites of the dried fish, I add more branches to the fire when a thought stops me.

"Have you ever spoken in an Arliean accent or even heard one?"

The light sways on her face as she thinks about the question before shaking her head.

I sit back against the rock and wrap my cloak closer. "The Arliean accent is a strange pull of vowels. The words sound as if they're dancing just like this fire."

She blinks.

I provide her with an example. "When you talk with this accent, you almost have to speak from the middle of your mouth. The words have to pass on the roof of your mouth to create the drawn out sounds."

Her mouth soon mimics mine as I show her the placement of my tongue when pronouncing different words. Speaking the common language with the Arliean way of pronunciation is one that took months to master during the only mission I was paid to do across the border. I feel confident in my abilities to jump back into that persona.

Biting back a chuckle, I watch her try to practice the words that come out with strained breaths. I take a rabbit off the skewer, rip off a leg, and hand it to her.

She takes a bite after it cools. "This is really delicious."

It's bland and void of any seasoning herbs, but it's the first meal today with any substantial content.

I smile warmly. "I'm glad you like it." Watching her rip off another piece helps my next bite taste better.

After we have sucked the meat off of every bone, we return to practicing the Arliean way of speaking.

"I know you want to laugh," she smiles as she uses her half-butchered accent. Amusement dances on my face as I toss my bones in the fire.

"The attempt is a good start, but we'll keep practicing. The Arliean people are naturally suspicious and unfriendly, so any indication that something is wrong won't go well for us."

Her face flashes a sliver of disappointment before leaning back against the rock at her back. Stars through the tree branches tower over us and glimmer like small shiny stones. The night sky is almost as beautiful as her looking up at it. The feeling I can't explain rises up again, and I let it linger a while longer.

After several minutes, Lylah settles onto her bedroll, wrapping her cloak around her, and wiggles closer to the fire.

"Good night, Ellis," she murmurs.

"Good night, Lylah," I murmur back.

It's the third day since our departure from the palace and what was promised to be a short trip is not looking so short after all.

Lylah has become more comfortable on her horse and doesn't have a hard time keeping up with my pace anymore. We depart west from our camping spot, allowing us to stay hidden in the woods while making significant progress towards the border.

A raindrop falls on my cheek and I squint up. Storm clouds form overhead and a distant lightning strike brightens the darkening sky. I motion for us to take shelter under a large tree in case it starts pouring any second.

"Did you see that lightning?" Lylah asks as her eyes brighten.

"Yeah but it might be to our advantage though," I say as I guide my horse under the tree. I look around for any movement. Lylah's brows scrunch, worries no doubt running through her mind.

I get the map from the saddlebag and lay it down on the dry grass.

"Here." I point to a line on the map just above the Volsan mountains. "This is the border. Now, I'm assuming this whole area is crawling with troops from both sides. The cover of rain might be the best way to cross the border unseen. Only a few soldiers will patrol in this weather."

Lylah scans the map as I talk, seeming to analyze my strategy. "Where do we cross that'll have the least chance at to being seen?"

I consider her question and point on the map again. "My best guess is we'll have to go west for several miles and cross here. The soldiers would be assembled more along the main road and probably have a checkpoint set up. We need to get as far away from this village here as soon as possible. I think that's where the Narvidian soldiers are being stationed out of."

"Yes, the king and his councilmen were talking about sending more soldiers and supplies there."

Good to know. Looking around one final time, I suggest another idea. "We should walk our horses the rest of the way to stay quiet and more out of sight."

She nods and I fold up the map before it has a chance to get wet. We walk west several miles in thick brush and towering pine trees before pivoting north. The rain picks up and its rapidly falling droplets on our hoods beat like a steady drum. Visibility is low, forcing us to take our time guiding the horses. Rain waterfalls off my hood, but I focus on any irregular shapes, colors or movement.

I glance over at Lylah and her eyes are just as alert. Both of us scan every direction for any bright Narvidium blue or radiant Arliean red uniforms. With only noise being the crunching of leaves and branches beneath us, we walk what I estimate to be an hour and spot no one.

"Do you think we passed the border yet?" Lylah asks loudly enough for only me to hear.

The landscape still looks like Narvidium, but that would be also be true of Arliea near the border. I nod in response. We get back on the horses again to trot slowly northeast towards the main road leading to Point Theane.

A bolt of lightning flashes across the sky. A loud crackle follows mere seconds later. Lylah lets out a muffled scream as her horse bucks her off and takes off galloping in the direction we came from.

Fear pulsates in my chest as my mare begins rearing. I don't hesitate jumping down in one swift motion. I try to calm her long enough to loosen the pack from the saddle, which lands on the ground with ease. The reins fall out of my hands when one more thunderous boom sends my horse in the same direction as the other.

"Are you okay?" I run to Lylah, my mind focusing completely on the possibility she could be hurt. Lylah sits up quickly and I stretch out my hand to pull her up.

"Yes. Thankfully, I landed on my backside. My forehead brushed up against a broken branch though." She begins wiping leaves and twigs from her cloak when I spot a thick trail of blood dripping down her face.

My heart leaps into my throat.

I move closer to inspect it, my finger trailing along her smooth skin. She stops and peers up at me with those pools of blue that threaten to unravel my resolve to not wrap her in my arms.

"It's not too deep, but I imagine you'll have a good-sized bruise around it." I clear my throat as I step back.

She brushes the blood off with the sleeve of her cloak. "It doesn't hurt. Plus, it'll heal fast." Looking around, her voice is shaky when she speaks again. "What are we going to do? We lost our horses and one of our packs."

What does she mean it will heal fast?

I steady my heartbeat and a plan begins to form. "We'll walk to the main road. Hopefully find someone who might let us in their wagon and offer to pay for a ride to the nearest town."

It's really the only plan there is. Rain continues to pour as I sling the pack over my shoulder and lead the way. The pack is heavier than I expected, but I don't let that show. Lylah's footsteps crunch behind me as we make our way through the towering maze of pine trees and dense grass.

Walking back to the main road takes another hour. Wet clothes cling to every part of my body. Rain sweeps along the dirt-packed road, creating deep trenches in places where the water flows downward. We walk along the edge, careful to avoid them and the large puddles.

"What's that?" Lylah points to something in the road ahead. I'm confident we had crossed the border, but the rapidly moving bodies I spotted seconds before her still set me on edge.

"Stay behind me and if anything happens, run towards the forest when I tell you."

Lylah's hood moves, which I assume is a nod.

The blurry figures come into clearer view as we approach. It's a wagon stuck in the mud and a team of horses struggling to get traction to pull it out. Several men are pushing from behind while a woman and a smaller figure stand off to the side under some trees.

A man spots us and yells out, "Ay, you there!"

I fidget with a dagger in the folds of my cloak. This could be a robbery setup but the genuine concern on their faces eliminates that line of thinking.

"Can you help us with our wagon?" He shouts over the rain.

Immediately, the accent is Arliean with the thick emphasis on their vowels making it easy to identify. I swallow the lump in my throat. I know how to make my accent sound like I'm an Arliean native, but Lylah hasn't had enough time to make it convincing.

"Sure, I can help. Can I put my saddle bag in your wagon to keep it dry?" The Arliean accent sounds slightly foreign on my tongue that even Lylah gives me a sideways glance.

The man with a wide brim hat nods, takes the bag from me, and places it just past the slit in canvas opening of the wagon. With a nod, we get to work on pushing it out of the mud. A few collected tries later, the horses manage to pull the wagon to a drier spot as the raging rain begins to slow.

"Name's Joweck," the man grins out as he sticks a hand out to me. I shake it and motion for Lylah to come from where I left her a little ways back.

"Nice to meet you Joweck, name's Ellis and this is my wife, Lylah." The words flow freely from my mouth as I'd spent the last several minutes rehearsing them. No need to disguise our names out here. No one knows who we are, and it's easier than remembering fake ones.

Lylah smiles and opens her mouth to say something.

I immediately interrupt her. "My wife is unable to speak, unfortunately. A horrible accident several years ago took that away from her."

Lylah conforms to my story with minimal hesitation, as I hoped she would. Her lips press together in a tight line as if to stop herself from speaking. She gives me a searching look before smiling back at the man and the two figures approaching.

"Oh goodness, that's so terrible!" A woman's voice exclaims as she joins Joweck. They interlock arms and she pats his arm softly.

Joweck motions to the woman. "This is my wife, Molia."

We exchange greetings and he motions past his wife to what I assume are their children. The two older sons seem slightly younger than us and to a young girl about the age of ten. They greet us before the two older sons go back to securing the wagon.

Joweck hands me my saddle pack from the wagon. "Here's your pack. We're most grateful for your help."

"Much appreciated," I say as I take them with minimal expression, knowing the bags of gold coins are in this pack. "Our horses got spooked during the thunderstorm and took off. We lost a pack as well. We just need to get into town and purchase another horse."

A few seconds pass as Joweck and his wife look at each other in silent communication. Their eyes say everything they need to in the absence of words. I hope to have that with someone someday.

Flashes of red flicker in my left peripheral vision. My whole body tenses. My hand grips the hard leather of the pack and the other instinctively moves to Lylah's lower back as I nudge her closer.

She follows my line of sight and stiffens as well. The clacking of horse hooves approach as Joweck releases his wife and greets four Arliean soldiers.

"Good day to you," the one in the front says.

"Good day," Joweck greets back with a nod which I mirror.

The soldier's trained eyes sweep across the scene before them. "Having some trouble with your wagon?" He asks and shifts in the saddle but my mind is already playing out all of the ways this situation could go wrong.

"Just had a wheel stuck, but all's fine now." Joweck laughs slightly and shakes his head. "Terrible time to go foraging for mushrooms."

Mushrooms? That's what they are doing out here?

The glistening metal of their swords and painted red armor makes this conversation feel like hours instead of minutes. I casually scout out the best direction we can head towards if things turn for the worst.

Drizzle continues to fall as a traveler passes going north and dips his head politely.

"My, what a large family you have." The soldier nods towards the sons who have stopped what they're doing and us. The little girl clings to her mother's skirt, only peeking out occasionally.

"I do have a beautiful family," Joweck beams, "But these two are just fellow travelers who were kind enough to help us with the wagon."

We are now visible to them.

I speak up, "Our horses got spooked by the lightning and the stupid animals took off into the forest. Threw my wife right off."

Lylah leans into me and I rub her back as if I'm comforting her.

The soldier's eyes move across the smeared blood on her face. "Horses and lightning. They don't always mix well."

He straightens in his saddle and gathers his reins. "We best be off. You all have a safe journey home."

"And to you as well," Joweck says as we watch them take off riding south towards the border.

My hand falls from Lylah's back and she steps away just a fraction.

"We best be getting home," Molia says to Joweck and I couldn't agree more. We need to get moving before we run into more soldiers.

Joweck turns to us. "We can take you to the next town if you'd like. It's the least we can do for your help." Joweck's words are like sweet music to my ears. After losing the horses, the mission just became a little harder, but not impossible.

"We'd appreciate that," I say and Lylah nods in agreement.

Molia motions to Lylah. "Come child, you look soaked to the bone. You and your husband can sit in the wagon with us. I best take a look at that nasty gash on your forehead."

And just like that, we make it into Arliea.

Chapter 17
Lylah

My forehead throbs with every bump as we head into the nearest village. I observe the sights through a small hole in the wagon covering. Smoke curls from chimneys and children kick around a straw and cloth ball similar to what we played with in the orphanage. A cow roams beside us, biting green tufts of grass growing on the edge of the muddy dirt road.

"Come here, child," Molia instructs before taking my face in her hands and gently pours water from a leather pouch onto it. Cool water drips into my hair, but I don't move as she uses a soft rag to dry my face. Next, she rubs some kind of ointment from a small circular tin. The cut still throbs but it subsides from the numbing properties of the medicine.

"There you go," she says and smiles warmly. I can't help but smile back, thankfully remembering that I'm not supposed to speak. My smile is short-lived as the cold finally gets to me and I shudder. The wet clothes cling to every crevice and I feel blisters forming between my thighs.

She gestures to the right with her eyes. "With two boys, I have to carry ointments with me. They're always getting hurt and we can't risk an infection in our little town with no accessible healer."

I nod but continue to look out. Exhaustion is creeping in slowly. Everyone else in the wagon keeps to themselves, including Ellis, who sits next to me with his arm around my waist. His hand is firm with every bump that nearly throws me against his chest.

I try to think of anything else but the warmth that's spreading across my lower back. My best guess for Ellis' declaration of my muteness is I didn't perfect the accent convincingly enough last night. I don't mind being mute, but it's tiring keeping myself from blowing our cover in enemy territory.

But being married to each other? That was the other part of the lie he told. I can guess that reason too. Less suspicious with a married couple traveling than a man and woman who are unwed. He could've said we were brother and sister, but I suppose that's less believable with our appearances.

The wagon comes to a halt and Ellis helps me down as the family gathers to say goodbye.

"We're so grateful for your help." Joweck shakes Ellis' hand. "If you would like to stay at the inn, the keeper is a friendly host and a kind man." He pauses before looking at his wife. "But Molia and I would be more than willing to provide you shelter for the night as another way of saying thank you. We have a small bedroom that you and your wife are more than welcome to use."

I turn to gauge his reaction. Ellis shifts beside me as the thoughts spin behind those exquisite eyes like a racing wagon wheel, most likely trying to foresee every angle and possibility.

He finally answers, "Your offer is very generous. We'll need a horse to get us the rest of the way to Point Theane. Would you have one we can buy from you?"

Joweck's face lights up in a wide, toothy grin. "We have several healthy stock horses that'll suit you well. Come stay the night and I'll show you what we have."

Ellis glances at me briefly, as if to get my approval. I give him a small nod. They are our best chance of getting a quality horse and not derailing too much further from our trip. Their warmth and kindness also makes me feel safer with them.

"We'd be honored to be your guests." Ellis puts his arm around me again and surprisingly, I don't stiffen as I had before. I know we have to sell this story, but the wide smile on my face is genuine.

Their farm is just a short ways from town, tucked away in a secluded part of the forest. A small meadow sits by a limestone brick house with red shutters. A barn is off from the main house with a fenced grassy field. The view feels like a dream in contrast to the taverns, outdoor camping, and hard riding we've done for the past three days.

The family unloads the wagon while Molia escorts Ellis and me inside their home. A cream-colored dog walks lazily to greet us at the door, tail slowly wagging with almost a grin on its shaggy face.

Molia turns to yell outside. "Bonnie, come get this dog out of the house before supper! You know how I feel about having him in the house. It's an outdoor dog after all."

Bonnie, the little girls, played with a cloth doll the entire time while giving me a shy smile. Her blue eyes go round with excitement when she runs through the door and throws her arms around the dog's neck. The dog doesn't seem to mind the yelling and the two take off running down the rocky path toward the barn.

"Bonnie gets lonely sometimes being the only girl and likes to have the dog in the house for company." Shaking her head, Molia lets out a big sigh. "The dog hair is what gets to me. All over the furniture and blankets." She bends down to light the already assembled stack of wood in the fireplace.

Ellis turns to me. "I'm going to head outside and see if I can help them with anything. Could you stay here and help Molia with things?"

I squint my eyes, yelling at him in my head for leaving me alone, but I nod and smile pleasantly with Molia watching so closely.

As soon as Ellis leaves, Molia pats my arm. "Oh dear, you're soaked to the bone. Let's get some dry clothes for you."

She opens a small cabinet in the hallway and rustles through various items. There are piles of linens, hats, and shoes, but she pulls out a light red tunic dress.

"Here," she holds it up towards me as if assessing the fit. "I'm a little bit taller than you, but this should fit."

She motions me toward a room where I can change before I can silently protest. I close the door behind me and shiver as I peel off my cold wet clothes, but leave only my undergarments and corset. The dry dress slips on with little resistance. It's a bit loose around the chest area, but it instantly makes me feel warmer.

Draping my heavy wet clothes over my arm, I venture out into the cozy living room.

"Much better I reckon," Molia says before grabbing my clothes. "Here, let me take those."

She lays each piece of my dress and cloak on a wire rack in front of the roaring fire. With the intensity of the fire, everything should be dry by morning.

"I'm thinking some beef stew will warm us right up." Molia guides me to the kitchen just beyond the living room. Pots hang on the wall to my left and vegetables in woven baskets sit on an oiled wooden counter that appears to be well-used with its divots and scratches. Small vases of wildflowers sit on sill of the small window that looks out over a luscious garden.

The thought of any hot food makes my mouth water. We hadn't eaten anything since breakfast which was a few handfuls of nuts and another apple. I help Molia chop carrots, celery, onions, garlic and meat for the stew. While we work, she talks about her family, how she met her husband and the children she loves dearly. I find that being mute has its perks because I enjoy just listening and not having to think of lies to tell her about my pretend life or pretend marriage.

Cooking is peaceful as well. The smell of the vegetables roasting and dried herbs being sprinkled in gives me a delight I didn't know I could get from such a simple thing. As her fingers masterfully slice a thick cut of meat and skim away the fat parts, I'm filled with a sense of awe. I try to hide it quickly to make it seem like I cook for my husband every meal.

My throat tightens when I glance over at her. Small strands of brunette hair with streaks of gray fall around her face and only her nose is flushed from the steam of the boiling water. But only one thought plagues my mind. Is this what it's like having a mother that teaches you how to cook?

The orphanage life is not what other normal children get to experience in their upbringing. While we helped in the kitchens sometimes, there were designated cooks who would prepare our meals. Most of them were local mothers who got paid to make vast quantities of food and leave afterwards to go home to their own children. The skill of cooking a meal from start to finish is not something I was taught before I was kicked out.

I imagine that if I had a normal upbringing, this would be a typical day in the kitchen with my mother. Tears swell in my eyes, but I blink them away quickly. Thankfully, she doesn't notice and moves on to another story.

After the stew is finished, we set the table and light candles around the room as darkness settles outside. My mind wanders to the elegant dinners I'd grown accustomed to at the palace, but this is different. Something about this feels more intimate and inviting than the palace's cold walls ever did.

The others walk in from dimming light outside and find their seats. Moments later, Ellis and I sit next to each other, sharing a meal with strangers who kindly took us in and made us a part of their family for just a night. They laugh and talk in a way that's genuinely loving and gentle.

I smile through the entire dinner, soaking in this feeling I never want to let go of. Ellis smothers a thick layer of butter on a slice of bread and passes it to me. Joweck tells stories of the village we are in, the various town jokes that have been passed down from generation to generation. Ellis and I listen intently between spoonfuls of soup that's bursting with savory flavors of roasted carrots and tender beef. Ellis glances at me from time to time with a look he's never worn before. Contentment is the only word that comes close to describing it.

After dinner, Molia motions for us to follow her. "You both must be so tired from your journey. Let me show you to your room."

The room is not at all what I expect. A large bed is pressed up along the wall in the center with a fur sewn blanket sprawling out across it. The two fur rugs on the floor are from some kind of short-haired animal. Another fireplace is positioned by the door with various jars of fresh flowers, a wooden box and a few books.

Ellis turns to Molia. "Thank you, this is incredibly kind of you."

I nod in agreement and give her my biggest smile. A smile from a full heart, and tears threaten to pool again. The day must have stirred my emotions. She gives us both a warm smile back before closing the door behind her.

Our pack is already on the bed when Ellis explores the room. I don't hesitate flopping down onto the soft fur blanket. Every muscle in my body aching from the unexpected turns of the day and falling off the horse certainly didn't help anything.

Ellis lights the fire with a flick of a dagger against a flint stone he finds on the mantle. Wood being consumed by flames has become a comforting sight the last few days.

"Let me see that cut on your face." Ellis' deep voice interrupts the sleep threatening to pull me under.

I sit up with a groan but let him look at it. His fingers lift my chin towards the light.

"Looks like it's healing. The ointment she put on it seems to have brought the swelling down."

Ellis' face is close to mine as he inspects further. His hot breath on my cheek sends a chill through me.

"Are you cold?" He asks before pulling his hands back. I'm sure the chill has nothing to do with the heat overtaking my body.

I nod, afraid that my voice can be heard. My eyes shift towards the fire and I lean back against the wall. Ellis settles on the bed next to me and we watch the flames together. The awkwardness is there for a few moments before a comfortable familiarity sinks in again.

"Thank you for helping me today. I know the horses running off was less than ideal." Ellis catches my eyes in a sideways glance before turning back. The firm lines of his jaw accentuated by the firelight and it makes me want to trace my finger across his stubbled face. A blush floods my cheeks, and thankfully, the light in the room is too distorted for him to notice.

I keep my voice down. "You're welcome... husband."

A smile creeps on his face, and his fingers glide through his auburn hair.

"Yeah, about that. I'm sorry if I put you in this uncomfortable situation. I came up with the mute story without really thinking and I knew you couldn't fake an Arliean accent that fast. The wife part was so they couldn't question us traveling together and keep onlookers away." A muscle in his brow twitches. "Their sons in particular."

Joweck and Molia's sons have barely looked at me since we met. They seem to be very shy in nature, so the fact he would be weary of that makes me smirk.

"I figured that was the reason for the Arliean accent part," I whisper with a playful tone. "Not so much about their sons though."

Ellis shifts to a more comfortable position. "You never know. Better to not get their hopes up. In small towns like this, eligible women tend to be hunted like animals."

Hunted like animals? I giggle softly, but decide to let it go. He's tasked with protecting me. I guess that means from anyone who might get the wrong idea.

"Has it been hard pretending to be mute?" He asks softly, tilting his head towards me.

I gravitate to him. "I just have to be more aware of myself so I don't accidentally say anything to blow our cover." A pause rests between us. "Am I expected to be mute the rest of the trip into Point Theane?"

Ellis lets out a tired laugh, a deep rumbling sound from his chest. It sparks overwhelming joy in me as soon as I hear it. "No. Once we get on the road again, we can practice the Arliean accent more. Hopefully, you'll be able to speak it more convincingly. We just didn't get to over the noise of the rain."

I slide down into the pillows. "Good, I would hate to not be able to talk when we meet the shopkeeper."

Our mission floods back amid this perfect moment. The king has been far from my mind most of the time, but everything comes stumbling back with one sentence from my own lips. The weight of every expectation press on my shoulders again.

His voice draws me back. "We should be about a day's ride from Point Theane. We'll have to ask around about the shop that Finnon spoke of. I hope it's still there or our search is going to take a lot longer."

My mind snaps to Ellis' freedom hanging in the balance. The thought makes my heart sink. He must be anxious to get back to the life he was living before he rescued me that day. Will he leave as soon as we get back?

Ellis gets up from the bed.

"I'll sleep on the floor," he says as he begins tossing one of the pillows on the fur rug.

"No need," I whisper as I sit up abruptly. "There's plenty of space on the bed for both of us."

He pauses, hesitancy seeming to tighten his lips. I hold his gaze, hoping to ease his mind. Is sharing a bed with me such an awful idea? I don't let the hurt seep onto my face.

The light sways in his eyes. Seconds tick by and my stomach churns with anticipation.

Finally, Ellis settles to the edge of the bed and begins taking off his boots. Moving to my side as well, Ellis begins to organizing his cloak on the nightstand for easy access to his daggers.

"Stay facing that way," I mutter to him. "I need to take this dress off. I have another garment under it so don't worry about being uncomfortable." The dress Molia gave me will be simpler to take off with fewer strings than mine.

He doesn't acknowledge my words but stays facing away from me. I reach behind and tug on the strings to loosen the corset in the back. Once I fold the dress and place it on my nightstand, I finally crawl under the safely of the covers.

"You can move around now," I whisper as I tug the blanket up to my chin and turn away. I hear some shuffling before he finds a comfortable position under the blankets.

Moments go by as the exhaustion of the day rocks me into a blissful sleep.

Chapter 18
Ellis

The fire has long died out when I open my eyes to find golden light pouring in. A rooster crows close by the window while I rub the sleep out of my eyes. I look over at Lylah. Her hair glows from a ray of sun cast across her head. The cut on her forehead is almost gone, but the purple blue has darkened.

She looked so peaceful in her sleep while I laid awake, getting up to stoke the fire, and analyzing every sound in the house, ready to strike at any second. My nerves are more on edge out here in enemy territory. Experience has taught me that even the smallest thing can easily cause things to spin out of my control.

Last night was the first time we shared a bed. It felt as unfamiliar as looking at yourself in the mirror after months without one. Her changing last night was no different. Sneaking a sideways look was as tempting as scooting closer to her. Holding her was an invasive thought I had to keep in check.

Get it together Ellis, you're better than this.

Reminding myself of the prize at the end of this trip is the only thing that kept my eyes forward. But her genuine smile on a rare occasion makes me want to be closer to her. We may have had very similar roots, but our lives now are very different. She's to lead a life of politics and high society with rulers of kingdoms seeking her attention while I'm only a lowly man for hire, working dangerous jobs to keep myself fed. Gaining my freedom will mean that we part ways, likely forever. I have no place in her new world.

She stirs as I sit on the edge of the bed, putting on my boots that have now dried. The first order of business this morning is to find Joweck and purchase the horse from him. Point Theane is only a day's ride, the conclusion of this part of our journey so close to finally being behind us.

"Where are you going?" her small rasped voice asks behind me.

I brave a glance in her direction and find her up on her elbows. Her eyes squint at the light with her wavy blonde hair falling down around her shoulders.

"I'm going to see if Joweck is up so I can buy that horse I looked at last night."

Without looking back again, I walk out of our room and towards the kitchen. Molia has already started on breakfast when I round the corner to the vast room. The wonderful smell of meat sizzling wafts from her metal pan into my nostrils.

Her face lights up as soon as she sees me. "How was your sleep?"

"It was very comfortable." I imitate a warm smile. "Thank you again for letting us stay."

My eyes jump to the two folded blankets sitting on top of their sofa. My mind goes back to the room and to a fleeting thought I had last night that our room was too nice to be a guest room. The pieces fall into place. They let us sleep in their room. They cleared out of the room to have enough space to house us. Their kindness is unheard of and their openness to strangers is overwhelming. A knot lodges itself in my throat and I can't bring myself to acknowledge it to Molia because I don't know how.

"You're most welcome, young man. You and your bride are welcome back anytime." She resumes cooking before turning back. "Oh, and Joweck is in the barn."

When I step inside the impressive, well-built wooden structure, Joweck is brushing the fur of the animal I looked at yesterday. I wish I could get us two horses, but we don't have enough Arliean coins for both, a resupply in Point Theane, and the journey back.

"Ah, good morning," Joweck greets me with a grin on his wrinkled face. "He'll be ready for you in just a moment. And it would be useless to sell you a horse with no riding gear, so he's all saddled and ready to go."

The hay beneath my feet crunches as I shift. Sweat forms beneath my tunic at the thoughtful gesture. I know everything about taking something that isn't mine, but nothing about receiving something as a gift.

"Umm..." I start to say and reach for more Arliean coins, "We couldn't possibly take them for free. I can spare a few extra coins to purchase them from you."

He throws up his hand. "Your response is a good enough payment for me. That's all I need to know about what kind of man you are. You and your wife are folks who seem like you just need a little bit of help. The Mighty One has blessed us with more than we need, so we're happy to share."

The Mighty One? I decide not to ask in case every Arliean know of this. My chest tightens. I'm not as good of a person as he thinks I am.

"When do you plan on leaving?" His question cuts through my chaotic thoughts.

"As soon as we can," I say as I rub my fingers through my messy hair. "We have some urgent business in the city and must take full advantage of the daylight. Here are the coins we discussed earlier and a few extra. We're grateful for your generosity."

Joweck takes the pouch of coins, puts it in his pocket, and continues brushing the horse.

I frown slightly. "Aren't you going to count them?"

"No." He shakes his head as he adds, "I trust that it's all there."

I counted the coins several times last night when Lylah was asleep to make sure I had enough to match his offer. The way he doesn't hesitate to trust me, a stranger he only met yesterday, is utterly foreign to me.

As the sun begins climbing higher into the sky, I make sure the stallion is prepped for the long day, checking all the straps, and tying our pack down. The ride with two people will be as uncomfortable as it will be difficult, but we'll have to make do with what we have.

Molia wraps up some pork cutlets and fresh bread in a cloth and hands it to Lylah, who is now dressed in her dried clothes. Although, the red dress from last night made her fit right in with this humble lifestyle. Like she was born to live on a farm among a large family.

I settle into the saddle first. Thankfully, it's flatter in the front and the back with more plushness than the Narvidian high-sided saddles. I reach to pull Lylah up to settle in front of me while allowing her feet access to the stirrup. After several tries with different ways to stretch her skirt over the horse, we finally work out how to position ourselves against each other in the most comfortable way.

I lean in over her shoulder and say quietly, "I'll need to have my arms around you like this so I can reach the reins."

She nods and her braid whisks across my face.

Joweck and his family wave us off with best wishes as we trot down their dirt road onto one of the main traveling routes I memorized on the map. The sun crests over the swaying trees and the light blue sky promises better weather.

I nudge the horse into a steady canter as we settle into the rhythm of the new horse. Lylah's back clashes against my chest before I push her against me so we can move as one. Even though I wish we could be on separate horses, our current setup is the most ideal for our situation. I can use my arms and body to protect her if we have to halt, the horse jerks hard, or we have to gallop.

The space between us fills with the numbing sound of hooves hitting the ground and the wind rushing past our faces. Green leaves turning to fiery orange and shades of consuming red the further north we travel. Hills and peaking mountains narrow on both sides as the road inclines into mountain passes.

My mind eventually wanders from the scenery to her. To the way her bright blue eyes observe our surroundings with wonder and curiosity. I return my focus to the swaying branches we pass, and the boulders jetting out on both sides of the road. I just need to think of everything and anything other than the rocking of her hips against my lap.

I shake my head quickly. Heat rushes to my face. Good thing she can't see me.

We stop in time for lunch and my stomach grumbles at the thought of pan fried pork on slices of fresh bread. Lylah unwraps the meal as we sit on a fallen tree log off the path of the main road.

I don't blame her quietness as she sits stiffly and tries to hide her winces. I can't begin to imagine what sitting halfway on me and the front of the saddle is like on her body.

Eventually, I break the silence. "We should be about five hours from the city. I know we can find a cheap inn we can head to when we get through the gates. Then we can start asking around for the shop tonight if you'd like."

Her face lights up at the suggestion. Poking around at night will be a safer option anyway. I doubt I'll be recognized here after so many years, but it's good to be extra cautious regardless of the maybes.

She looks out at the trees in deep thought. I wonder where her mind goes when she's silent like that.

"You said you've been to Arliea before?" Her eyes find mine as if trying to piece together a mystery.

"I did a job here once," I answer as I rub my neck. "A big job."

She looks at me, expectantly waiting to tell her the story. I haven't been open with her about my past, but this part of my life doesn't open old wounds too much.

"I stole something from King Meadon. A ruby necklace, I think."

"No, you didn't," she gasps out as she covers her mouth with her hand.

"I definitely did, five years ago now. Snuck in and back out but the guards chased me all the way off of the city walls into the river." Somehow, I feel proud telling that story. At the young age of fourteen, I outsmarted the guards and made it out with my first ever stolen object.

I smile as I lift up my right pant leg. "That's how I got this scar. A jagged rock got me in the end."

Her eyes sweep over the long scar that spans the side of my calf. I had to get ten stitches and didn't have any of Finnon's special numbing salve when my skin was being sewn back together.

"Wow, that sounds like a crazy story." She lets out a laugh. "Who taught you how to do that type of work?"

"I had a good mentor." My smile quickly falls. He was a good mentor who taught me everything I know, but we parted on bad terms. No use dwelling on it now after so many years.

Her smile falls too. I wish I could tell her everything about my life, but I'm afraid my deepest secret will cause her to never look at me the same way again. I killed a man and there's no coming back from that. His lifeless eyes still haunt my dreams, and sometimes, my waking moments too.

I change the topic. "You may have to remain mute while we're in the city."

The sadness that clouds her eyes twists knots in my chest. I promised her last night that we would get more time to practice, but I was too lost in my own thoughts to think of practicing more. It's too risky to walk into that city and not be certain she can shrug off any unconvinced onlookers. With the tensions between our kingdoms so high, I would rather not end up in another prison or beaten in a dark alley.

Once the horse has grazed on enough grass, we mount up and set off north. He should get us to the city with some strength still left. We trot for the remainder of the day as I hold onto Lylah tighter to keep her from sliding off. She leans into me more and a gloved hand rests on my hand that's around her waist. We mold more into each other as the day progresses, depending on the other to stay upright.

The city comes into view shortly as the sun begins its descent. I slow our pace. Tall towers spike up towards the sky, with guard towers well positioned along the massive walls. Merchants and sellers line the sides of the only stone bridge leading into the city, pushing goods and vegetables in our directions while speaking loudly over each other. Lylah's eyes are alive with amazement as she takes in the new place with all of its smells, sights, and sounds.

The river flows freely below us the further we make our way across the bridge. Everything here is so different from Narvidium, especially the stone houses built into the wall. But most of all, like the point of an arrow, the royal castle rests at the city's tallest center. Its own towers reaching towards the cloudless sky. From what I remember seeing inside of the palace walls, all five mage's statues jetted out in a semicircle with what I assumed was Movak in the front. Their chiseled figure, though hauntingly beautiful, stood guarding the royal grounds.

We stay on the horse when I see a few of the other travelers doing the same and walk past the gates with only a nod from the guards. Not much for security or checking people, but I'm not complaining. I forgot how crowded this city is and the further in we go, the harder it is guiding the horse without almost running over someone.

Leaning towards Lylah's ear, I say, "We'll have to get off and lead him the rest of the way."

We dismount with minimal struggle, except for the stiffness that makes my bones feel like solid stone. Lylah stays in front of me while I take the reins and we make our way towards the center of the maze of cobbled roads and buildings. With each face we pass, the diversity is evident. The Ladonne descendents are known for loving color. They immediately stand out in their bright colored tunics and dresses, which contrasts dramatically against their pale skin, narrowed eyes and black hair.

I turn towards the Crooked Pig, an inn I've heard is discrete and being rundown enough that we won't draw any unnecessary attention. It's not much to look at when we finally find it. A bar is nestled towards the back when we enter and tables with chairs made of oak are placed randomly throughout the rest of the downstairs room. The poorly lit space only has a single candlestick melted onto each table and several more on the bar counter. Patrons sit talking in clusters and an occasional smack of a fist on a table causes Lylah to tense.

A Ladonnian bar keeper eyes us as we walk in. Braided black hair rests on his chest against a bright purple tunic. Their cultural belief, from what I've been told, is that long hair symbolizes wealth and good fortune.

"Are you the owner of the stallion in my stable?"

I nod in reply. His eyes drift to Lylah and pauses on the bruise on her forehead. My stomach churns as he gives a squinting glare back at me. I'm almost certain he thinks I caused that bruise. On purpose.

In most cities, it isn't uncommon for a man to beat his wife. In Arliea, there are laws against this, and the women can actually press charges against a man for hitting her. From what I understand, this was signed into law at the time of the last Fire Mage.

"Did he hit you?" The man asks, leaning on his arms with eyes solely on Lylah.

"I-" I try to interject, but he holds his finger out at me. The size of his forearms alone make the words in my throat lose sound.

Lylah's hands fly up. "Oh, goodness no. I fell from my horse and a branch scraped me." Surprisingly, her attempt at an Arliean accent isn't not bad at all. To our luck, the commotion in the room disguises any imperfections.

"If you're afraid of him hurting you if you say anything, let me know right now. I'll throw him out and make sure he never walks again." His voice turns deep as the threat sharpens.

"No, I'm quite sure," Lylah retorts before stepping in front of me. A unexpected twist of circumstances putting her in the protector role.

The answer seems to satisfy him, and his mood lightens.

He turns towards me. "That'll be three gold pieces if you want to put your horse in my stable and six on top of that for a room tonight." Wiping the cups with a cloth, he continues watching me with narrowing eyes.

I dig through my pocket for the Arliean gold coins and put some down on the bar. "Let us stay two nights and I'll give you fifteen right now for the room and the horse."

He appears to consider it, but there's no denying the gold coins gleaming in the dim light. Cheering erupts from a nearby card game. He takes the coins and shows us to our room with little hesitation. The room is not luxurious by any means, but enough for us to sleep under a dry roof. There are two beds this time, and I sigh with relief.

A key appears between two gruff fingers. "I expect this key back to me in two days."

Agreeing, I take the key. Before he turns to leave, I stop him briefly. "My wife and I are looking for an apothecary. Is there one in the city?"

The bar keeper lets out an irritated chuckle. "Apothecary? We have several. There's several a few streets north of us towards the square and popular among the locals. I've heard that if she takes an interest in you, she tells you your future."

Lylah gives me a quick glance as the man exits the room. "Sounds like a good place to start."

Chapter 19
Ellis

Thieving has always been a lonely life, especially for the past several years. No one to keep you company during times of uncertainty. No one to help you make a decision when a second opinion could offer insight from an angle you didn't see. Having Lylah beside me during this trip has highlighted just how much having a companion can keep my dark thoughts away. Instead of spiraling into my broken mind for company, I take solace in watching Lylah experience things for the first time. I find myself content in the small moments when she smiles or laughs just like she is now.

The apothecary the bar keeper mentioned lights the dark street with a tall candles displayed in the window. Lylah takes a deep breath and opens the door to the small shop. I've learned that her nervousness always shows on her shoulders as they rise higher than normal. Her lips press together in a thinner line with each step. I can't imagine what this moment could mean for her. For our world.

A single bronze bell that hangs from the doorknob sings when we step inside.

The contrast of the dark streets to the red glow of the shop is notable with hot coals simmering in the fireplace and more candles melting on the mantle. Bookshelves line the left side with various bones tied on strings hang from spines of leather-bound books. Shiny gems are perfectly arranged on the counter as we make our way deeper into the space. Bird feathers of all colors lay in a wooden bowl with more bones of every shape and size.

A chill runs up my spine and I suddenly feel on edge. There's a weird energy in this room that I can't describe.

An older lady emerges from behind a curtain that must be to the rest of the shop and gives me a slow, wandering look before tearing her eyes away to study Lylah. A colorful scarf ties back gray streaks of hair while dark eyes conclude we are unfamiliar faces.

Several long seconds creep by before the lady finally speaks. "Welcome in." Her long fingers interlock as she smiles widely. "What can I help you find? We sell only the most exclusive items in all of Point Theane, so you've come to the right place."

Lylah glances sideways at me before pretending to look through the vast selection of feathers and holds them up to the candlelight.

I keep my voice firm. "My wife is in need of a salve that can prevent infection." My Arliean accent is flawless as she nods her head unsuspectingly and looks through several jars of liquid she has on the shelves behind her.

"Ah yes, this one will do. A bit of rosehip and chamomile oil will heal almost anything." Setting the jar on the counter, her smile reappears, but it doesn't seem genuine in the slightest.

"Do you need anything else, young man?" She looks at me for a long while before her eyes gravitate to Lylah again. Her eyebrows scrunch together before looking down.

I casually sidestep to block her view of Lylah. "No, just that should be fine."

Something is definitely off about her. I can feel it in my bones as clearly as I can sense the seasons change. Maybe what the bar keeper was saying about fortune telling has some merit to it. I've heard of people who had unnatural abilities, like talking to the dead. No one knew how, only speculating on different theories that were never proven.

The Arliean woman moves around the counter toward Lylah who takes a few steps back, bumping into a shelf that creaks.

"Something about you is so warm. I see this light around you I've never seen before. Here, give me your hands." The woman reaches out to take Lylah's hands with wide eyes.

Instinctively, my hand hovers over a dagger. Everything inside me is telling me to leave this shop right now, but Lylah places her hands in the woman's palms cautiously. The woman goes perfectly still. Her eyes widen unnaturally and tears begin to stream down her face.

Lylah jerks her hands away and steps closer to me.

"What's happening to her?" She whispers as she takes hold of the crook of my arm.

"I think we need to leave," I say sternly, "Now." I toss a coin on the counter and grab the salve before turning to leave.

A voice behind us speaks in a deep rumble. "Blood and weeping will come pouring down upon you. Five come together and one sees the true end. King against king will fight for fire and fire will destroy it all."

Lylah turns to look back at the shop keeper but I push her out of the door. A coldness settles in my bones that's not related to the night chill. The way her mood shifted was unlike anything I've ever seen.

"Wait, we need to go back!" Lylah exclaims loudly. A dog barks in the distance. I lead us out of the street and into a darkened alleyway.

"No, we don't." I rack my hands through my hair and look around to make sure no one heard her Narvidian accent in the crisp air.

Lylah searches my face. "What she said, what did it mean? I need to know. What if that was Maureen?" Lylah tries to push past me, but I gently nudge her into the stone wall behind her.

"No, we can't go back there. I shouldn't have let her touch you. People like her are dangerous. Something dark was in there."

Confusion radiates from her eyes and she tries to push past me again.

I hiss out a frustrated sigh and push her harder into the wall this time. "Listen to me. You can't go back there. We need to get away from here as soon as possible."

Lylah avoids my eyes and crosses arms over her chest. She certainly doesn't make this easy but I pin her against the wall with both hands, blocking her in.

"I made a deal to keep you safe," I say in a low rasp. "You need to trust me when I tell you that I don't feel right about that shop or that woman." I lean in closer and her eyes search mine for a brief moment before turning her head away. After a few minutes, I step away when she doesn't try to get past me.

We make our way back to the tavern, walking several streets over, but I'm pretty sure I lead us too far from where the inn should be. I pause to look at the buildings but it's too dark to tell them apart.

"What?" Lylah asks quietly as I analyze the cross streets.

I groan. "I think I missed a street and now this doesn't look familiar."

She lets out a tired humph before turning to look around too.

A silent creak of a wooden sign swaying to the right catches my attention. Dried flowers hang in the window and jars of crushed plants indicate it may be another apothecary. We can look in quickly to check it off our list. If the other shopkeeper went to the city guards, it would get us off the street.

Lylah doesn't say anything when I open the door for her, but looks around curiously. More dried herbs hang from wooden racks suspended high above us and a strong floral scent I can't identify floats in the air the further we venture in.

A woman with bright brown eyes stares intently at us from behind the counter, only shifting briefly to give us a genuinely warm smile. Her skin is a deep shade of umber with full lips that accentuate her face. Raven colored strands of curly hair surround her face like a halo.

Her voice is like velvet when she says, "Welcome. Is there anything I can help you find?"

Lylah remains quiet as she looks around at the jars of dried flowers and stones scattered on varied bookcases. Something about this place feels warm and inviting, unlike the coldness of the other one.

I decide to take a gamble, my Arliean accent focused. "We're looking for someone. Perhaps you may know of her." Maybe it's better to just get to the point. "Maureen Loumon."

The smile disappears briefly from the woman's face, but she recovers almost immediately. I narrow my eyes as I catch the slight reaction.

"That name doesn't sound familiar." Her eyes meet mine with matching narrowed eyes.

"Well, in that case, we would like some herbs for a cut." I pause briefly. "Preferably something that's numbing and can prevent infection."

Lylah moves to stand beside me as she observes the woman as

well with the cut on her face barely a line now. The shopkeeper pulls various jars from the shelves and combines them all in a stone bowl, pouring them with practiced motion.

Her steady hands make a paste as I try again. "The person we're looking for is an old friend of someone we know. He told us we can find her here in the city." I look around and spot a door that must lead to the back.

I eye it curiously when she draws my attention back at her. "Like I said before, that name doesn't sound familiar to me."

"You know something, and you recognized that name when I said it." I phrase gently, not wanting to come across as threatening. My patience is wearing thin as my weariness from the journey grows. Navigating these delicate situations is not my strong suit and there's only so much dancing around the issue I can do.

She continues pounding but says nothing. After a few minutes of silence, she hands me the jar of paste. "Put this on the cut twice a day and it'll start healing as soon as tomorrow. I recommend leaving it on the cut when possible for faster healing."

I hand her a coin. "We're staying at the Crooked Pig if something jogs your memory. Finnon is the one who sent us."

Something flashes in her eyes at the mention of Finnon. "I hope you have a good night and come back if you need more." Her smile is forced this time, and she waves as we leave.

We find our way back to the inn after a passerby kindly explains which street to take.

"She knows something." I declare once we're inside the bar.

"Agreed. She definitely didn't want us saying Maureen's name and seemed very uncomfortable when you kept asking her," Lylah says softly so only I can hear. I put a two coins on the counter for a few bowls of potato mash and carrots.

The room is rowdy with laughter and conversation. But here's no singing like I've come to expect in a Narvidian tavern. I motion for us to head upstairs with our meal, and Lylah nods tiredly.

We settle into our separate beds under the glow from several candles around the small room. Each spoonful of the hot meal travels down my throat and settles warmly in my stomach.

"Here." I grab the jar the last shopkeeper made for us and move towards Lylah. She holds perfectly still as I smear some on her forehead. The deep purple bruise looks painful and I definitely know what those feel like.

Lylah looks at me through thick lashes. "You know I can put it on myself."

My fingers close the lid. "You definitely can if you would like next time. I just... figured it would be easier if I did it for you."

She murmurs a thank you.

"How did it heal so quickly?" I ask her, my eyebrows furrow. It has healed abnormally fast for only happening a few days ago.

"Mages heal faster, according to Finnon." A sigh escapes her. "Why does it almost always have to be my face?"

A knock interrupts my response. We exchange a frown and stare at the door. I grip a dagger between my fingers as I open it just a crack. To my surprise, the girl from the shop stands in the hallway with a cloak and hood on. She looks over her shoulder quickly before I gesture for her to come in.

Once inside, her eyes settle on Lylah, who's now sitting on the edge of her bed.

The girl speaks first. "Finnon is an old family friend of my grandmother, the one you asked about. Why do you seek her?"

Silence fills the room. Flickering of the candles being the only movement for several seconds. We didn't discuss how we would answer this question, so I let Lylah take the lead.

"We're seeking information, answers that we believe Maureen has." Lylah stands and walks closer to her.

The girl shifts under her cloak and steps back. "That accent is not Arliean."

I close my eyes at the mistake. No other way now but forward.

The shopkeeper pulls off her hood. The light reflects slightly across her flushed cheeks. "Information about what?"

"We found a letter from Maureen to a woman named Viana. We just want to ask her some questions." Lylah studies the girl for any reaction, but she doesn't give much to interpret. I respect the skill it takes to control her expressions like she's doing now.

"We can't speak here." The girl flips her hood back on. "This is already a risk. Come by the shop tomorrow morning and you can meet my grandmother. She urged me to come find you after I mentioned someone stopped by knowing Finnon."

Lylah and I look at each other before agreeing. It feels like we're one step closer to finding out the answers we came here for and getting out of this horrible city.

She turns abruptly at the door. "I'm Sourina, by the way."

"Pleasure to meet you." Lylah smiles at the name, "I'm Lylah and this is my..." She pauses and chews her lip. There's no reason for me to be her pretend husband in this case.

I speak up quickly. "Ellis."

She gives us a quick smile before heading out of the door and disappearing down the pitch-black hallway.

Chapter 20
Lylah

My eyes snap open at the first hint of morning through the torn window curtains. I only feel slightly refreshed after the anticipation of today kept me up most of the night. Sleep never pulled me under for long. I wrap the wool blanket over me, trying to ignore my racing thoughts, but it's useless.

I push my hair out of my face but inhale hints of jasmine from a small strand. Before going to sleep last night, I was smelling like a farm animal. Thankfully, Ellis and I utilized the bathing room downstairs. The hot water washed everything away, the soreness of my muscles, grime and sweat, and even some of the weirdness from last night. Ellis stood guard at the door until I was dressed and escorted me back.

Fragmented thoughts analyze the first shop keeper's words over and over. She spoke of five which is easy to guess with there being five mages. But she said that one will see a true end. Will one of us be killed in battle or assassinated? Just manifesting these powers put a target on my back. Our backs really.

Scents of baked bread and roasting meat wake me again in a few hours. I wait eagerly for Ellis to finally wake up before we get dressed in silence. He turns away first before I slip on my dress, tugging on the strings in the back to tighten my bodice. After I say I'm done, he pulls back his blanket and swings his leg to the ground with a groan. It's my turn to look away quickly, but something out of the corner of my eye captures my attention. I turn to keep myself from staring too long at what appear to be long, scarred lines spread across his back and some even snake to his chest.

He rubs his eyes and smoothes his hair. "I haven't slept that deeply in a long time."

"Must be nice," I groan as I try to smooth out the wrinkled parts of my skirt.

Questions swirl as I chew my lip. Finally, I give in and turn back to him. "How did you get those scars?"

Ellis goes rigid before slipping on his tunic shirt over the lines, which disappear from view.

"We don't have enough time to go over every one," he answers in a low voice. I feel my stomach drop slightly at the assumption he would tell me. At this very moment, I would give up everything just to know who or what caused such damage to him.

When we get downstairs for breakfast, the sight before us isn't much to be desired. Heaps of drunk men lay on the floor and piles of thrown up food are obstacles we navigate around to find the only empty and semi-clean table.

The bar keeper from last night is nowhere to be seen, but a middle-aged woman brings over plates of roasted pork, slices of warm bread, and glasses of fresh goat's milk. Ellis pays the woman two coins for the bowls and we take large bites until every crumb is gone.

A short walk to the shop reveals only a few townsfolk in the streets. Back home, Rinmor is always bustling with people as soon as the sun rises. The usual sight of sailors going out to their ships with cargo or vendors setting out their goods in the markets is nowhere to be seen here. Point Theane is soundless as cold dew lingers.

Sourina greets us after we knock on the green shop door. "Come in," she says as she gestures with a wave of a hand, a turquoise colored bracelet jingling on her wrist.

I instantly admire her rosy cheeks and dark, curly hair. Her beauty and gracefulness strikes something familiar in me. I know I'll never be as beautiful or graceful. No matter how many elegant dresses and fancy hairstyles I have, her natural beauty will always catch the eyes of everyone in any room. Even Ellis' eyes lingered on her last night when we first walked in.

Sourina leads us to the back of the shop, where an elderly lady sits on a sofa with a quilted blanket spread over her lap. Her white hair is styled in twisted braids at the nape of her neck. Wrinkled lines highlight her gray eyes as she stares peacefully at the fire in the stone fireplace.

"Grandmama, these are the folks who came into the shop yesterday," Sourina says softly as she lays a gentle hand on her shoulder. "Remember, Finnon sent them."

The old woman's rich brown face lights up at the mention of Finnon. They clearly had some kind of history, even though what he said about Maureen was brief. Their expressions when remembering each other almost hints at a romantic past.

"Finnon..." Maureen tests the name on her tongue and gives a small laugh. "What does that old houger want from me?"

I take a seat on the olive green sofa next to Maureen. "Finnon is a healer for the Narvidian king. He sent us to find you."

"Come here, child. Give me your hand." She turns to look at me and stretches her hand out to me.

I give her my hand hesitantly, but somewhere deep down, I feel safe with her. Ellis shifts behind me but doesn't protest.

"I know what you are." Maureen smiles widely, tears pooling in her eyes.

Inhaling sharply, I straighten. "You do?"

"You're the Fire Mage, of course." Patting my hand, her gray eyes searching mine and it feels familiar somehow. A tear slides down her cheek.

"Grandmama?" Sourina appears on the other side. "What do

you mean she's the Fire Mage?"

Maureen closes her eyes. "Can't you feel that warm red glow around her, Sourina?"

Sourina nods. "Yes, I felt it as soon as she stepped into the shop yesterday, but I didn't know what it was."

"Her power is quite strong. I haven't felt this before but I recognize how it's described to feel." Maureen opens her eyes to look at me, truly look at me as if I'm the only person in the room. Her hand cups my cheek and I can't help but lean into it.

"What does it feel like?" I shift to the edge of the seat, my excitement blooming in my veins.

Maureen's eyes crinkle as she smiles. "It feels like when the sun is beaming down on you on a hot summer day. Like all the evil has been sucked from the world." Her hand drops from my face before moving to smooth out her blanket. "It feels like hope."

There's sadness laced in her voice when she speaks again. "Sourina and I are the only ones left now who know how to sense a mage's powers. A gift given to our family to protect. Although, some try to imitate it by smoking dried herbs which give them false illusions."

I search for the right words. "I found one of your old letters in the king's library. You wrote to your daughter about secrets your family had passed down. Is sensing a mage's powers one of them?"

Maureen moves her focus back to the fire. "Ah yes, I was writing to Viana, my only daughter. She was a stubborn girl who ran away from home. I wrote the letter in hopes it would find its way to her. She came back less than a year later, pregnant." Sourina pats

Maureen's shoulder. "She died during childbirth, but gave me the greatest gift of all. My Sourina."

"I'm so sorry to hear that," I say and chew my lip. "Reading your letter gave me hope that you can teach me everything you know about Movak and the other four mages. About my powers."

Maureen turns to hold my gaze with eyes full of compassion. Ellis settles into a chair in the back of the room. Sourina observes us hesitantly before taking a seat next to him.

"Almost everything about the mages was moved to the Mage's Tower in the Balgorn Sea. There's little accurate written material left around the kingdoms. My ancestors were the ones who trained the mages when they were coming into their powers and fought beside them in every battle. They protected the texts by moving them so no one could destroy or distort their history."

I let the words soak in, fighting back tears that threaten to sink me deeper into disappointment. "Every book and scroll was moved to the tower?"

"Yes."

I push the despair away. "I nearly burned a girl alive about a month ago by accident and I haven't been able to summon fire since. King Addard sent us to you in hopes of learning what it means and how to control my powers."

"King Addard..." Maureen chuckles in return. "Tragic childhood that one. Be wary of kings. They seek only power and power always finds a way to corrupt."

The king certainly has a tragic past, but the second part makes my nose scrunch. The time I've spent with the king, there's been nothing corrupt about him and only shown me kindness and mercy.

"Only an emotional response can trigger a mage's powers." She continues again, disrupting my thoughts. "The first five mages were used by the Arliean king to control and take over the neighboring kingdom of Ladonne, which they did eventually conquer. After decades of fighting, the mages promised to keep the balance of power across the remaining four kingdoms by handling all manners of political disputes. My ancestors were there through it all." Pride radiates in her words.

Hope stirs in my chest again. This is the first time I feel connected to them. I'll finally have my answers.

Maureen's eyes turn grim and she looks deep into my soul. "Be careful not to let the fire burn you from the inside out. Fire burns everything in its path, whether you want it to or not. A wildfire is just as destructive as a fireplace being lit."

A chill turns down my arms, but I scoot closer. "Can you teach me?"

Maureen laughs, her mood completely flipping. "Oh child, I'm an old woman now. I don't have the strength to teach you."

My face falls and tears threaten to surface as I stare into the dancing flames. "The answers you seek are in the Mages Tower, warded to not visible to anyone but those who have the key. My Sourina will show you the way." Maureen's wrinkled hand encloses mine.

"Me, Grandmama?" Sourina's voice shakes as she stands.

"Yes, my sweet darling. I've passed down everything to you. You know the stories and truths," Maureen says tenderly and blinking back tears.

"Grandmama, I can't go with them. I have to stay here and take care of you," Sourina says before moving to crouch down beside her.

"This destiny is yours." Maureen pats her cheek gently. "I feel my time is quickly coming to an end. My bones have ached for such a long time. I'm ready for the afterlife and to be greeted by my ancestors and my Viana."

Glistening tears roll down Sourina's face. Ellis shifts behind us slightly, a short dagger shimmering as it twirls in his hands.

Sourina crooks out with a shaky breath. "Grandmama, don't talk like that. You're going to live longer, you have so much more to teach me about plants and minerals."

Maureen rubs her tears away with a gentle touch. "Your mother was my greatest accomplishment but you're my greatest gift and so much like her. It's like I had a second chance at raising her again." She smiles. "Your spirit always has our ancestor's guidance and protection. There's a greater life out there for you than what this shop and this city have to offer."

Sourina lets out a soft cry as Maureen continues, "Take the sacred book, journals, and the other items I showed you from the chest. You'll need them for what comes ahead."

She nods as another sob racks her shoulders. "I don't want to go. Grandmama, my life is complete having you in it. I belong here with you."

"Oh darling girl, you have an amazing life ahead of you. A life full of loss and love, betrayal and heartbreak. I feel the struggles you'll face, but you're ready to give it your all."

As they rest their foreheads against each other, soft words pass between them. Words that are too quiet for me to hear.

I look back at Ellis again. His dagger twists faster with eyebrows drawn so tightly. He catches my glance and gives me a rare smile laced with a sliver of emotion I don't expect to see. Sadness and uncertainty.

Sourina's sobs become louder as our eye contact breaks. Maureen's face is peaceful, her eyes closed as if sleeping. Sourina shakes her shoulders and calls out her name, but her grandmother is dead.

Chapter 21
Ellis

Large displays of emotion always make me uncomfortable. The sound of Sourina's desperate sobs as she shakes her grandmother's dead body is at the top of my list at the moment. Spinning the dagger in my hands faster, I eye the scene before me. Lylah has her hand clasped over her mouth as Sourina cries out harder and harder. The room echoes her grief, and it stirs the grief I thought was long buried.

Getting up quickly, I walk out to the front room of the shop. The scenery outside has already changed, with townsfolk scurrying past the windows holding baskets of vegetables and various breads.

I pace in the small space, feeling unsettled by the whole situation. I twirl another dagger in my other hand as my chest tightens. Lylah approaches me while eyeing me closely, too closely before another figure follows behind.

A voice pulls me out of my darkening mind. Sourina stands in the light, her eyes swollen from her tears.

"I..." she starts before taking a shaky breath, "She's gone." A few more tears rolls down her face and I want to run out of here as fast as possible. "I can't believe she's really gone."

Time ticks by before Sourina straightens her shoulders and inhales a deeper breath. "I'll have her body prepared for the ceremony." She turns to Lylah. "Will you two come? She would've wanted the Fire Mage to be there."

Lylah looks briefly at me before nodding. "If you wish us to be there, we'll come."

Sourina glances between us as if remembering we are foreigners. "Here, we believe that preparing the body with oils and spices allows for entry into the afterlife with beauty. The embalmers will prepare her body for the pyre in our sacred burning grounds."

Their ceremony practices differ vastly from Narvidium. We believe that the body should be returned to the earth from which we take all things. To repay the debt, we give our most beloved thing, the bodies of our loved ones.

She wipes her face with her sleeve. "We'll do it tonight and leave tomorrow morning. Meet me at the embalmer's shop by the northern wall."

I inhale sharply and say, "We'll gather supplies until then. We may not have enough Arliean coins for two horses. But Lylah and I can ride the same one and purchase another for you. It may slow us down, but we'll make it work."

Sourina walks wordlessly to a stack of books behind the counter and pulls out a small ornately carved box. Opening the lid, she takes out a leather pouch. Round flat pieces shift as she places the pouch in my hand.

Never in my life have I had people just hand me large pouches full of coins like this. The king trusted me to use them for our mission, just like Sourina trusts me to use them now for our journey back. This is all completely new to me and makes me feel inadequate.

With her eyes on mine and a rasped voice, she states, "This should be enough to purchase my horse and all the supplies we may need." She takes a step back. "It was my grandmother's dying wish I go with you. That's what I'll do. Remember to meet me before the sun sets." Her skirts twirl as she steps back into the other room.

Almost in desperation, I usher Lylah out into the street. Feeling grateful for the fresh air and a plan I can work towards, I push every other thought aside.

We find the horse stables first, after asking locals for directions, for two new horses. The owner is a hard man to bargain with, but I talk him down into giving us two horses for almost the price of one using flattery and convincing lies. I tell him the horses are going to carry a nobleman on a mission assigned by King Meadon. To sell the lie, I reveal to him him that the nobleman is looking to add a few horses to his stables, but only if he finds the best deal in the city. The seller eagerly agrees, no doubt wanting to show off his best stock for someone so close to the king. He has several used saddles at a reasonable price, which I inspect for a long time, as if to make sure it's to the nobleman's liking.

Next, Lylah and I head through several streets before we find the central market, which turns out to be three times bigger than the one in Rinmor. Breathing the crisp air only calms me slightly before I hyperfocus on what we still need to get. Buying supplies at the market is much easier with the horses as we stuff the packs full of various breads, fruit, nuts, dried meats and firm vegetables that can make the trip. We barter with a merchant a few stalls down for three bed rolls.

Lylah continues to the next stall as I slowly follow, watching every figure around her. A man wrapped in furs says something to another merchant under his breath. At first, I don't notice what they're saying, but their topic piques my interest.

"Did you hear? They're sending more troops to the southern border. They found a horse with no rider roaming around the woods." The man says between sips of something from a leather flask.

The woman leans closer. "I heard Narvidium is sending assassins to kill the king."

My stomach clenches. Lylah lingers a few moments on a red scarf that an older lady holds up, her fingers grazing over the silk-like material.

"How much?" I ask the woman, my thoughts still thinking over the conversation I overheard. If they found the horses, the city must be on high alert. As if on cue, a cluster of guards pass us and I pivot my back to them. She retreats her hand from the scarf, grips my arm, and shakes her head.

The woman smiles. "Only four coins. It's made from Korrim's finest silk by an excellent craftsman in Marvoe."

I hand her the coins and Lylah's eyes widen as she accepts the flowing red scarf.

"I'll look so beautiful around your hair." The old lady struggles to stand, but gestures for Lylah to step forward. "Here, let me show you how to best put it on."

I watch as wrinkled fingers loosely wrap it around Lylah's head and tucks some of her hair under the fabric. Lylah gives the woman a smile before we turn to walk back towards the inn, taking our time to enjoy the sunlight that doesn't provide any warmth.

Lylah touches the scarf and smiles up at me warmly. "Thank you."

"You're welcome." I fidget with the reins as the horses follow behind. Giving gifts to a girl can be seen as a show of romantic interest in Narvidium. That's definitely not what's happening here and I hope she doesn't get that impression. "If Arliea is anything like Narvidium, women wear head coverings during funeral proceedings."

"Oh... I'm glad we could find one in time then." Her face falls briefly before tugging the scarf around her reddened cheeks.

Lunch is quiet when we get back to the inn later that day. The Ladonnian bar keeper nods at the tossed coins, including extra for the two horses in his stable, and brings us whatever is on the menu. Lylah seems to be lost in thought as we sit in the far corner, away from any prying eyes.

"Lylah?" I wave my hand in front of her face and she shakes her head as if finding her way back from a distant world.

"Sorry," she mutters and takes a spoonful of vegetable mash and roasted chicken. "I'm so hungry though. This looks delicious."

I can tell. She practically rips the meat clean off the bone and licks her finger. I catch myself smiling at her change in demeanor away from palace life. I like this Lylah better than the one who puts on an impenetrable mask of etiquette.

I take a bite of my chicken as well and continue my line of thought. "When we leave tomorrow, I'm thinking we take the road towards the east this time, along the coastline. What do you–"

"Do you remember your family?" Lylah looks up with a gaze so intense it practically sears a hole through me.

"What?" The question twists my insides.

She drops the chicken bone onto the plate with a thud. "I don't remember my parents. I was dropped off when I was a baby. But not a moment goes by that I don't wonder why they did it or even if I look like them." She looks down and pushes the plate away with one swift movement.

"This is my only possible connection to them." She takes out the compass from her pocket. It's not worth anything but to her, it means everything. Unexpected guilt rises up in my throat that I took such a beloved object. I can only imagine what those few days were like without it.

"What makes you think about them now?" I ask as I put my bone down slowly.

"Seeing Sourina with her grandmother. The shared love in their eyes. I want to know what that feels like." Lylah's voice cracks slightly and she clears her throat. "I'm sorry. I don't know what's come over me."

"It's okay to want that, I think," I say, even though I don't believe the words. It's not okay to want to feel loved. Love gets you killed or worse, puts people in danger. Love sometimes tells you to leave the house and never come back. Love disappears when you wake up.

Lylah stands quickly. "I'm going to head up to the room. Please continue eating. I didn't mean to disturb your meal."

I watch her walk across the bar and up the stairs. When I look at the empty chair, the air feels cold and tense without her near me.

Later that night, a man lights the lanterns on the street as the sun descends behind the houses. We quicken our steps as we walk north towards the embalmer's shop after some directions from the local folks who give us odd looks. The shop is a smaller cottage than what I was envisioning, with a wooden sign dangling above a chipped red door. A lone wagon and horse stand waiting outside with a two men. Lylah moves the scarf over her head like the old woman showed her and nods.

I knock on the door and someone shouts, "Come in!" Lylah goes first and I follow closely behind. Overwhelmingly strong aromas of flowers and cinnamon swirl in the air as soon as we're inside.

"You're here." Sourina's voice floods with relief in the small space. Thick dark curls peek out from under a pulled back red veil. She fidgets with a large pouch similar to the one she gave me to purchase her supplies. "I know this is last minute but I appreciate you being here."

A lump lodges itself in my throat as the lurking dread of tonight finally arrives. If it's anything like Narvidium, there will likely be mourners there.

She turns back to the shopkeeper and sets down the coins. The shopkeeper shakes her head slowly. "Oh my dear girl, I'm so sorry for your loss. Embalming and burning of the body are of the old ways. The popular preference now is by burial."

"It's more of an honor to embalm. You know it's what she would have wanted." She lifts her own scarf over her curls. "You've prepared everything?"

"Yes, dear." The shopkeeper looks through parchments before pausing, "Maureen was a well loved healer in this community. You know how many bushels of herbs I've purchased from her." She pats Sourina's arm. "It's mighty fast for a burning ceremony. Typically, the embalming process would be a few days, not hours. Is everything okay?"

Sourina's veil sways. "Yes, there's some urgent business I must take care of out of town. The shop will be closed until then I get back, but you're welcome to anything in there. I know my grandmother gave you a key." The shopkeeper nods. "Would you be able to keep an eye on things for me while I'm gone?"

The gray hairs around the woman's eyes move as she adjusts the spectacles on her face. "Of course, dear." She glances down at her papers again. "We've prepared everything exactly how you asked for."

It doesn't take long before Lylah, Sourina and I follow the horse drawn wagon up the cobbled road. Several others join behind us when a flat circular patch of grass comes into view. The city walls disappear into the growing shadows behind a pile of logs stacked to eye level in the middle. Enormous oak trees similar to our great oak tree in Rinmor canopy this sacred place.

The driver slowly halts the wagon in front of the unlit pyre. Two other men lift Maureen's body wrapped in red cloth and place it on the wood. Only her face is visible while her her eyes are smeared with a wax-like substance.

Sourina steps out from between us and moves to her grandmother's side. Touching her cheek, a stifled sob escapes Sourina's clenched lips. I flex my jaw, wanting to be anywhere but here. Out of the corner of my eye, a woman dressed in a decorative red robe begins to hum. Her fingers pluck gently at a two stringed instrument I don't recognize.

The melody soon wraps around us when Sourina takes a torch from the embalmer's shop owner and lights the pyre. Red flames engulf the body as she stumbles back slightly and Lylah reaches to catch her.

Beautiful lyrical words spill out of the woman with each stroke across her strings and thrums in my chest.

May her body be accepted,
For she's one among selected,
The stars welcome her upward soul,
And depart this life as whole,
Oh, bathe her in beauty, beauty.

Lylah wipes her eyes as the fire's orange glow flicks across her face. Old emotions seep out as I look up at specks of light floating up towards a cloudless starry night.

Chapter 22
Ellis

Sourina appears the next morning when she said she would with two cloth sacks ready to go. Puffiness surrounds her eyes as if she spent every minute crying since her grandmother's funeral ceremony.

I take her bags and strap them to her horse, avoiding the pits of sorrow in her eyes. Emotions... they're better handled by someone who isn't me.

Riding out of the city in the early morning is refreshing and I relax as soon as we're across the bridge. The gloomy morning air rushing through my hair means we're closer to being outside of Arliean borders.

Both of them ride side by side behind me. Pride swells in my chest to see Lylah's riding abilities tremendously improving in the short time. But Sourina soon proves to be as equally skilled after becoming more comfortable with her new horse.

Last night, I decided that perhaps going east would be better so we can be closer to the Narvidium border. According to the chatter in the market yesterday, as far away from where I assume they found one of our horses. The water's edge and the various fishing towns along the way will give us plenty of places to camp.

By the time we find a decent place to stop, everything in my body hurts. We've been pushing ourselves to get as far away from Point Theane as possible before the sun rises higher over the trees. I get an apple and walnuts to snack on from my pack. Sourina does the same, but Lylah decides to lay in the short grass that's barely hanging on to shades of summer. Tiny red birds chirp above us, their small but beautiful melody gives this place serenity. We take in the various views, separated by our own world of thoughts.

I glance over at Lylah as her question floods my mind again. Yesterday, her sudden curiosity brought back invading memories of my family. Nothing good can come from thinking about them, but she cracked open the chest of emotion I keep buried deep inside and right now, I can't seem to quite close it again.

"Where's the border from here?" Sourina's voice cuts through.

I take the map out from my cloak and lay it out on the ground in front of us. Lylah rolls onto her side to see. I trace my finger across the thick black line that stretches over the middle section and up on the eastern side.

"If I'm calculating right, we're about here. This black line is the border," I state. Sourina's eyebrows scrunch tighter the longer she stares at the map.

"From what I've heard," she looks up at me, "there are soldiers from both sides all along this road and on the east. How do you plan for us to sneak across?" Her tone seems to suggest my incompetence.

I clench my jaw and hold her gaze. "This isn't my first time going across the border and it won't be my last."

Sourina glares back at me, clearly annoyed. "I wasn't trying to insult you, relax, but that doesn't answer my question."

Lylah eyes us with a neutral expression and pops a few almonds in her mouth. The gash on her forehead is completely gone and the bruise vanished like it was never there.

"The way we came across is around the troops this way through the forest off the main road." I nod at Lylah. "It didn't go as planned. Thunder scared our horses, and they took off."

Sourina studies the map, her finger gliding across the paper in calculated motions.

I continue my line of thought while refraining from rolling my eyes. "When we were at the market yesterday, I overheard some merchants talking about more troops being sent to the southern border because I think they found one of our horses."

Lylah sits up a bit. "Really?"

"Yeah. That's why we need to cross the border as soon as we can."

Sourina points to the map. "There's an old castle on this ridge line here. It's on the cliffside along the ocean over here. I doubt anyone has been up there in decades. We can go that way and then come down the other side through this mountain pass into Rinmor."

Lylah kneels by the map now and asks, "If there's a castle here and a shorter route to the border, why didn't King Addard tell us about it or Finnon?"

Sourina takes a bite of her dried meat and shrugs. "How should I know? It was owned by the royal family, apparently as a vacation spot before the Arlieans destroyed it. I doubt the king has been there since everything happened and probably forgot about it."

"How do you know?" I ask as I stare at the area she's talking about. There isn't even a mark on the map or any indication of anything there.

"I read about it."

Whatever she read could be wrong too. "I say we continue diagonally along this side. Cross the border tomorrow where there's bound to be minimal soldiers and camp overnight along the coast." I sigh and rub my stubbed chin. "After that, we head south towards the castle for the second night. If it's still there. We should be able to make it back to the palace on the third day."

They nod in agreement to the proposed plan and we get back on the road. Sitting has already made me nervous. I don't want to be in enemy territory any longer than we have to. After a few hours, I motion for us to ride southeast towards the Narvidium border and cut through the forest. Just before darkness starts creeping across the sky, we search for space big enough for us and the horses.

Setting up camp is a welcome venture after a long day of slow riding through dense forest. We roll out the bed rolls on the ground and tie the horses loose enough for them to graze, but not loose enough that they can take off in the middle of the night. My stiff arms gather sticks and dried wood for a small fire and find some kind of game to eat. Sourina wanders off in the dim light to forage for things to add to our meal.

It doesn't take long for me to come back with four squirrels in my hands. Sourina appears shortly after with wild onions. Lylah uses a stick to skewer the onions and turnips from our pack and adjusts them over the fire. I get the squirrels cooking as well, the combined smells make my stomach rumble.

"That squirrel was cooked perfectly," Lylah says after we finish eating and toss the picked-over carcasses into the fire.

Sourina sits back against a tree. "Agreed."

I sit back against a tree stump, hunger no longer sinking its teeth into me. An owl hoots in the distance and trees crack as they sway back and forth.

Lylah takes off her boots and rubs her feet through her stockings. Sourina stands and walks towards the horses, pine needles and leaves rustling loudly beneath her. She emerges from the darkness moments later holding a thick leather-bound book and sits next to Lylah.

"This is my grandmother's book. It has been passed down for

generations." Sourina's features gleam in the light when she turns to Lylah. "There's a lot to go over."

Lylah slips her boots back on. "What's something I can learn right now?" Her eyes are wide with anticipation. This is her moment to learn from the sources since Maureen said everything else is in the Mage's Tower.

"Oh, this is neat." She tilts the book down towards the firelight. "One of the other four mages was from Narvidium. Her name was Bella, and she grew up in a northern town."

Lylah nods. "Bella is well known in our kingdom. She could move objects with her mind."

"Correct." Sourina flips to another page. "The other four mages were a great asset to Movak in the wars they fought. Some texts even say they were like a family. It's assumed that the four mages who emerge this time will have amazing powers to help you with whatever comes next. I'm not sure if their powers will be the same as what the others had."

Lylah stares at the fire. It's hard to comprehend that four strangers will be a huge part of her future.

She scoots closer. "Does it mention anything about how to generate my fire? I've been trying since the one incident, but nothing has been happening." Lylah holds her palms out in front of her. "When I do this, nothing happens."

"Woah," I exclaim and dodge out of the way. "Watch where you are trying to point your hands." I saw Jesimie's burned body be taken out of the library on a stretcher. It was a gruesome sight.

"Whoops." Lylah tucks her hands under her legs and gives me an apologetic look.

Sourina briefly looks up. "Yeah, let's try not to burn down the entire forest. Especially if you don't have control yet." Pages turn as Sourina studies the book. "It seems that summoning fire was easy for Movak. He was a natural as soon as he first summoned it so I don't see anything here about it."

Lylah's face contorts slightly, discouragement clearly written on her face. Movak was the only other person like her and for him to summon fire right away must be crushing to hear.

An arm nudges her. "Hey, don't think anything of it. You'll summon fire and learn how to control it in no time. It just means we get to figure it out together."

"Thank you for the encouragement," Lylah replies with a smile but nothing about it seems heartfelt. I can tell that Sourina is trying to comfort her, but I don't think it's working. I just wish Lylah believed those words as much as we did.

Chapter 23
Ellis

Sourina leads the way the next morning. We ride cautiously towards the border, on high alert as we analyze every tree and rock for possible soldiers. Crossing the border is easier than I thought. Only a few people are moving in the far distance, but we walk the horses slowly so not to attract any attention. Even if the Arlieans sent more soldiers to the border, they would arrive long after we were gone.

The second night, we stay in a small village that hugs the coastline. Small fishing boats rock in the water, tied to a small wooden dock. A kind gentleman points to a sizable cottage that occasionally hosts travelers. A widow whose husband died in the war welcomes us into her home with a delicious supper and tea with cakes afterwards. Thankfully, I didn't have to share a room with anyone this time.

The next day's ride was mentally easier, each minute bringing us closer to Rinmor. The roaring sound of waves hitting the shoreline echoes up the cliffs we ride on top of. This scenery is flatter than I've seen so far on this trip; the only trees are a distance away, outlining the forest to our right. Tall blades of grass sway in a rhythmic dance beneath us.

Just as my back begins cramping, we arrive at a shadowy castle-like figure against the darkening orange sky. A crumbling stone wall disappears into blackness with an iron gate that lays crooked off one hinge.

Sourina speaks up as we trot past the gate. "The castle shouldn't be too far up the stairs. It's going to be hard maneuvering in the dark, so maybe we camp out down here until first light?"

I fidget with my reins and eye the darkness for any clues of what to do. "We could camp here but I don't like the openness. There are many other things that are still dangerous."

"You are right about that," a male voice says from the darkness. Torches begin lighting rapidly around us. We're completely surrounded by men with outstretched swords and a several drawn bows aimed at our chests. Lylah grips her reins beside me as her horse takes a step back. Fear radiates in her eyes as the figures block us in on all sides. Sourina is the first to get down from her horse with her hands raised.

"Now, that's what I like to see," the same man grins as he inspects our gear and horses.

I instinctively grab my daggers.

"I suggest you put your daggers away." His words catches me off guard. "I would hate for someone to get hurt."

Did he see me reach for them? How did he guess they were daggers and not something else?

They tie my hands first, the greatest threat between the three of us. I look at faces I can just barely make out, hoping to get any kind of clue of who they are, but none of them are familiar.

Lylah and Sourina are bound next before we're shoved up the stairs towards the stone castle sitting high on the cliffside. The light from the torches only illuminating sections of the dark exterior. Lylah struggles against the bonds, her small frame fighting against the men holding her wrists.

"It's going to be okay," I say to her and when I manage to catch her eyes, it's like she didn't hear me. We ascend one stone stair at a time into what appears to be the main entrance.

"Trust me," I mouth to her, but this is one of the few moments I've ever felt helpless.

Torch flames allow me to see our captors more clearly. The man holding my restraints is of muscular build, towering over me with immense strength. The pungent smell of his sweat-soaked shirt is overpowering.

I have to take the chance, no matter how slim.

Taking a deep breath, I jab my elbow into his side and knock him off balance. In the next second, I kick in his right knee as it bends back unnaturally. His screams of agony rings in my ear but I tune it out. With one swift motion, I relieve him of his blade strapped to his side and push him down the stairs with a forceful shove of my shoulder. I eye my next target with tunnel focus and try to throw him off balance with my foot before he swipes a long silver blade at me. Dodging it is muscle memory before another glint from a blade catches my eye.

A voice halts me mid-motion.

"I imagine slitting her throat would be like cutting through butter." The man from earlier is holding onto Lylah with a curved blade at her neck.

His slender, pointed nose is more visible now in the brighter light. Long wavy black hair outlines his face, which stops at his chest. A scar runs down the side of his neck before disappearing into his shirt collar.

My stomach drops at the sight of her against his blade. A small trail of blood begins rolling down her smooth olive skin. I drop my blade immediately and it pings off the stone and down several stairs.

Narrowing his eyes at me, he removes the blade from her neck slowly. I let out a quiet sigh of relief. Her shoulders drop before the man pushes her roughly towards the entrance. My jaw clenches at the sight of her being caught in this uncertain situation. My need to protect her runs deeper than I imagined. Is it my threatened freedom that's behind this tightness in my chest?

I glance back at Sourina, but her face remains rigid. She glares up at me with anger clearly brewing in her eyes before a new guard jerks my bound hands, forcing me to look ahead. I don't know what she's angry at me for when she's the one who suggested this castle in the first place.

Iron doors reach up into the starry sky and creak as they open. I take in every detail I can gather from the limited light with every step into the vast open entry room and its stone carved walls and pillars reaching up past the darkness. Wooden crates line the borders of light while more men gather in clusters whispering to each other.

The room goes silent in a matter of seconds as soon as the scarred man stops in the middle. This doesn't seem to faze him when he circles Lylah for a split second before coming to me. Everyone in the room seems to collectively step forward to watch the commotion.

"Your reputation is quite legendary around here." The man strokes the stubble on his face. I keep my composure nuetral as I try to suppress every urge in my body to find a way to slit his throat.

"I don't know what you're talking about," I flatly say while keeping my eyes trained on him.

"We haven't met yet, Ellis, but I've seen you from a distance. We work for some of the same people." In the light, his dark brown eyes hide behind wavy hair. His confidence seems to be anchored in the mystery of who he is.

My voice is even when I respond. "We're travelers on our way to Rinmor wanting to find shelter for the night." The men holding our bound hands shift slightly, their boots echoing in the vast space.

The man makes his way to Sourina and observes her cold brown eyes staring back at him. "I was planning to let you go all, but meeting you Ellis was far more intriguing." The man takes slow steps to come back into my field of vision.

I meet his gaze as hatred boils. "What do you want?"

"I currently don't want anything. Only to say it is a privilege to have you as a guest in my castle," He proclaims loudly as he gestures around him.

His castle? This castle belongs to the royal family. He's merely a trespasser who claimed it as his own.

"Do you bind all of your guests?" The rope around my hands stirs more anger in me. I force it down.

After a few moments, the scarred man nods at the men behind us who slice the rope off our hands. Lylah rubs her wrists and glares at him before wiping the trail of blood with the back of her cloak sleeve.

"I'm Taramin and this is my crew." He flashes a smile that's neither happy or playful. "You're welcome to join us for the night and free to leave in the morning. What kind of host would I be if I didn't offer you a warm meal and beds to sleep in?"

Considering it for a few seconds, I nod my head and give a strained smile. He won't let us out of here without accepting his invitation. There's a purpose to this game he's secretly playing. I just don't know what it is yet.

Taramin leads us further into the castle and rounds a corner to open doors that lead into a dining room, resembling the one in the Rinmor palace. Long rows of handmade tables and benches occupied by laughing and talking figures fill the room. As soon as we enter, every voice hushes to an absolute silence. Every head turns in our direction.

"Proceed." Taramin waves his hand towards the shadows and talking fills the dining hall once more. We make our way to the fire place where a giant iron pot hangs over a raging fire and the smells coming from the pot make my stomach growl.

A man dressed in a gray tunic stands by the pot and stirs whatever is in it before serving us each a bowl. We take them and sit at an empty table. Heads turn to look at us, but I only stare at the bowl of soup and relish the heat on my face. If anyone is stupid enough to attack us when I'm this hungry, they'll experience pain they never imagined.

Taramin pats me on the back and I stiffen. "I have a few things to take care of. Enjoy the soup and Flop over there will make sure you get to your beds for the night." He gestures to a man sitting at an adjacent table who dips his head in acknowledgement. "Also, I hope allowing you to keep your daggers is a sign of good faith between us. Breaking the knee on one of my men was an unforeseen loss that I'll choose to ignore for now." His teeth flash into a sly smile. "I'll just have to count you in my debt."

I swallow hard. Something tells me I don't want to be in his debt. A problem for another day.

He turns to go before stopping. "Do say hi to the Shadow Dealer for me."

I stiffen again at the mention of the Shadow Dealer. We wait until Taramin is out of the room before our shoulders collectively relax. Sourina digs into her soup first and nods her head before taking another huge bite. Lylah follows suit, but I observe the surrounding figures. Faces aged with time sit alongside those young and inexperienced.

Sourina brings my attention back. "Do you think we can trust him?"

I take a bite. "Never trust anyone."

She looks around thoughtfully. "I think we should leave as early as possible tomorrow. We can still hit the mountain pass down into Rinmor and be there by late afternoon."

I nod at her suggestion. Slurping of soup fills the next few minutes, along with the chatter hovering around us.

Sourina sighs as she sits back. "That was excellent soup. Best I ever had I think."

"Food always tastes better when you've had a long day," Lylah says as her wooden spoon scrapes the bottom of the bowl.

I lean back as well. My fingertips linger near my daggers, every shadow uncertain. Sourina stares ahead, seeming to be lost in thought while Lylah lays her head down on the table.

"Are you okay?" I ask after a few moments.

Lylah looks up at me, startled. "Yeah, I'm okay." My eyes shift down to her neck where the blood has smeared across and dried.

A pause stretches between us.

Over the noise of the room, I hear her small voice say, "I'm scared."

A dagger falls into my hand at the ready, but deep down, I know that's not what she means. I don't say anything, but allow her space to elaborate if she wants to. If I've learned anything from spending this past week with her is that she'll speak when she's ready.

She shrugs. "I guess I'm scared of my future. Only a month ago, I was no one, but now I feel like this massive weight rests on my shoulders. I hold this power inside me, and what if I end up hurting someone else?"

Sourina leans towards her. "I know what that weight feels like. My grandmother always told me how important our family is and the responsibility we hold. Let me just tell you now that it never goes away."

Lylah's shoulders sag at the words and I twist the dagger in my fingers between the folds of the cloak. I don't think Sourina or I truly know what she's going through and perhaps we never will.

We sit like that, the fire's blazing light around us and the weight of the world on all our shoulders.

Chapter 24
Lylah

The next morning, our horses and all our supplies are waiting for us as promised. Even Taramin comes out to wave us goodbye with a grin disguised as friendly. Something is very off about him. The fact that he let us go so easily with a brief and cryptic conversation is more unsettling. But I'm too tired to analyze it right now.

Ellis leads the way across the clifftop plains with the ocean waves crashing down below. The ocean this far north is a different kind of beauty than off the shores of Rinmor. More wild and unpredictable. Several jagged rocks shoot out from the water through the mist which I can only guess to be the North Ribs. I've never seen them in person, but the maps I've looked at in the library illustrated their approximate location. I look one last time before we turn west towards the mountain pass.

I've come to look forward to the way wind rushes through my hair. The beauty here is unmatched by anything I've ever seen, the lively greenery of the Volsan mountain forest beginning to mold around us. Being in the saddle this long starts to feel like I'm one with it after so many days of soreness.

Before the sun begins dipping down from its high place in the sky, the city of Rinmor emerges out of the horizon. As we get closer, the familiar smell of the ocean brings out an unexpected smile on my face. In front of me, Ellis' body seems to relax as we almost race to the gate. The horses neigh as we push them harder to reach home.

The road thickens with travelers on their way to the port for what most people come to Rinmor for: a chance at profitable business deals. King's guards line the main gate entrance as we approach, checking each traveler's bags and wagon beds. They weren't here before but it makes sense for the king to increase security with the growing tensions.

We wait patiently in the line of people, every horse and wagon in front of us weighed down with sacks of goods. The guards stop Sourina first and open her horse's saddle bags.

Ellis steps in to stop him. "Look, she's only a scholar on her way to see the king."

The soldier pauses at the mention of the king but pushes his way past Ellis and takes out a few books. He scans the pages before putting them back in the bag roughly. He inspects the other side, which is only filled with jars of herbs and cloth-wrapped plants, roots and all.

Sourina shifts uncomfortably next to me as she fidgets with her sleeve. To a stranger, she would appear to be a scholar or healer, but those items are the only ones she selected to bring with her from home. Books she probably explored with her grandmother, each page holding special memories.

The soldier puts the jars back as they clink against each other. Sourina clenches her hands into fists. I move in front of her to keep her from making any sudden movements that may provoke the soldiers.

"Move along." The soldier's voice is gruff as he gestures us forward.

Ellis nods stiffly, and we mount our horses again before making our way through the familiar sights and smells of the port city.

My stomach churns with anticipation about seeing the king, his intense stare and contemplating eyes flash in my mind. The feeling is immediately accompanied by an unexpected sting of sadness as I look over at Ellis, who's only focused on the road ahead.

What will he do when he gets his freedom? Are these few moments riding side by side the last ones I get to spend with him?

The palace and the cliff it's carved into are shadowed in the afternoon light. As we approach, tower guards let us pass after some questioning. The grounds are eerily quiet with only the sound of whistling wind against harsh edges of stone.

"Welcome back!" Finnon exclaims as he emerges from between the rounded pillars of the main entrance and the lifeless rose vines that cling to them.

"Finnon," I smile tiredly as I get down from my horse and step towards him. "It's good to see you."

He takes my hands and gives them a gentle squeeze. "We were so worried. Two days ago, one of the horses you took was escorted here from the border."

Ellis interjects as he adjusts the straps of his saddlebags. "We were going around the armies at the border when a thunderstorm hit and spooked the horses. Arlieans found the other one."

Finnon's eyes go wide as if imagining the scene before him. Sourina moves around her horse to unstrap her packs.

"Let the servants do that," Finnon scolds, before she catches his gaze.

"Maureen?" Finnon freezes and his eyes sweep across her face for a few second.

"How do you know my grandmother?"

"My name is Finnon." He gives a wide smile. "She was a very special lady to me. You look just like she did many years ago." He moves closer to Sourina, and somehow he appears younger.

"She spoke of you often," she says and inhales sharply. "She passed away a few days ago. Before we left Point Theane."

Finnon's lips press together as he hugs Sourina suddenly. Sourina stiffens but wraps her arms around him. "I am so sorry to hear that. She was truly a marvelous person."

Ellis stops beside me and clears his throat. "Finnon, I need to see the king."

My stomach drops with those words. Is he leaving right now?

"Ellis... " His name rolls off my tongue in a whisper.

Finnon shakes his head. "The king is indisposed at the moment and will be unavailable until tonight. He has requested that you all join him for dinner in the dining hall."

Finnon motions for several servants to get the horses. Sourina follows Finnon as he leads the way through the arched entrance doors. Ellis and I stay standing on the wide cobble path. I should be glad to be back but a sliver of my heart feels unsettled.

He dips his head slightly, "You did great. On the trip, I mean."

"Are you–" I begin to say as my mouth moves ahead of my mind.

He interrupts me, "I'll see you tonight." I don't even get to finish my question when he turns and strides away.

The maids take their time bathing me, scrubbing every inch of my body as dirt and sweat spirals down to the bottom of the gold tub. Lavender stocks and rose petals float on the warm water in this peaceful moment that doesn't seem real. As they move to lather my hair in expensive oils and soaps, I feel truly clean for the first time since I left.

They put me in a dress made of forest green fabric that flows from my curves but thick enough for the colder weather. I don't complain about the tightness of the fabric as I want to because this is my life now. It feels weird being back in this persona when I haven't cared about how I looked the last week. I watch as they pin my hair in a pile of curls on my head before applying a deeper red powder to my lips and cheeks.

"Do you require anything else, milady?" One of them ask as they glance at me through the mirror on my vanity desk.

"No, I don't need anything at the moment. You may go." My voice sounds softer from the last time I was in this room. Before I felt intoxicated by the power being in this room provided, but today, I sit here unsure of who I am. The last week has changed me in a way I can't begin to process right now.

The maids bow and leave.

Once all alone again, the reflection looking back at me has empty eyes and sagging shoulders. I inspect her slightly hollowed cheekbones, full lips and some blonde strands that swirl down. My streak of ginger is pulled back and hidden behind the rest of my hair.

A knock startles me and when I open the door, Ellis stands at the door in formal attire. A jaw muscle clenches as he runs his eyes over my body before meeting my gaze.

"You look…" Ellis mutters slowly before clearing his throat, "Clean."

I smile at the odd comment and the thud from the door closing echos in the hallway. "You look clean as well."

I can't help but compliment him in the same way. The difference between our traveling selves is like night and day. His stubbed jaw is now smooth and the mess of curls that I've grown used to are now slicked back with oil.

He offers me his arm and I take it hesitantly. The formality of this exchange grows in the pit of my stomach. Everything we've gone through seems like it never happened, and I'm not willing to let it all go yet.

"It feels strange being back here after our trip." I break the silence with the most obvious thought we must share.

Ellis looks around at anything but me. At the walls and the various paintings framed in gold. Even the torches that light our path through the maze of hallways that take longer for me to remember.

"Yeah, I suppose it is," he murmurs but doesn't initiate any other conversation. I don't make another attempt either.

The dining room is set for a small gathering with tall candlesticks and a dark linen tablecloth. The exquisite centerpiece is a delectably seared swordfish on a silver platter. Smaller plates of sautéed vegetables, a variety of baked rolls, and delicate porcelain bowls filled with sauces scatter across the table in an intricate display.

Sourina is already seated when we arrive so Ellis pulls out the seat for me between her and where the king will be. Ellis takes the seat across from Sourina and immediately sips whatever liquid is in the gold goblet.

"This is quite the extravagant display of food, isn't it?" Sourina exclaims as she gapes at the giant swordfish topped with browned onions and peppers. I'm not sure she has ever seen this much luxurious food in one place before. The anticipation of trying each dish clearly reflects in her eyes.

"Yes, the king enjoys elaborate dinners," I say as I place the cloth napkin on my lap.

Right as I mention the king, the double doors to the dining room open and a guard announces his arrival. King Addard doesn't have the extravagant crown on his head and no royal robe trailing behind him tonight. Finnon follows close behind him with a grin as his warm eyes connect with each of us.

"Welcome back. I am so glad to see you all back safely." King Addard states as a servant pulls out his chair at the head of the table. Finnon seats himself across from me before an awkward silence envelops as servants come to cut the flakey meat off the fish and scoop the various dishes onto our plates.

We wait as is customary for the king to take the first bite. When he does, the servants all exit, leaving us with the privacy to talk freely.

King Addard sips his wine while glancing at me, but shifts his dark gaze to Sourina. "Did you find what you were looking for?"

I jump slightly. "My apologies, Your Majesty. This is Sourina Loumon. She is the granddaughter of Maureen Loumon, who wrote those letters we discovered in the library. She has come to teach me what her family has passed down about my powers and the mages."

The king gives Sourina a small nod, which she returns with an uncertain smile. I'm sure she feels nervous being in the presence of a king, an enemy king no less, but at least tonight is less rigid.

"You are welcome to stay in my palace during your training with Lylah. I look forward to seeing what you can teach her," he says while cutting a piece of fish on his plate with graceful movements.

Talking ceases temporarily while we each enjoy the next several bites.

"So tell me, Ellis," the king directs his attention to Ellis next. "How was being in Arliea? Did you have any trouble getting inside their borders?"

Ellis places his fork on the plate before answering. "Yes, we had some trouble and unfortunately, we lost both of the horses we departed with. Despite that, we made it into Arliea quite easily by walking. The armies don't stretch out across the entire border, so we were able to find a stretch with no soldiers."

King Addard nods. "Yes, Finnon informed me when the soldiers found one of my horses a few days ago. It seems that you were able to purchase more horses."

After a quick sip of wine, Ellis explains how the Arliean gold the king provided was enough for a bargain with a man we helped along the road. Ellis proceeds to tell the story of Joweck and his family, how they housed us and fed us the night we were soaking wet from the storm with no horse and barely any supplies.

Sourina listens with interest while Ellis outlines our trip with minimal detail, saying just enough to satisfy the king's questions. Surprisingly, he leaves out the part about the crew we ran into at the abandoned castle only last night. His jaw tenses as he finishes the story. But I've learned to pick up on his little mannerisms like the brow scrunch he has now is him battling with himself.

"My sympathies on your grandmother's passing," the king says solemnly. Sourina dips her head at his genuine words before finishing the last few bits of food on her plate.

Dessert arrives in the form of a large assortment of berry and fruit tarts with various whipped cream flower designs on them. As I take a small bite, I nearly moan at the well balanced tartness and sweet notes of the cream. It's the first sweet thing I've eaten in a week and I have to remind myself where I am.

Ellis picks at his tart with his fork after only taking one taste. His distant mood and the realization this is likely our last meal makes me lose my appetite. But I take another bite anyway, if only to keep myself from thinking about him leaving.

Chapter 25
Lylah

"Quit moving around," Sourina grunts at me and her voice radiates the lingering frustration of the afternoon. With my eyes closed, it makes it hard to take her seriously. We sit outside under a large evergreen tree in the East Gardens of the palace with the wind lazily curling around us.

Sourina was banging on my door at dawn this morning to start our first lesson. I slid further under the covers before a servant got her a key to my suites. King Addard made it clear that my training would start right away, but anxiety pooled at the unknown.

"Focus on your breathing," she says in a soothing tone, each word phrased like a beautiful poem. "Focus on the birds chirping around us. Feel the wind in your hair... on your face."

I scrunch my nose and force myself to focus. The grass beneath us provides some cushion from the firm ground as I stretch out both hands to feel each blade skim my fingertips. A stronger gust of wind pushes loose strands of hair across my face in long ribbons. I hear an echo of a bird's wings flapping.

Deep breath in.

Deep breath out.

My body feels heavy and light at the same time with each breath. My tangled thoughts begin to unravel.

"Good," Sourina whispers. "Reach further inside yourself for warmth. Like you're stretching your hands out towards a fire."

I attempt to mentally reach down inside my body for some source of warmth, but I don't understand what it's supposed to feel like. A small burst of heat suddenly radiates up my arm and I jerk away.

"No," Sourina says gently. "Don't push it away but invite it in."

I try to remember how it was in the library, the only other time I felt that warmth which started me on this wild journey. My breathing accelerates as the smell of burning flesh cuts through my mind and the feel of the knife slicing through my arm like fresh bread. Hopelessness claws at my chest as it did that day and many of the days since. I strain to focus on the warmth as if it's a friend and not an enemy.

Small burst pulses in my left arm this time and climb slowly to my shoulder. A burning sensation spreads across my chest. Every muscle in my body clenches tightly.

I gasp as the air starts evaporating from my lungs and my breathing turns shallow and rapid. I grasp the grass before my shoulders begin to shake.

"Lylah!" a voice is shouting, but it's so distant I barely sense where it's coming from.

After what feels like an eternity, the voice yells again, "Lylah!" My shoulders shake violently and the heat inside my chest begins to slowly crawl back from where it came.

"Open your eyes... please." I recognize Sourina's voice when I slowly crack open my eyes. She leans over me with a firm expression, but with eyes full of fear.

She rubs her forehead and presses her face into her hands. "Oh, Lylah."

I glance up at the sky in a dazed moment before sitting up from the lying position I find myself in.

"What happened?" I ask as I look around.

An uneven sign escapes her. "You almost passed out from not having any air in your lungs. You were gasping for breath for at least three minutes or longer."

"I was on the ground for that long?"

The worry in her face confirms it as she wraps her arms around herself.

I struggle up from the ground and dust the grass from my dress.

The stories of Movak's ease with wielding nips at me. I want to try again and again until I get it right. No matter the cost.

"We're done practicing for today," Sourina says firmly as she gathers all of her books, rolls of parchment, and walks back inside without another word. Her curls bobbing up and down with each fleeing step.

I decide to stay longer in the East Gardens after my breathing settles back to a steady rhythm again. Guards post themselves at every corner, but far enough away that I don't feel like they're following my every movement. My dress is plain today with no exquisite detailing, which I prefer these days. I almost look like I don't belong roaming in the king's gardens, but scrubbing his floors again.

Some of the flowers have started to lose their petals while other more resilient flowers remain open to the world. A cluster of statues captures my attention as they stand like solemn guards, paying tribute to the people they represent. I step closer to the marble statue in the middle. At the foot of the statue are letters pressed into sheets of metal spelling out words I can't quite distinguish. Moss and vines have started to climb up the stone as he stands stoic with a long robe and a sword at his hip. The towering figure appears to be contemplating something challenging with his head tilted towards the right.

"That's Movak Torgin," King Addard's voice states behind me. "The first Fire Mage."

My head snaps back to look at him with my mouth gaping open. "This was Movak?" It makes sense now. I've seen this figure in the southern square with Bella but didn't know who he was at the time.

The king steps forward as we admire the impeccable craftsmanship of the statue side by side. I feel as though Movak is standing right in front of me instead of us being separated by two hundred years.

"Yes. He was a gifted fighter and served the kingdoms very well with his skills in politics, royal affairs, and war." There's something off in his tone, as if scoffing at Movak's achievements. "It's okay to accept that your service to the kingdoms will look different than that of Movak and his mages. I know you will be a great Fire Mage as well."

Mastering my powers will be more difficult than I ever imagined. That much became evident only moments ago with Sourina. But maybe there's truth in his words, Movak and I will never be the same. Maybe it's time I stop comparing myself to him.

"Thank you," I mutter unenthusiastically.

"How are your lessons going?"

"It's been harder than I thought." I don't look at him, but clench my jaw instead. "Sourina has been trying to teach me from her grandmother's book, which has apparently been passed down in her family since Movak. But we're both doing the best we can." I pause, feeling envy rise up. "The book says Movak was a natural and could wield fire after his first try."

Movak's statue doesn't look contemplative anymore but smug, as if mocking me.

"I became king when I was only four years old. My entire family slaughtered right in front of me." He pauses and I turn to him.

"Things may seem daunting, but we bravely find the strength to do what we must."

Our eyes meet for a moment and the raw pain there is undeniable. The scenes of his family no doubt flashing in front of those golden eyes. His shoulders sag for just sliver of a second before his kingly demeanor slides into place and wipes away any evidence he even showed emotion at all.

"I'm so sorry about your family." The words are more of a whisper than I intend. The empathetic part of me wants to reach out to him, but I keep my hands at my sides.

A sad smile creeps across his lips. "Don't stay out here too long or you will catch a cold."

Chapter 26
Ellis

"Come in."

King Addard sits at the desk in his study as I enter. I bow before choosing to stand in a relaxed but alert stance in front of him. The room is the same as when I last saw it, on a mundane afternoon when I was offered the terms for my freedom. But standing here right now, I feel changed in a way I can't quite place.

He shuffles some papers around before looking up. "You managed to get everyone back safely, including the most important people in the kingdoms right now. For that, you have my gratitude."

A part of me wants to say that we almost didn't make it back and tell him of the crew hiding in the old castle to the north, but I clench my jaw tightly and nod instead. It's a near failure I'm not ready to admit with my freedom so close.

He lifts a quill up from the desk and dips it in a small gold pot of ink before scribbling something across a flattened piece of parchment. Melted wax follows suit along with a metal stamp which he presses into the hardening liquid.

"As promised," he holds the parchment out to me. "Your freedom."

I take it with zero hesitation, roll it up and tuck it behind my back beneath my shirt. He raises an eyebrow slightly but doesn't say anything.

"I do have a proposition for you if you are interested. I would assume it would pay way more than what you could find on the streets." King Addard puts the quill down and stands.

I wait as he moves towards the window and looks out across the roofs of houses in the far distance, towards the sea. His robe and crown are nowhere to be seen today. The man in front of me can almost be mistaken for a wealthy merchant or elite member of society, not the king that he is. If I saw him on the streets, he would make for an easy target.

"Your Majesty?" My eyebrows rise in curiosity as my trained eyes linger on him.

The silence is uncomfortable before he speaks. "Lylah needs a skilled bodyguard until she is ready to be on her own. The powers of the Fire Mage run in her veins, but she hasn't yet harnessed their full potential. Which means right now, she is vulnerable."

The proposition is not something I saw coming.

"May I have a few days to think about it?" I shift on my feet, not sure how he takes to being asked to wait. I want to have time to think over the details before I subject myself to another contract.

"Take a few days to think but the offer will not stand for long." He glances back at me briefly. "Even these walls can't hold off the enemy. Her safety is in jeopardy. I would think fast if I were you."

Something heavy presses down on my chest at those words. I bow on my way out but he doesn't look at me again.

Once I'm back in the room I've been staying in, I ask a servant to get me a satchel which I use to pack the few clothing items that belong to me. The fancy dinner wear is not to my taste nor will I need it out in the city. The old Ellis would have taken them and sold each one for a profit but I leave them hanging on the ornate wooden hangers.

Walking out of the gates and into the crowded streets is something I thought I wouldn't do so soon. Rinmor is just the same as how I left it. Townsfolk move up and down the streets with their wagons as mothers usher their children out of the way. I eye every single person that I pass. The Shadow Dealer will find out I'm in the city soon. If he hasn't already.

I head straight to my room by the docks. Carther has likely come and gone during the time I've been away. Walking through the living room indicates that I'm right. There's no teacup by the fire and the usual warmth of the room is now darkened by drawn curtains.

Once up the stairs to my room, it's exactly as I left it, with my neatly made bed and the small desk by the window overlooking the harbor. Its surface is still scattered with my scrolls and knives needing sharpening on the grinding rock. I set my satchel down on the desk and dust springs up in the visible sun rays.

A firm knock suddenly echoes in the room and hushed voices sound below my window. Every nerve in my body comes alive. I grip one of my daggers between my fingers.

"Oh, Ellis." The taunting voice is one I recognize. How did he even get in?

I move soundlessly to retrieve my bag. Glancing at the window, I guess the distance to the ground when I remember a small ledge that could give me enough leverage to get up on the roof without risking broken bones. I unlatch the window so I can escape with just a few movements.

Taking a few deep breaths, I open the door. Men pour into the compact space of my bedroom. Our eyes meet as the Shadow Dealer steps through the small door. He gives a chuckle before stopping a few feet away while his men form a half circle, blocking the only obvious exit.

"Ellis, Ellis... you've been a hard man to find this past month."

I stand my ground as he glares down at me with a chilling demeanor. Looking at his full muscular build, I never understood why he needed bodyguards. He must take them everywhere to show his strength in employed men at his disposal. My heart rate quickens as he steps even closer. I step back into my desk and the contents on top rattle.

"Your last job was incomplete. You know how I feel about that." He crosses arms across his chest. His blue eyes are sharp, like his disappointed stare can cut right through me.

I gulp audibly. The job he's referring to took a turn when I rescued a certain girl from uncertain outcomes.

My voice sounds charming as I reply, "You and I have had a close working relationship for quite some time. Trust is one of the well established things between us." I smile with a confidence I don't feel, but an illusion is the best way to make sure these dealings go smoothly.

"I had trusted you to get the job done, but the item you were assigned to retrieve wasn't in my hands by the deadline."

I nod stiffly. "I ran into an issue that night and I couldn't complete the assignment. I had to...." I search for the right words. "Pay off a debt."

He drums his fingers on his other arm. The silence increases my uncomfortability and jumping out the window sounds more appealing. "My men held bets and concluded you ran off with it."

I calculate my exit route more precisely. The tone of his words shrouded in a thin veil of threats.

"In the past, you've hired me for far more expensive and enticing items. Why would I take this one?" The logic makes perfect sense to me and I hope it buys me more time to think.

In just two strides, he has a knife to my throat. I don't fight his blade because trying to escape now will be a death sentence.

Matching his blazing glare, a thought comes to me. "Taramin said to tell you hello." The words sound unnatural on my tongue, but the Shadow Dealer freezes. His knife wavers slightly.

"What did you just say?"

"Taramin said to tell you hello," I repeat the words as color drains from his face.

His knife lowers before sheathing it behind his back, nodding to his men who promptly back out of the room.

"You have one last chance to get me that pocket watch." He looks down at me just long enough to make me feel like a child. "You're in luck. Sir Winhester's ship docked this morning and we all know where he's going to be tonight." He pauses. "If you fail again, our next encounter will not be so merciful. I have yet to cut off a finger or two this week."

I nod slightly before he stalks out of the room, allowing me to breathe again.

I find myself on the same fence post in front of the same tavern as when I had chosen my morals over my job. It's colder tonight than that night and thankfully, no girl to rescue that'll result in my arrest and servitude.

Shaking the memories out of my head, I focus on the passersby.

The plan I had that same night is the same one I'm sticking with on such short notice. A tavern full of drunk witnesses who won't remember anything except for memories of good music and a jolly time is the best cover.

I jump down from my onlooking position and enter the tavern where a stiff scent of mead and baked bread rushes past my nose. The threats from the Shadow Dealer drive me to find a seat at a table in the back and order the delicious drink from the woman carrying them on her tray.

She gives me a seductive smile as she sets it down, her assets on full display to sample, but I politely take out a coin from my pocket and put it in her hand. The woman doesn't hide her disappointment before walking away.

A table next to me begins playing a betting card game which I join, pretending to slur my words and make subtle comments about the many coins needing to be relieved from my pockets. The game is easy to manipulate as I facilitate some wins and some losses. My game companions laugh as they slam their mead cups onto the wooden table and exclaim when a winning hand is revealed.

I mimic their sluggish movements when a door swings open and three figures walk through the small tavern entrance. A few sideways glances are exchanged as Sir Winhester adjusts what little hair he has left on his head. After looking around, the merchant claims a nearby empty table in my line of vision.

Taking a long swig, I inspect the two bodyguards over the rim of my cup. They both carry themselves as if they're hired hands from the dock who've only been in a few fights. Their eyes scan their surroundings for long minutes before relaxing after not perceiving any apparent threats.

I wait about an hour or so, observing the various factors that could hinder my success. Sir Winhester has managed to drink more than I thought was humanly possible for a man of his short stature. His words only starting to blend together in the last few minutes. The bodyguards begin indulging in a few beverages as well, making it easy for me to get invited to their table for a card game. Stories of the sea quickly spill out of them the longer we play. Their quests to seek the most exotic items become a favored topic.

Sir Winhester recalls loudly, "I once possessed a beautiful sapphire necklace that lived nestled deep in the breasts of the Murvoan queen!"

The men laugh at his claim. I raise my cup to join in. "To the Murvoan queen's supple breasts!"

"I'll drink to that." The merchant lifts his cup higher and drinks it in one breath. My eyes briefly land on the glimmering gold chain that secures the pocket watch. What is so important about this pocket watch?

One of the ladies glides over to the merchant with a pouty lip while pushing up her breasts. "What about my supple breasts?"

His eyes widen at the view and inserts several dekari between them. "They're also lovely, my darling. I'll be well acquainted with them tonight."

I take the opportunity to put down my cards and watch their

outburst of shock as I take the winnings from the middle.

"Looks like this is all mine. Sorry, gentlemen." I pretend to drunkenly stuff the mound of gold coins into my trouser pockets but purposefully miss a few and they roll under the table.

"Ya cheated!" One of the guards exclaims as he slams both hands on the table. The drinks jump in their places and slush onto the scuffed wood.

I sloppily laugh it off and continue to stuff my pockets. "You're just jealous you aren't as good of a player!"

The other guard grabs me by my collar and throws me into Sir Winhester, who spills his drink all over himself. I stagger into his chest again but relieve him of the watch before I'm slammed down on the table.

"Hey, not in my tavern! Take it outside," the bartender shouts over the ruckus. Everyone takes a minute to compose themselves when the watch lands into the safety of my cloak sleeve.

I stand up slowly and pretend to lose my balance. "Here, just as a sign of good faith."

A handful of gold coins are shoveled out of my pocket and scatter across the playing table. The men nod in satisfaction and sit down to resume the game. I say my goodbyes and walk out of the tavern with exactly what I came for.

Chapter 27
Ellis

"Take a seat." The Shadow Dealer motions with his eyes to the seat in front of him. "You're making them uneasy."

Two guards stand on either side of him as he inspects the watch with a circular magnifying glass, taking his time reviewing every surface. I shake off their intimidations and decline the offer to sit. Every exit out of this warehouse running on repeat in my head as I watch him.

"You actually lifted this right out of his pocket without him suspecting a thing?" He sits back in his black leather chair and genuinely smiles up at me. A rare sight I never thought I would see. I nod smugly at the veiled compliment. He doesn't hand those out very often either.

The Shadow Dealer places the pocket watch on a satin cloth in front of him. "Did you know that this pocket watch once belonged to King Founar?"

I shake my head.

"It's rumored to hold a secret." He sighs and folds the cloth around the watch. "I'm not sure what that is yet, but the thrill of figuring it out is usually the best part."

I never thought I would hold such a historical artifact, different from the gems and other precious items I usually steal.

He tilts his stubbled jaw line toward me. "You still owe me a secret."

I blink. I completely forgot that with each payout, I must share a secret with him I may have come across. His rates are higher, not only because of the level of job but the secret you bring back. It's one way the Shadow Dealer holds on to his control. Thoughts spin uncontrollably as I think through what I can tell him. Since my capture, I've learned lots of secrets, but none that would be good in his hands.

"The Mage's Tower." It feels like I spit out the words.

He sits up in his chair.

"What about it?" He asks with a tone on the edge of demanding and curious.

"I'm working on a lead for a big job, something on my own. I may have found something that reveals its location but it'll take more time to gain trust." The lie is easy to tell, but it cuts too close to a truth I need to protect.

The Shadow Dealer rubs his chin. "I'll accept that for now, but I expect to hear more." His eyes scan mine as if saying something only I can understand. For sparing my life, he expects me to cut him in on whatever I'm working on.

The Mage's Tower is whispered to hold secrets, scrolls that only exist there, and precious items that once belonged to the last mages. All confirmed by Maureen. The score from the tower would be more than enough to live like a king.

I simply nod. I'm not willing to verbally agree to anything.

"You're free to go."

I turn to leave, wishing my legs could move faster without seeming like I'm running out.

His voice halts me midstep. "Ellis, you're always welcome to join my crew. I've said it before, but the offer still stands."

I pause briefly before walking out of his warehouse, through the secret entrance and into the busy streets of Rinmor. Working for the Shadow Dealer has never been my plan. The life of being indebted to someone until death doesn't rank high in my goals. He's a hard man and his men work even harder to run his business. I never want to be under his thumb besides the few jobs I do for him. He pays me better than he does anyone else for my skill set. That's more than enough for me.

I make my way to the market as I often did before my arrest. Every few minutes, I side glance over my shoulder for anyone that may be trailing me. With the semi-fake secret I told the Shadow Dealer, I wouldn't blame him for having a few of his men follow me.

Liem Street is popular for its long rows of merchants and farmers who come everyday, despite the extreme cold and heat, to sell their goods. The selection of produce today are only the things that can be harvested during winter season like cabbage, beets, and turnips. I stop at a farmer's stand and hold up a dirt dusted carrot. No one sticks out of the ordinary when I glance around casually while patting my satchel gently to feel the journal I grabbed last minute.

"The carrots were hand picked this mornin'." The man smiles and holds up a cabbage. "If ya buy a cabbage, I'll throw in a few carrots for free."

There's a sliver of desperation in his voice as he holds up the green vegetable to me. Imagining the mouths he has to feed at home, I pay for the produce and a hand woven basket. I find a decent selection of apples down a few stalls and purchase those as well.

Missing the last month from my normal route lodges an anxious knot in my chest. Has my mother been okay these past weeks? I pause when I pass by an older woman selling colorful garden roses, the yellows and purples standing out in the gray surroundings. Handing her a dekari, I add the flowers to my basket.

The familiarity of my old routine briefly satisfies the impending loneliness that has started to creep in the last few nights. My days have been quiet and filled with lurking thoughts of the palace and Lylah. Her blue eyes swim in my vision every time I close mine, haunting my sleeping hours and shadowing my waking ones.

Will she be mad at me for leaving without so much as a word to her? I chew the inside of my lip, a habit I can't seem to break lately. Accepting the job at the palace will allow me to stay close to her. If I don't take the job, someone else will and I'll never be able to see her again.

"Do ya have some spare coins?" A small voice breaks through the tension building in my shoulders. Round bright blue eyes peek around the corner from the alleyway as a little girl steps out into the light. Matted hair surround her dirt-smudged face while her tiny hands tug on a tattered shirt that's too big.

I kneel on the hard dirt path and set my basket down. "What's your name?" My voice is oddly gentle.

"Ella." She tugs harder on her shirt before meeting my gaze again.

"Well, Ella, I have a few apples if you'd like them." I show her the bright red apples and watch her eyes light up.

"Thanks, mister," she says excitedly as she takes them. She's busy trying to put the apples in her pants pocket when something gold catches her attention. Two dekari stick up between my fingers.

"Here. Make sure you stay out of trouble with these." Ella nods and gives a smile unlike anything I've ever witnessed before clenching them tightly and taking off skipping down the alleyway.

Is that what Lylah looked like when she was a child? I can almost picture her begging on the street just like Ella had.

Shaking the thoughts away, I pick up my basket of goods and head to the one place I know I shouldn't go. My chest tightens again with each step and wish no one is home.

I pause before knocking on the familiar blue chipped door. The stone house with a straw roof on the edge of the city is one I'm not used to seeing in the daytime, but this will likely be the only opportunity for a while. Seeing the small garden down the dirt path brings back happy memories until the view of the ocean lodges a lump in my throat.

The door creaks open and my body freezes.

"Ellis?"

The voice pools anxiety in my stomach as I grip onto the basket harder, nearly snapping the bent twigs. I haven't heard my name being said that way in almost six years.

"Hi, Mom," I crook out.

Tears cloud her eyes as she ushers me in. Uncertainly wreaks havoc in my mind along with a mixture of emotions. Some I haven't felt in a very long time.

"How have you been?" She asks as stands in the entryway of my childhood home and motions me inside. The smell of the wood fire blazing in the hearth reminds me of when father was alive. Playing with him around the house and heading down to the beach to learn about the ocean and its creatures are all core memories here.

I set the basket down on the kitchen table. "I brought some food for you."

She inspects the food and narrows her green eyes. "You're the one that kept leaving the food baskets on the doorstep over the years?"

I meet her gaze reluctantly but nod. We haven't seen each other in six years and some of that was my fault. She was never supposed to find out it was me, but something about today made me homesick.

A tear slides down my mother's cheek as she clenches my face between her wrinkling hands in one swift motion. "I've been looking for you all around town over the years. I didn't know how to contact you after you left."

A firm expression slips into place. "You told me to leave and never come back. That's exactly what I did."

She retracts her hands and steps away slowly.

Her voice is small when she speaks again. "You killed someone, Ellis, when you were only twelve. I was scared." A small speck of fear still flashes in her eyes.

My heart beats faster at those true words. I did kill someone, but the past can't be undone.

"I knew I shouldn't have come." My jaw flexes as I take a few strides towards the door but she tugs at my arm.

"I... I just want to look at you a little longer," her voice breaks as another tear slides down her face. I stand where I am, not wanting to move, but unsure of what to do.

"You've changed so much," she observes and wipes her face with the back of her dress sleeve. "I wish your father was here."

My stomach drops at the mention of him. I miss my father but I know he wouldn't have been proud of me. I'm callused to the world unlike he was. His compassion for people always led his actions. He would have given up his last dekari if it meant helping someone in need.

I turn towards the door again. "I'll be gone for a while. I don't know when I'll be back."

"Ellis, please." She lets out a small cry. "You don't have to do those things anymore. Come live with me. We can build a new life together, away from all of those bad people. I have some money saved. We can make an honest living."

I feel like a child again, wanting her approval. "This new job is unlike anything I've ever done. It actually means something real. I can't tell you what it is, but it's dangerous, just in a different way."

She clasps her hands together and looks at me through teary eyes that could pierce a hole in my chest. "I know you'll always make your own decisions. You're a man now. But I'm still your mother and I'm allowed to worry about you."

"I know, Mom. I'm planning on doing something that matters. Something you would be proud of me for." I kiss her on the cheek and she wraps her arms around me.

"I'm always here, Ellis."

I pull away first. "I need to go before it gets dark."

She pats my arm and turns towards the metal pot hanging over the fire. "Well, stay for dinner, and then you can go. I just started a chicken roast and I know how much you love mashed potatoes."

I smile and agree to stay for dinner.

"Good to see you are back." The king says the next day as we stand in the dining hall waiting for the others to join us.

"You made a good offer," I reply, but don't look at him.

"My guards didn't alert me that you came through the gate."

"That's because I didn't. You have a few security vulnerabilities to say the least."

"Good to know," he replies rigidly.

I turn to him. "We'll have to discuss the terms of my employment if I'm to be her personal guard. My employment won't be cheap."

The king chuckles. "I expected nothing less."

Before I have a chance to say anything else, Lylah walks in with the most stunning dress that pins me in place. The silver and red details of the fabric mimic star-like patterns as it trails on the ground behind her. Her eyes find mine as they widen, and her lips part only briefly before walking past me.

Sourina follows after her in a forest green tunic dress. Her curls are pinned back away from her face. She gives me a small smile, which I return, and pull out the chair for her. Lylah is already seated when I try to catch her glance again.

The food brought out on silver and gold trays is as extravagant as usual, with dishes of roasted pork and candied beets. Never in my life have I eaten so many spoonfuls of caviar, but the briny beads of flavor have grown to my liking.

Lylah looks everywhere but at me, mostly with a clenched jaw and stiff shoulders. The tension radiating off her is palpable as she stabs her pork and scrape the silver knife across the porcelain plate.

No one reacts to the odd behavior, but continue to talk about various topics like the weather and next steps in Lylah's training.

Since the moment I met her, we've formed an unspoken connection that has caught me by surprise. A part of me imagined Lylah would be upset for not saying anything to her when I left, but I was only gone for three days. She's acting like I disappeared for months.

"Dinner was delicious, thank you, Your Majesty." Lylah bats her eyelashes ever so slightly at him.

The dessert in front of me suddenly loses its flavor and I push it away.

King Addard scoots his seat back and announces that he has some work to complete tonight and will see us in the morning. "Ellis, tomorrow morning at eight in my study." I nod as leaves.

Lylah excuses herself and heads through the double doors with quickened steps. I give her a few minutes head start before deciding to go after her.

Sourina taps my arm as I pass. "She's not doing well."

I pause, furrowing my brows. "What do you mean?"

"Her powers... It's like they're being blocked by something. My guess is something in her mind is blocking her connection to them. We've been working nonstop since you left and I've only had to stop her from killing herself six times."

My heart nearly stops at those words. "What?"

"She's stubborn and feels like she has to master it instantly. When she tries to use her powers, they're getting trapped in her chest, close to her heart. Several times she has pushed herself past her limit and passed out from the exertion on the wrong areas of her body." Sourina wears a worried expression, deepened by the candlelight hue. If what she says is true, it's definitely concerning.

"Is there any way to get her to clear the blockage in her mind, so to speak?" I never thought I would say a sentence like that in my life.

"Yes, I've been reading about it in my grandmother's journal. An emotional block can limit a mage's powers. Only they can clear it if they overcome whatever they're feeling. I guess a few of the other mages had to."

I shift on my heels and rub my hands through my hair. "Well, how do we do that?"

"Not we. You. I've only known her for a short time, but I've seen her connection with you. Something is seriously bothering her and I'm hoping," Sourina pauses, "she will face it with you."

She gives me an encouraging smile, but I feel like she just asked me to pluck the stars out of the sky. Emotions and talking about people's feelings are the last things I'm good at. My method of dealing with emotions usually involves punching something or throwing daggers into flesh.

"Please, just give it a try," Sourina pleads with her eyes, gripping my arm harder.

"Fine, but you owe me for this," I say loud enough for her to hear before heading out to find Lylah.

Chapter 28
Lylah

The night sky doesn't give me the same kind of peace tonight as it usually does. My fears bubble up like a spring overflowing. My mind splits in a thousand directions, thinking of everything all at once.

Being in this palace without Ellis had been harder than I anticipated. I knew he would leave, I just didn't think it would be so soon and without even saying goodbye. I thought I had prepared myself once we got back from Arliea, but not enough it seemed. Now he's back, and I can't help but feel anger and relief all at the same time.

One emotion fighting for control over the other.

"The city looks beautiful from up here." The familiar voice quiets my racing thoughts for only a few moments. I don't say anything but lean on the rock wall and look out over the twinkling lights of candles burning in the lamp posts far below.

"I know you're upset with me over how I left." Ellis steps beside me and rests his forearms on the wall too. The air around me doesn't feel so cold anymore.

An unexpected tear slides down my face. I wipe it away quickly.

He continues, his voice shifting to a softer tone. "I'm sorry I didn't say goodbye." A sigh escapes his lips, "I... just needed to take care of some things and give myself time to think."

Another tear falls.

"The king gave me my freedom declaration and all I could think about was how fast I could get out of here. I longed for my freedom every minute of every day and when I got it, I took off without looking back."

I force myself to look at his face, but it's unreadable. Of course it is.

"I thought you and I were friends." The words come out in a whisper and another tear rolls down my cheek. Why am I this weak? Crying like a little girl feeling abandoned again?

Ellis finally looks at me. "I'm so sorry I hurt you. I never intended to do that." He doesn't acknowledge that we were friends, which makes my heart sink lower.

I nod at his words, believing them for the first time. I know I would have run too if I was in his position, but he came back. This last month has proven that he could never physically hurt me. But my heart is more fragile.

"Why did you come back?" The question has been burning in my mind ever since I saw him in the dining room tonight. His slicked back hair and formal wear doesn't suit him, but still makes my stomach flutter. My anger won in the end, and I had breezed past him like he was merely a servant.

"The king offered me a job." Ellis lets out a tired smile towards the city. "I needed time to think about it."

I stand straighter and the cold stone on my forearms gets warmer.

"What job?"

"To be your personal bodyguard," he says but avoids my gaze.

Those words make my heart squeeze with happiness until I realize he's hesitant. Keeping me safe will have a life or death outcome to the job. His hesitancy is expected, but more hurt claws at me.

I keep my face neutral. "I guess the king trusts you with my life," I say as I look down at my fidgeting fingers.

He inhales the night air, "Do you trust me with your life?"

"Yes." I mean it with my whole heart, regardless of the current state of my emotions.

We stand in silence as a few dried leaves rustle across the stone walkway beneath our feet. For the first time, I hear the noise of the city, with the ships ringing their bells, and taverns coming alive with singing and dancing. It feels so far away from here but yet so close.

"Sourina told me about your progress over the last three days." His words are soft and not the normal sternness.

I scoff. "What progress? I've been trying to follow her instructions, but I can't seem to get it." I take in a deep, shaky breath. "A few weeks ago, I was a nobody. A lone orphan girl who was trying to survive, and now, I have to be this person with these powers." I shake my head and my throat tightens. "Why me?"

Ellis brushes a loose strand of hair from my face. Our eyes lock and my stomach flips in surprise. His greenish-blue eyes flicker to my lips for a fraction of a second before meeting my gaze again.

"Talk to me. Tell me what's truly bothering you," Ellis says with a whisper. I don't want this moment to end, but the intensity of his gaze stirs my already swirling thoughts. What would his lips feel like?

I look down at my hands again as my fears spill out. "I'm scared that I'm not good enough for what I need to do. I'm scared everyone will see me for the fraud that I am. Someone who can't live up to Movak and the great things he has done."

A sob escapes me, and everything begins to unravel. "I'm afraid I'll always be as alone as I have been my whole life. No one to love me. Everyone always scheming behind my back."

"Keep going." His hand is close to mine on the stone, and I focus on the inches between our fingertips.

"These powers," I hold up at my hands. "I'm afraid of hurting someone. Afraid of hurting you." I can't look at him. Not after saying those words out loud.

"Lylah..." My name escapes his lips in the most tender way. The sweet sound sends a shiver down my spine.

I force my eyes closed and continue, "I'm scared of the future. Where I'm going to go and what I'm going to do. The voice that constantly whispers things I've heard my whole life. About being worthless, not amounting to anything. Always being a failure."

Another sob shakes me as my legs give in and I collapse into Ellis. The truth to my words crushing me beyond the strength to stand for the first time in my life. The kids at the orphanage leaving invisible cuts from their hateful words. The maids attacking me in the library, leaving physical wounds. Even though the scars healed, I'll never forget they were there.

"Woah, I got you." Ellis holds me up as I sob into his shirt. His arms wrap around my shoulders and we stay like that for a few minutes. The rigid muscles of his body enfold me so tightly that I never want to leave the arms of the only person I've ever felt safe with.

Ellis's chest vibrates as he says, "You're not a failure and never worthless. You're your own person and will never be like Movak. Make the powers your own and don't listen to the stories they tell about him. They are over exaggerated and probably not even true. Soon enough, you'll be just as unstoppable as he was."

The warmth of his embrace soothes me so I stay here for as long as possible before he gently pushes my shoulders away.

Words stumble over themselves as I laugh. "I'm so sorry. I'm pretty sure I ruined your shirt." I try to brush away the charcoal that was on my eyes, which has now seeped into his beige shirt.

He gives a small smile. "Don't worry, the maids can clean it." Chuckling, he says, "Never thought I would ever say that."

I take the moment to force my feet to step further away from him. "Thank you for coming out here and listening to me."

Ellis clenches his jaw. "Any time." He clears his throat and returns to his neutral expression. "Goodnight Lylah, I'll come see you tomorrow during your practice."

I nod and for the first time, my mind feels the lightest it has ever been.

Chapter 29
Ellis

"You will be paid twenty dekari a week." King Addard glides his ink pen across the parchment on his desk as we negotiate the terms of my employment.

"Make it twenty-five dekari weekly, and I'll train her as well."

"Train her?" His eyes brows rise into his hairline, his pen pausing on the sheet.

"She'll need to learn how to protect herself if I'm not able to get to her or we are separated. Training in the skills of daggers, sword fighting and other maneuvers is what we should be offering her." I was tossing and turning last night trying to figure out what my terms would be and this is a firm condition.

Teaching Lylah to protect herself will not only make her stronger, but more confident. Especially when she enters into a world that will try to kill her for who she is. Some will be rulers afraid of the power she brings to the Narvidium kingdom and not their own. And others will be those who are afraid of what they don't understand.

He scratches his freshly shaved face. "I can see the logic of your proposal and I agree. She will need to learn that eventually. Why not do it as soon as we can before we introduce her to the kingdoms?"

Relief washes over me. I was nervous he wouldn't see the wisdom in my request.

"We will hold a ball in a month's time. Do you think you can have her trained by then?" He doesn't look up from his desk.

I gulp at the timeline. "A month, Your Majesty? She hasn't even manifested fire yet." That hardly seems like a reasonable enough time for her to master everything she needs to learn.

"Our annual winter Solstice Ball will be held here in the palace with every ruler on this continent and beyond invited to witness this miracle. I expect her to be ready." The stern tone of his voice states the resoluteness of his decision.

I clench my jaw and bite back the words that want to come out. "Do Sourina and Lylah know about this?"

King Addard looks up from his writing. "Yes, they were told a few days ago."

Why has he accelerated this timeline? It's no wonder Lylah was practically having a mental breakdown. Every corner of the world is about to come to gawk at her. And she has to be ready for it.

He continues, "You can stay in the room where you are now. It's far enough from Lylah, but still close in case anything happens." He jots that down on the parchment. "You will eat downstairs with the higher level servants like Finnon, Maggis, Eliera and the guard captain. Finnon can show you the way during lunch hours."

I agree with eating separately because it makes sense. I'm not a guest anymore, but a paid employee. At least I don't have to be in the same room as the servants who caused harm to Lylah and snickered behind her back. If I had my way, I would cut each of their tongues out myself now that I'm free.

"Now, tell me about the vulnerabilities you mentioned earlier. I will have them repaired immediately."

His golden eyes hold mine as I recount the weaknesses I noticed earlier. "Parts of the palace wall on the west side are crumbling enough that a person running up it could get inside the walls easily."

His quill moves quickly on a fresh piece of parchment.

"Your guards don't patrol the wall in a frequent enough pattern. Most of the wall is left unguarded, so any intruder could slip in unnoticed. If Lylah is to be announced as the Fire Mage and this is where she will reside, this place is not equipped to hold off that kind of threat on her life." When I slipped in last night, I didn't see a guard anywhere on the west side. Most of them had gathered at the gate playing cards in the main guard tower.

"Is there a leader of your palace guard that gives them orders?" I ask.

King Addard replies thoughtfully. "Yes, Frax is my guard captain. You can meet with him after we are done here about the guard issues. I will see to it that a stonemason repairs the wall immediately."

I recall a few other smaller areas that could be reinforced, but conclude that I'll inspect in the daylight.

"I believe our employment agreement is finished." He holds it up to me before pausing. "Lastly, Ellis, your relationship with her will be professional from now on. You are not her friend or her confidante. You are only here to keep her safe and train her. We can't take her focus off of what she will need to accomplish."

I nod stiffly. I knew he was going to say something about our unique relationship, so I'm already prepared. I have to keep her at a distance but her question of friendship torments that resolve. Her red teary eyes from last night flash in my mind, but I force the memory away.

"I understand."

"Good," he says firmly before setting down his quill. "Is there anything else we need to discuss?" I shake my head. The pay and terms are to my satisfaction.

I walk out of his office with a new purpose. There's a question that has lingered ever since we got back from Arliea as I make my way to the kitchens. The familiar smell of roasting vegetables and loud clashes of a butcher knife hitting against a wooden block grips me unexpectedly. I didn't like the scrubbing part, but being in this kitchen made me feel like I was part of a group. A team.

"Ellis," Jorge gruffly says as he sets down his knife. "To what do I owe the pleasure?"

I can't help but smile at the sight of his sleeves rolled up past his bulging biceps. The unshaven stubble on his jaw indicates the week has been busy. Maggis always prefers the servants to be clean shaven.

I get right to the point. "I'm hoping you can clarify something for me. I know you still get news from your crew who are loyal to you." I lean against the door frame as I watch his eyes flash me a warning.

"I don't get any news. Not sure where ya heard that from." He picks up the knife and resumes chopping the carrots and celery.

"I'm not stupid. Every Wednesday you get a letter hidden in the vegetable crate delivery. You always make sure you're the first to accept the delivery." I watch with amusement at the way my words make his eyes close briefly and sigh.

He doesn't look up when he speaks again. "Fine. I do get updates from my crew. They're on the Ravage now."

"The Ravage? I thought it was a merchant ship now, part of the trading route that goes to Korrim for silk and marble."

Jorge squints at me. "It is. Doesn't mean the crew on it are particularly loyal to its captain."

I connect the dots. "You're the original captain of the Ravage?"

He nods. It makes sense now why he has so many enemies. A captain of the Ravage rarely keeps his life for long, with the ship being the strongest and oldest in the waters.

"I used to be part of its crew." The words come out just loud enough for only him to hear.

"Before or after she was taken?"

"During." The word leaves a knot in my throat.

"I'm glad ya made it out. The reports were... not easy to read." His shoulders are less tense now. Maybe because now, we hold common ground.

"Taramin, have you heard of him?" The name leaves a foul taste after I say it.

His eyes snap to me. "How do you know that name?"

He knows something about him. How interesting. "I had the misfortune of meeting him not too long ago. Everyone seems to know who he is, but I've never heard of him before."

"Be careful. He's cunnin', that one," he instructs as he shakes his head. "Managed to overtake the Brekas island with his band of misfits recently and plans on moving into Rinmor."

"The Shadow Dealer won't like that," I comment with a shiver at what he would do to Taramin if he steps foot in Rinmor. But the Shadow Dealer did have a peculiar look in his eyes when I mentioned him earlier.

"No, I don't think he will," Jorge grumbles out while placing a skillet on the open flames and tosses in more wood in the hatch below.

"Do you think he'll be a threat to the king?" I chew on my lip as I remember the amount of men that were visible that night. No telling how many were lurking in the shadows.

"If ya're worried about the girl everyone seems to be whispering about, I think she'll be fine." He uses his hands to curve the steam rising from the skillet towards his face. A pinch of salt from a glass jar goes into the pot as he stirs the contents.

"It's not about the girl," I say, but it comes out defensive for some reason.

He scoffs. "Like ya worry about the king's safety."

"I'm employed by him." I retort.

"I am too. Doesn't mean that I worry about whether the big bad Taramin is going to break into the palace." He stirs the steaming vegetables again, and the delicious smells make my stomach growl.

So he's a threat if Jorge said it like that. I roll my eyes and walk back out.

"Come back any time," Jorge calls out before a deep laugh rumbles behind me.

Chapter 30
Ellis

A few days have passed since I talked with Jorge, and something about Taramin continues to unnerve me. The darkness in his eyes and fake hospitality eats away at me as I try to figure out why he keeps my mind hostage.

On the western lawn, Lylah and Sourina are practicing various breathing techniques. For what Lylah has to accomplish, breathing will be vital to controlling her powers and learning the combat moves I'll teach her later on.

Lylah puffs out irritated breaths, her voice clearly heard from where I'm standing by the palace wall. "I'm having a hard time moving the heat from my center towards the palm of my hands."

Sourina catches my gaze briefly before snapping her attention back to Lylah. "That's because you're forcing it. Fire is a wild thing you can't control." She moves one arm in a graceful motion across her chest. "Let it flow naturally."

"When I try to let it flow naturally, you say it's too close to my heart. Your directions are confusing." The frustration is evident and I understand what it's like. I had to go through similar exercises when I was training, the fear of not being able to do it constantly gnawing at me.

I decide to walk the perimeter instead, checking for any oddities in the security while they train. A few guards pass by but don't greet me at all. Their eyes are mostly fixed on Lylah, her brows scrunch in concentration as I usher the guards past. Our conversation from that night comes to mind unexpectedly, but I can tell her shoulders sit a little higher today.

"Try again," Sourina instructs as she clasps her grandmother's book close to her chest.

Lylah takes a deep breath and closes her eyes. I straighten as her hand glows red and a jet of orange-hued flames shoots out.

"Lylah! You did it!" Sourina jumps up and down. Lylah looks down at her hands in amazement before glancing sideways at me. I give her a proud smile and she celebrates briefly before calling fire out of her hands over and over again.

Different guards pass by more frequently to gawk at the Fire

Mage. I instruct them to move along, but I can't help and smile at their curiosity. We're truly witnessing a miracle of the last two centuries.

After an hour or so, Clouds have begun to move in as Lylah makes her way to me, wiping her forehead with her sleeve. The sun has started to step down in the sky. A few golden rays catch the blonde wisps of hair that have come undone from her braid. Her dress is not ornate today, just plain and functional for the occasion.

"Did you see me use my powers?" Lylah asks with excitement laced in her voice.

"I did. I always knew you could do it."

"Thank you." Awkward seconds pass before she continues, "It takes a lot more energy than I anticipated and even raises my body's temperature. I feel like I've been standing in a furnace for hours." The beads of sweat on her forehead are unmistakable and the drenched spots on her gown around her arms show the exertion.

"I wonder if raising your body's temperature like that is harmful to you or if your body differs from ours to withstand it?" My growing list of safety concerns is going to have to be more than just attacks from the enemy but from herself. What if she pushes herself too far? Do we even know what too far is? What if she hurts herself and I'm helpless to save her?

"According to Maureen's book, the mage's bodies were born with differences to their specific powers. That's what the healers back then noticed when they tended to their wounds." She scrunches her nose and stares out over the city. I wonder if she misses being out there as much as I do instead of being stuck behind these cold, gray walls.

"Anyway," she turns to me. "I'm starving. Are you coming for dinner? I didn't see you at any of the meals the past few days."

Her blue eyes are round with so much expectation that I have to look away. "I won't be eating in the king's dining halls with you anymore. I'm a paid employee now. I eat with the other staff downstairs."

"What?" Her brows furrow with questions, but the king said it and I must obey.

"We'll see each other during training hours, and I'll be around when you're outside to make sure you're safe. I'll always be by your side when you leave the palace walls."

"I guess that makes sense," Lylah breathes out quietly. She doesn't attempt to hide the sadness in her voice. I'm relieved to be out of the stiff dress shirts and proper royal manners all the time. The taste of fine dining is missed though, the higher-level servants only get a fraction of what the king eats. But being around fellow peers and other guards will help me learn my place. I'll always be a thief who doesn't belong in the world of royalty and mages. I'll spend my life safeguarding her.

"The king is a generous man. I know it must be for the best." Her face shows that she believes those words but I don't put wealthy, powerful men on pedestals like she continues to do.

I don't answer but escort her back inside the safety of the palace.

AWAKENING FIRE

Winter creeps in as we settle into our new routine, the chill of the air biting at our cheeks more and more with each passing day. I've completely transformed the palace guard and their views of security. The task was overwhelming, to say the least. Most of them were young men whose fathers didn't make it back from the war. A similar enough tale as mine, the fatherless hole in their lives just as big. Their eyes constantly searching for a purpose, a place to belong just like me, and I could earn their respect easily.

It was the older men that survived the war who didn't feel like a nineteen-year-old boy should be telling them anything. They had survived the war, after all; they knew what was best. Their eye rolls and scoffing were irritating every time I would try to show them how a thief like me might try to sneak into this place. The guard captain was among them, aged in his views and not nearly capable enough of keeping up with the demands of securing a palace at our current threat level.

After a talk with the king, a few of my suggestions went into practice, which allowed for the old guard captain to be retired and a new captain to be appointed in his place. The improvement already brought a new wave of morale through the guards, which was refreshing to see.

Lylah has quickly increased her skills with summoning fire and can call it out with a second's notice. Her control over the unpredictable element is impressive with daily practice. The king has observed a few lessons from his study window that overlook the west garden now dusted with fresh snow.

Our first lesson in combat training starts this afternoon and, oddly enough, I'm nervous. All the skills I've learned over years were by trial and error under the threat of death. A few voyages had forced me to earn my keep fighting to survive and a few mutinies taught me to always watch my back.

How do I put those lessons into practical application for a young woman with no background or instinct to harm or kill if necessary?

"Are you ready to fight your first Fire Mage?" Lylah says as she wraps the red scarf I bought her in Point Theane tighter around her head. The flecks of falling snow catch on her braided hair and settle on the tips of her long lashes. The red flush of her lips is twisted in a smirk.

I toss her a wooden stick and she catches it with ease. "Cockiness is never a good look."

Sourina sits on the steps leading up to the western entrance with her book in tow while shielding the ancient pages from dropping snow with her cloak. I glance up at the king standing in the window, looking down as well.

I clear my throat and twirl the stick in my hand, measuring the weight and curve of the wood. "The first thing in self-defense is knowing your weapon. Sometimes, you'll only have mere seconds to calculate what you're using."

Lylah considers my words and inspects the stick too. Her eyes hover over the piece with analytical eyes as if she's studying a piece of art.

"Next, you want to know your stance and the strengths of different points of your body. The fire you wield will be stronger for it when your body can be used as an anchor." I stand in front of her with my feet spread in attack form. One foot behind me and one foot planted firmly in front with the stick sword at my side.

Lylah copies my movements. I walk around her and shove between her shoulders with my hand.

"Hey!" she exclaims but catches her balance quickly.

I ignore her. "In any situation, this basic move neutralizes your balance when the unexpected comes. It also allows you to move more freely."

She huffs but continues to listen, her eyes following mine intensely.

"What's the most vulnerable part of your body?" Snowflakes dance around us as I await her answer.

"My head," Lylah responds after some thought.

"Your head is very important, but your heart is the center of life. You'll bleed out in minutes the closer the wound is to your center. When in an attack, your center mass, chest, and stomach will be the first place they go after. If they aim to kill, a sword through the heart is the fastest."

Her mouth perches. She adjusts the stick sword in her hands and recenters her body to the way I showed her. I lift my pretend sword and settle into my stance in front of her. I strike towards her center and step forward to use the momentum to disorient her.

The stick lands squarely at her chest with her sword barely lifted halfway to meet mine.

"That's not fair. You didn't give me any warning." Lylah rubs her cloak where the stick landed.

I step back and readjust myself. "Do you think your enemy will pause to warn you?"

She doesn't answer and returns to the stance while lifting the sword higher towards me.

"Try again."

She nods, determination burning fiercely in her eyes.

I step forward with my opposite leg this time and thrust my sword towards her shoulder. She blocks my advance with her stick with a satisfying clash.

"That's better. You anticipated the move and predicted where it would land. That'll become a great skill to master while we train." A mixture of pride and relief floods my chest. Now, it's time to force it to be muscle memory for her.

Lylah smiles and nods for us to continue. I swing the sword again towards her ribs on the left, but she shields herself with her arm.

"Now your arm has a big gash. Move sideways if you want to have more time to use your sword to block."

She rubs her arm. "Do that again slowly so I can practice stepping sideways." We run through the moves again and she sidesteps before thrusting her sword to meet my blade, but misses.

Her nostrils flare. "Again."

I swing my sword again, but this time she meets my blade with hers. A bright smile lights up her face at the success. I can't help smiling too. She's a natural at picking things up quickly, but I already figured that out during our trip to Arliea.

The rest of the afternoon consists of us acting out various moves in repetition until Lylah complains about her aching muscles.

"Same time tomorrow?" I ask as I take the training stick from her.

She smiles. "Same time tomorrow."

Chapter 31
Lylah

Three weeks have passed since the king announced he had sent letters out to every ruler about the Solstice Ball. The big event that'll be used to officially introduce me to the world. The day he brought Sourina and me into his office to tell us, I fought the panic threatening to consume me. I thought I would have more time to train at my own comfort level, but we had a month. Every day, I tried to push those thoughts from my mind as much as possible and threw myself into getting ready.

Each training session with Sourina and Ellis amplified and left me barely standing each time. Afterwards, the maids bathed me in goat milk and rose petals, and I fell asleep as soon as my head hit the goose feather pillows. I ate my breakfast and lunch quickly, with decorum when the king was present, so I could have as much daylight to practice sparring and wielding fire. The powers have been growing stronger, and thankfully, so has my confidence.

After a whole week of training hard every day, my body and mind rebelled to the point of tears and sickness. With the king's permission, I designated one day of the week to rest. The only time I could almost put my Fire Mage persona on a shelf. Normally, I would sit in the library reading intriguing stories and taking occasional walks in the gardens, now completely covered in snow.

Luckily, today is my day to myself with no agenda. My fingers graze the spines of the leather-bound books in the library. As the day of the ball draws closer, I can't help but want to study more about Movak. The war he led on Ladonne has been plaguing my mind recently. The known history of the Ladonne kingdom states that they later surrendered and merged borders with Arliea.

But the more I think about their history, the more it makes no sense to me. If the mages were given their powers to protect the peace, why did they use them for a power-hungry king like King Lenthor? Did they know his agenda for conquering Ladonne? Or were they deceived?

It's already midday when I stop looking through books and huff out a loud breath. The books in here don't say anything of use and haven't for a while. Maureen's words flash through my mind, 'Almost everything about the mages was moved to the Mage's Tower. There's little written material left around the kingdoms.'

I groan and straighten my skirts. I'll have to ask Sourina if her book says anything about Movak's time in Ladonne or why they chose a side. Not wasting any more time, I want today to count for something more and go beyond the walls for the last time before the world invades my life.

"Your Majesty?" I peek my head into his study, where he tends to spend most of his time these days. I've barely seen him this last week. Finnon has been taking his meals to his study while I sit alone in the enormous dining room each night. Sometimes Sourina joins me but most of the time, she chooses to eat with Finnon.

King Addard's shirt is undone down to mid chest when I enter. His sleeves are rolled up as he moves around stacks of scrolls which cover every surface of his sizable mahogany desk. His black wavy hair is more tousled than normal, and a shortened glass goblet rests in his hand.

Wide golden eyes look up at me before he adjusts himself to sit more stiffly in the plush leather chair. Something must be bothering him if he has gotten to this state of disarray when normally he's so reserved and proper.

"Your Majesty, are you okay?" I observe the room with a fast glance and see more scrolls and books scattered behind me.

"Yes," he replies hesitantly as he rakes his hand through his black hair and takes a sip of the dark liquid.

His voice is strained when he speaks again. "I had asked the kingdom rulers to bring those they believed to be the other mages. Your protectors and partners in what's to come." King Addard takes a bigger gulp this time. "The ball is less than a week away and the letters are piling up with replies."

He grabs a handful of the letters and lets them fall to the desk again. "So many claims of power. I don't have enough hours in the day to analyze them all."

My mind spins at the four other potential mages who will be part of this journey. Time is ticking down until I meet them. What will they be like?

I fidget with my hands. "Do you need any help?"

"No, it is crucial you continue your training. They will demand a presentation of your abilities so you must be prepared." He pauses and says as if to no one, "Ellis has been working to secure the palace and increase troops in the surrounding towns. Korrim will arrive by ships, so the port has to be well patrolled."

"Ellis is the best at what he does," I reassure him as I step forward. He meets my gaze with a distant look. "And will make sure nothing happens that your guard and soldiers can't handle. What if we hold presentations of these so-called mages and make them demonstrate the powers they claim to possess?" It's the only idea I can come up with to make sure we weed out the imposters from the real mages. If I have to do a demonstration, why can't they?

"I was thinking the same thing." He sets down his glass and stands.

Another thought pops into my head. "Sourina can sense a mage's powers and could help with the process. I can ask her the next time I see her if you'd like."

He nods. "Yes, we can certainly use her when the time comes."

I smile at his acceptance of my ideas, but something is still troubling him. "Anything else I can help with?"

"Ah yes, I'm hosting a dinner party with all the councilmen and advisors tonight. They know of the Solstice Ball but nothing about our unusual guests. I would like to have you there by my side." King Addard rests his hands against the back of his chair and holds my gaze, a silent plea reflecting in them. I feel like a butterfly with my wings pinned in place.

"Anything you need of me, Your Majesty."

A few moments pass before he begins moving the scrolls around his desk again.

I lick my lips. "Your Majesty, I had a request before the dinner tonight." I fold my hands behind my back and fidget with the end of my braid.

"Yes?"

"This is my last free day before next week. I want to go into the city as me and not as *her*." Hope clings in my chest that he'll say yes.

"What do you want to do there?"

"I want to walk around the docks, smell the ocean breeze, and experience being someone normal one last time," I answer hesitantly. Honestly, I'm not sure what I want to do yet, but all of those options are on my list of possibilities. "Before people begin to recognize me."

"As long as you take Ellis with you, that's fine with me." King

Addard picks up his pen and begins writing. "Please be back in time to get ready for dinner."

I nearly skip out of the king's study and find Ellis within minutes walking up the eastern staircase.

"I want to go into the city and you're coming with me." My voice echoes in the stairway. This is my last chance to be me and I can't have him saying no.

"What do you want to do in the city?" Ellis raises an eyebrow.

"Where's your sense of adventure?" I say as I turn to go back up the stairs. I'll need an outfit that won't draw any attention. "The king has already approved it," I call over my shoulder.

"Fine, meet me by the eastern entrance," Ellis calls back, and I can't help but feel giddy. I instruct the maids to bring me an ordinary dress, and what they bring back doesn't disappoint. Upon inspection in the mirror, I look like a young girl ready to pick up winter produce from the market. The cloak draped over my shoulders should be enough to keep out the biting wind.

Ellis waits for me on the east side of the palace, where the crates of food get delivered from my understanding. He has replaced his guard uniform for the street clothes no doubt have been collecting dust these past few weeks. We slip out of the side gate with a small nod from Ellis up at the guards in the tower. They don't seem to question it.

The new layer of snow has already started to melt under the bright sun. Nothing is sweeter than the strong ocean air in my lungs. We make our way down to the harbor through the northern and central city square when I stop.

"What's wrong?" Ellis asks and looks around as if ready to fight.

I turn to him. "This is where you pickpocketed me."

His head tilts back, and he lets out a slight laugh. "Is that so?"

I point to the bakery that's to the left. "I had just come out of that bakery and you bumped into me. The next thing I knew, my compass was gone." I lift the compass out of its safe place in my pocket.

"I'm glad it was you." He smiles down at me.

My heart beats wildly. "Really?"

"Yes."

He elaborate further and continues towards the harbor, passing the ancient oak tree like he has seen it a thousand times. Clusters of people walk around the massive tree trunk in conversation, while others look at each mage's statue. I want to go over there to look at their statues again now that I have a deeper connection to them, but Ellis doesn't slow down.

The harbor is bustling with the movement of sailors in their patched coats. Seagulls fly overhead as the sun reflects brightly off the water's glassy surface. It's warmer today than it has been in weeks, which is a gift in itself. It's a perfect day to forget the emotional weight of the dinner tonight and the daunting festivities that are only a week away.

I grow more aware of Ellis' body next to me as we walk. He's glad it was me that day, but what does that really mean? Maybe we're friends after all, even though he never agreed to that in the gardens, nor mentioned it again just now. I can still remember the warmth of his breath on my lips. The tenderness of his finger as he wiped my tears away haunts my mind.

My eyes close briefly as I try to push those thoughts from my mind. We find ourselves at the docks, with its wood boards creaking beneath our feet the further we venture out towards the end. It truly is a beautiful sight, the rhythmic motion of the swaying ships in the water.

Ellis points at a ship to the left of us. "That's the Ravage. I worked on that ship seven years ago when I was first on my own. The captain laughed at a kid like me wanting to join his crew but I was determined."

I lean on the dock railing and watch the crew pull down the sails on the ship Ellis pointed to. Hearing him recount details of his travels with the Ravage is like reading an adventure book from the palace library.

"One night we were sailing under the cover of night when an unmarked ship appeared beside us. We sounded an alarm, but it was too late. The sailors were already swinging over to the ship with swords slashing." He pauses, as if seeing the scene right before him. "That was the first time I learned how to fight a real enemy, and saw friends die around me."

Silence engulfs us as I glance over at him, wishing for him to continue, but he remains quiet. A storm of emotions seems to be forming in those piercing eyes.

"What happened after that?" I say to the air between us.

He doesn't look at me. "Our crew was taken captive after suffering heavy losses. The ship sustained massive damage, but they took us to the Narvidium island of Brekas off the coast. But during that time, an unknown group had taken it over when the soldiers were called to guard the border during the Arliean war."

My brief history lessons covered the Brekas island. An island owned by the royal family with a small village to care for it, but I never knew it was ever invaded. My education was not like what other children with parents got who could afford to send them to school. There weren't enough teachers to cover all the orphans needing an education, so there was a rotating schedule. If you had friends, they would fill you in on what they learned on the day you didn't attend. Few ever filled me in.

Without hesitation, I put a hand on his shoulder. "I'm so sorry."

It feels odd to feel sorrow for something that didn't happen to you years ago, but his face twists, as if holding himself back from truly feeling. The death and chaos he witnessed that day still affects him.

He shrugs casually, like we returned to talking about the weather. "It happened a long time ago. The ship was repaired and sold to a commercial trading company."

I remain silent but wish I can provide the same comfort he did for me. I'm not sure what made him want to let me see into a fraction of his past, but I'm grateful that he did.

Chapter 32
Ellis

My heart pounds wildly in my chest as I watch the Ravage. She looks like the best-kept ship in the harbor with pristine sails and several new additions to make her faster.

A hand on my arm pulls me out of my spiraling thoughts.

"I want to show you something." Lylah gestures to follow her back into the city and towards the eastern edge of Rinmor. Poverty creeps in the further we venture into this sector. Fences leaning after harsh winters with no money to repair them and roofs caving in from years of neglect.

Opening up to her about my time on the Ravage was not something I planned on. Seeing the ship again after so many years brought back memories of the pools of blood and bodies that were scattered on her deck that night. Their lifeless eyes will haunt me for as long as I live.

My plans also didn't include this unexpected outing, but I can't complain. It's nice to be out of the palace walls for the first time since accepting the bodyguard position. Each day has blended into the next with almost no breaks. The days Lylah takes off from practice usually allow me to focus on other guard duties.

We approach a building I've never seen before. It's quite sizable compared to the others around it. The sign above the door reads 'Rinmor Children's Home No. 1'.

I glance at Lylah as her brows furrow in deep thought. Her posture changes from holding her head high to her shoulders to almost sinking as low as when I first laid eyes on her.

"Is this where you..." My voice fades the longer I look from her to the structure. Three children scream as they run around, chasing each other with sticks. They barely have coats or scarves on to keep them warm.

She swallows. "This is where I grew up."

Scanning the building, it wasn't impressive by any stretch of the imagination. Paint chips from the wooden siding under the now setting sun. The stairs leading up to the entrance buckle dramatically as children run up and down them.

"I left this horrible place without ever looking back the night I met you. The head mistress had given me three days to find work and a new place to live with only the dress I was wearing and a few dekari in my pocket. I wanted my life to mean more than ending up in the pleasure houses like so many of the girls before me."

My fists flex at imagining Lylah on the steps of a pleasure house luring men in by batting her long lashes and barely clothed. I know she would have done what she had to in order to survive, and I would've passed by without ever knowing her.

"Does the king support the orphanages in any way?" The question is ready to ignite instant fury if the answer is no.

"He does, but his councilmen take care of the details on the various welfare projects. Most of them likely pocket the coins that are given to feed, clothe, and educate the children. We certainly didn't benefit from that money." She spits out the words like they're poison. Her fists begin to glow red hot as she clenches them.

I look around nervously at the growing heat that suddenly radiates from her.

"Woah." I place myself in front of her, blocking out the view of the deteriorating building. "Take a deep breath."

Her teeth grit together. "I could burn it all down. Right now. No one else has to suffer."

A small flame shoots out from between her closed fingers.

"You would be killing countless children. Hell, this whole sector would go down in flames with just a single spark."

She ignores me and stares through me, her eyes beginning to glow red as well.

"Lylah, look at me."

She doesn't focus on me.

"Please, just look at me," I whisper desperately. I understand this rage but this isn't the time and definitely not the place.

Nothing.

I urgently grab both sides of her face and press her body to mine. Her skin is scalding, but I force my hands to stay where they are. Her blazing eyes finally shift to mine and we're weightless in a sliver of frozen time. I hold her as if she's a fragile but dangerous thing. Nothing else matters in this moment.

Heat beneath my fingers cools and her body relaxes.

I take a deep breath.

"I'm okay," she murmurs.

I step back and drop my hands from her face. The way she fit perfectly in them, her smooth skin against my rough palms carves into my memory.

Tears pool in her eyes at the horrors this place must hold for her. I want to wrap her into my arms and wipe away every tear that threatens to fall, but the king's words hold me in place.

She wipes at her eyes. "Thank you for being here with me." Lylah glances at me again, pink flushing her cheeks and nose, the redness still lingering in her eyes.

I need to get her out of here.

"We have a little bit more time before we need to head back to the palace. Is there anything else you want to see?" I look around at the various people passing by on the streets. They don't pay any attention to us which is a relief.

"Can we have a drink, just one, at a tavern? No missions, no obligations... just you and me." She wipes another tear away, and my chest hurts to see her in pain. Pain I can't fix.

I swallow at her words. "I know just the place."

The tavern by the docks called The Helm has been my favorite over the years. The owner, Benti, is a loyal lover of bribes when I need to scout out a target or get valuable information. Like I could be in two places at once, him at the bar listening and me listening from within the crowd. My life would've been very different if Sir Winhester had walked into that tavern instead of the one he did.

"Ellis!" A booming voice to my left draws my attention.

I smile and clasp Benti on the shoulder as we embrace. "It's always good to see you."

He scans my face with sweeping eyes. "I haven't seen ya around in quite some time."

"I've been busy." I look around at the tavern as almost every table is full of men having a drink after a hard day's work.

Benti's eyes divert to Lylah and I stiffen. He extends his hand, "Name's Benti, and who might ya be?"

Lylah takes his hand with slight hesitation. "Lylah."

"I can see why you've been busy," Benti laughs out as he walks behind the bar counter and leans against it. "What will ya be drinkin'? The usual?"

"The lady will take a mead and I'll take your golden ale." I pull out the stool for Lylah and take a seat next to her.

The large hand carved wooden mugs arrive shortly and I take a much needed sip. The subtle sweetness and smoothness of the liquid relaxes me. Lylah sips on hers, and I can't help but remember the first time she drank mead. Her nose had scrunched with disgust and she almost spit it out.

"This is exactly what I wanted," she says as she rests her head on her hand and observes the various conversations behind me. "Thank you for bringing me here." Her blonde hair stands out in this dark tavern, the smell of her flower soap is more intoxicating than the beverage I drink.

I clear my throat. "Sometimes you need a reward for hard work. You deserve it after all the training you've been doing."

"I don't feel like it has nearly been enough to make me ready." Lylah doesn't look up from her cup as her thumb rubs against it.

"All you can do is take it one day at a time. I don't think you ever feel truly ready."

She nods and takes a sip.

A nagging image invades my mind as we let the words linger. The condition of the orphanage makes my stomach twist in knots, especially seeing those children playing in such a horrible environment. They laughed like nothing was wrong, but everything was wrong.

"Will you mention the orphanage to the king now that you have his ear?" Despite the bitterness that springs up, Lylah does seem comfortable around him and could alert him easily to this negligence.

She sighs. "I've been trying to figure out how to approach the topic with him. After the ball, I want to tell him about the atrocities the kids go through." The sadness in her voice is evident as her hands curl tighter around her cup. "What I went through."

"I'll do whatever I can to help you," I say as I lean in, but I have no idea what I can do from my position in the palace. What I really want to do is teach every one of the councilmen who pocket the money a lesson.

"I know you will," she replies and drinks the rest of the mead.

The light diminishes outside. A lamplighter passes by with a torch and a ladder, lighting each street lamp on his route south.

"I need to get you back for the dinner," I say as I help her off the stool and usher her to the door.

"Is it that time already?" She questions as she sways a little bit. She waves back to Benti, who smiles back widely.

We make it back into the palace with little trouble. Lylah stumbles over a few steps as I help her up the stairs to our rooms.

"That mead was a lot stronger than I remember." She giggles to herself after catching herself on the last step. Not only was it stronger but the cup was a lot bigger. I should have limited her.

"Almost there," I say with my hand stretched out to catch her if she falls again.

Before she opens her bedroom door, she turns back to me. "Thank you for coming with me. I've never felt more free than I have today." Lylah glances up at me through thick lashes and a twinkle in her eyes.

I swallow slowly as my eyes scan over her full lips and flushed cheeks. She smells like wild flowers in the spring and I want to bury my face in her golden locks. Her blue eyes lure my head down as I search for a signal to stop.

Just for a moment, I'm tired of pretending I don't want her. I do want her, more than any treasure I've been hired to steal. I want her lips on mine. I want her fingers in my hair. I want to feel her soft skin beneath me...

The king's words stop me again as reason takes over. I force myself to take a step back. Raw disappointment flashes across her eyes, and I flinch. I almost throw everything away for just this one kiss. Battling the consequences versus a kiss where I allow every buried feeling from the first moment I met her to overtake me.

But it isn't worth the king removing me from her life forever. I have to settle for the contentment of just being near her.

I turn towards my room instead. Within time stopping seconds, she tugs at my shoulder and places her lips to my cheek. My heart nearly pounds out of my chest but I turn away quickly, allowing my feet to move first before my heart does.

"I'll see you at practice early tomorrow," I call out over my shoulder, fighting everything inside me to turn around and press her up against the door in an all-consuming kiss.

Chapter 33
Lylah

King Addard waits for me by the doors to the grand dining hall. He has put every effort into his outfit. The blue robe is lined with glossy black fur which is held together by clasps and a blue sapphire pendant the size of my fist. The crown on his head is glistening more than usual as if it's been freshly shined. A clean-shaven face gazes back at me with jet black hair combed back, every strand perfectly placed.

A warm smile blooms across his lips. "You look radiant."

I blush at the comment, but hold my head high as I take his extended hand. My dress is nearly black with red poppies embroidered on my bodice. Expert hands worked on this dress and I couldn't help but admire it for extended moments in the mirror before leaving my rooms.

My mind wanders to the one thing I shouldn't think about. Ellis' lips so close to mine only an hour ago. I could feel the warmth of his breath. I wanted him to kiss me, more than ever before. We've been dancing around the attraction we feel and I don't understand why he always stops himself when he's near me. Maybe I misread his feelings. Maybe he doesn't feel anything at all.

I shut away those thoughts. It's time to focus on what's in front me.

An invisible mask slips on as I try my best to relax my tense shoulders. The mask is one of confidence I don't feel, but I play a trick to make my body exhibit it. I imagine that I'm walking into a field of flowers and not a room full of graying men. I've met the councilmen and advisors before, but something about this time makes it more definite. They'll find out who I am for the first time, allowing me to get a taste of the chaos that'll rain down this time next week.

We enter together as Maggis announces us. Each person standing by the table bows when we enter. Every one of their eyes gravitate to me like the last time with a mixture of emotions. Some are confused. Some are curious. Most are simply surprised.

I look around for Sourina, but she's nowhere in sight. This isn't her preferred place to be and probably avoided it at all costs. I can picture her now, kicking her feet up in the library or mixing tonics with Finnon.

Over the weeks she's been here, she spends most of her free time in his healing rooms studying the polfoss flower once she found out about healing properties it possesses. Finnon seems to enjoy the company when I've gone to visit, a fun detour on my daily walk between lunch and training.

A servant helps me get seated next to the king. The meticulous details of royal etiquette have become second nature to me as I place my cloth napkin on my lap. Platters of roasted duck and masterful displays of side dishes fill the vacant spaces of the table. Everything ranging from charred cabbage wrapped fish to caviar on bread crisps.

"Your Majesty, we are most grateful for this sudden invitation, but we are curious as to the occasion." The advisor that speaks is one I recognize from the last dinner. He had joked previously that the king may be interested in one of his daughters.

The king takes his time biting into the perfectly browned duck breast smothered in a golden gravy. I'm sure he's buying time to figure out how to approach the revelation of why I'm here.

Silence.

"Last time, when Lylah was here at the table with us, I spoke about her being someone who is important to this kingdom." He doesn't shy away from glancing at each one of his advisors.

The room stills for a moment before he speaks again. "She is a Fire Mage."

His words induce loud gasps as shock consumes the air in the room. Every pair of eyes whip to me as I place my hands in my lap and meet their stares evenly. My heart feels like it's beating in my throat, but I force myself not to buckle under the weight of their stares.

"How is this possible?" states a man to my right and they all nod.

"Lylah manifested her powers about a month ago from an emotional event just like Movak had. Since then, she has been training to control her powers and recall them at a moment's notice."

He nods at me. I close my eyes to focus on calling out a speck of fire from inside me. I lift my palm up, eye level to the guests, and feel the heat radiating from between my shoulder blades and through my arm. A small flame dances on the center of my palm, earning even more gasps from around the table.

Weeks ago, I would've been too terrified to attempt this indoors. Working with Sourina on visualizing the heat in my body and the importance of controlling my emotions has made me more comfortable with small flames.

"This is incredible!" One of the councilmen exclaims. The food has all been forgotten as they push back their plates.

King Addard smiles. "Yes, it truly is." He pauses before sipping his evening wine. "The Solstice Ball is approaching in five days. I sent out letters to the rulers of every kingdom, announcing the manifestation of our Fire Mage. Rulers and their parties will begin to arrive in the next few days to attend our ball."

Whispers erupt simultaneously as they seem to process the unfolding events.

Sir Yorshie clenches his fist on the table. "As your advisors and councilmen, we are most surprised we were not told of this sooner."

The king tilts his chin to him. "I'm the king, and require no permission from you."

It suddenly feels cold in the room as I dab my face with th,e napkin. I know there's nothing on it but the sheer awkwardness of this dinner makes me need to do something with my hands.

"Are we equipped to take this kind of arrival? With your father, our city used to be more fortified, but we have not come close to the security we once had." Another advisor at the farthest end of the tables makes a good point. He hasn't met Ellis, who has worked to elevate this palace out of the crumbling state it's been in for decades.

"We have been working tirelessly to ensure the harbor is secure, the city, the palace and surrounding towns. No expense will be spared to make our kingdom shine in the presence of arriving royalty and diplomats."

The councilmen and advisors seem pleased with these updates. A voice pulls me from my thoughts as I take the last bite of the cabbage dish on my plate.

"My lady, do you have a companion to take you to the ball? My son would be an excellent fit to escort you." I haven't thought of an escort and the question catches me off guard.

A deep voice cuts through the air before I can respond. "Lylah will be attending the ball at my side, Councilman Remik."

I look apologetically towards the advisor, who adjusts his dark blue velvet vest nervously. He gives a polite nod to the king before taking big gulps of wine.

Chancing a gaze at the king, he gives me a sideways glance and a slight tilt of his chin. Maybe he knows I don't know the rules of these sort of events or that I need to be escorted, but I'm grateful for the rescue.

Dessert follows shortly in the form of a giant layered cake that gets placed in center of the table. Servants slice off pieces before placing them with a dollop of whipped strawberry cream on each plate.

Everyone enjoys the cake with little to no conversation as the night settles into farewells. Each of the guests come and kiss my hand while expressing their excitement. A few of them do seem genuinely excited, while others seem to try to hide a deep hunger for the power I wield. Just like everything else in their lives, they want nothing more than to own me like some sort of prized possession. Heat bites at my shoulders, flames wanting to roam over the men who make me uncomfortable, but I subdue it.

"You did great today." The king states as a servant takes his robe off and carries it out of the room. The crown remains nestled in his midnight colored hair as he escorts me back to a sitting room that houses a grand piano and a hearth three times the size of the one in my room. A roaring fire is already blazing in it, shadows dancing wildly across the room.

With a deep exhale, he sits in a plush sofa seat and motions for me to do the same. He pours a glass of clear golden liquid and offers me one. I take it but have a feeling it's a lot stronger than the mead I drank earlier.

"How was your outing?" He swirls the contents in his glass.

I think back on the day and smile. "It was exactly what I needed. I'm thankful you accepted my request."

"This kind of life is restricting. You are young and should experience freedom when you can." His shoulders sag at the comment and I can't help but wonder if he ever got those freedoms. He became king when he was only four with the help of his uncle, who reigned until King Addard was of age.

The obvious question slips out. "Do you have freedom as well, Your Majesty?" I feel like I don't know him at all except for the few instances we've interacted during meal times. He mostly keeps to himself.

He looks at me with a furrowed look as I allow myself to admire the strong lines of his face. A jaw muscle flexes as he seems to think about the question.

"I enjoy reading and studying history. Horseback riding has been a growing passion of mine. Collecting rare breeds for my stables brings me joy," he states while turning to look at the fire.

Those are more like hobbies and not so much freedom.

"Have you ever been outside of the palace walls?" I turn to look at the fire too, feeling my own flames yearning to be let loose.

He chuckles at my question and takes a long sip. I do the same, not sure where the courage to ask these prying questions is coming from. The liquid burns all the way down my throat and I try to control the shiver that threatens to shake me.

"Oh, what is that?" I try not to scrunch my face as I hold the glass up but he lets out a hearty laugh. The first genuine laugh I've ever heard from him.

"You should have seen the look on your face." He laughs again. "It is from Murvoe. Barrel aged huriso made from barley. I got it as a gift when the Murvoean king came for a diplomatic visit and thought to give it a try with you." He holds it up to the fire light.

"It's definitely something. They drink this for fun over there?" I set the glass down on the beautifully carved wooden table beside the sofa.

He smiles again. "Yes, it is their favorite beverage at meal times. Even the townsfolk drink a small cup every day. The king said they believe it wards off evil spirits."

I shudder at how it tasted in my mouth, but remember where I am. "Thank you, Your Majesty, for offering me such a kind gift. I think I'll stick to wine and mead if that's okay."

He chuckles and nods. This is the first time I'm talking to him outside of the normal royal protocol situations I've been in. I don't know what to do with myself so I just wait.

With his eyes on the flames, his says hoarsely, "I haven't been outside of these walls in almost five years. And before that, it was brief."

I don't say anything but feel only pity. With two summer palaces serving as a vacation spot he could escape to, I can't decide if it's the lack of time or desire. How can he rule his kingdom without ever stepping foot into it? I can imagine the brutal deaths of his family have brought fear. Narvidium needs the rule of their king as much as the king needs subjects to rule.

"Might I suggest we go outside the walls in the next few days? With fleets of ships arriving, wouldn't it be beneficial to alert your kingdom of what has happened?" I resort on sitting at the edge of the sofa with the warmth on my face.

He leans forward as well. "An announcement is needed, but we will need to take security measures. I want to announce the idea of you, but not quite you." The king chews on his lower lip as his eyes move rapidly with each passing second.

Setting down his glass loudly, he grins. "We shall have a decoy."

Chapter 34
Lylah

"Stop yawning."

The wool scarf around my neck is keeping me as warm as if I'm still in my comfy bed. Ellis glares at me and slashes a sword towards my left arm.

"I can't help it." We've been at it for hours already and I stayed up all night reading everything I could get my hands on. The anticipation of today and the coming days feels like someone is stepping on my chest and I can't find my way from under it.

I dodge his swing with a loud clash of metal. We've upgraded to real swords which have been sharpened. It made me nervous at first, but the thickness of my cloak has kept me from harm so far. Ellis has ramped up the intensity of our training, including running laps around the four gardens that surround the palace.

"Have you been practicing the breathing techniques I instructed you to do before every session?"

"Yes." No.

Running in the winter temperatures is more than enough to exercise my lungs to where my powers are practically burning right through them.

He combines a fast combo move while using his height advantage to force me backwards. I keep my balance with ease and throw a counter strike strictly out of muscle memory and connect with his right forearm. The sharpness of the blade catches his sleeve and slices the material open.

"Did you see that?" I exclaim as I turn excitedly to Sourina. Her curls spill out of the scarf wrapped around her head. The chilly morning has forced her to sit in a chair today instead of the cold stairs of the entrance.

She gives me an encouraging smile. "I didn't think I'd ever see the day you'd nick Ellis."

I can't help but take that as a compliment to my rapidly developing skills.

Ellis rolls his eyes as he examines his sleeve. He scoffs loudly. "She hardly nicked me."

"Just admit it." I almost jump up and down but restrain myself enough to just grin ear to ear. "I drew first blood."

Ellis finally nods as he inspects the cut closer. "Yeah, I can admit that."

"That's for all of the times you hit me with the wooden swords for weeks now. I have so many bruises on my arms and ribs from you," I retort quickly. It's true, even my maids have shown concern over the new purple bruises developing every time they bathe me. My rapid healing allows for the old ones to disappear and new ones to appear.

The greenish blue depths of his eyes darken. "I wasn't trying to hurt you."

"I know." I straighten. "It has helped me to learn to tolerate pain better, so it was worth it."

We go back to sparring when Sourina calls out, "Now add fire."

Ellis' eyes widen before scowling at her and grabs a wood shield he made in anticipation for this type of training.

I frown though. Containing the intensity of the flames is the hardest of all the things Sourina has been teaching me. Everything inside of me begs for the fire to be released in an all-consuming way. I stuff that feeling deep down, if only to not let it accidentally overtake me.

Clearing my mind, I focus on the heat that spreads to my fingertips. I throw one stream of fire aimed at his chest, but he uses the shield to divert the flames.

He ducks and yells from behind the shield, "Are you trying to singe off my hair!"

I let off the heat, and the flames disintegrate into the cold air. Deciding to use this rare opportunity to attack and catch him off guard, I swing my leg until my foot catches the back of his knee. He groans at the impact but recovers by not falling completely. With a swift swing, he jams the shield into my side as I slide back on a small patch of ice.

I rub my side but choose to throw a dagger towards his left shoulder. But he anticipates it and allows it to lodge in the shield.

"Good one," he ventures to his feet while rubbing his knee. "Using the flames as a distraction for a different form of attack."

I smirk at my almost successful plan.

"Truce." He holds his hands up before taking my sword. "How did last night go?" The throwing daggers remain secured behind my belt, perfectly placed for minimal delay in retrieving them like Ellis taught me.

"The king wants to parade me around Rinmor but using a decoy to break the news to the kingdom before everyone arrives." I watch their faces take in the news but Ellis doesn't seem surprised.

Sourina, on the other hand, stands quickly. "Couldn't that be potentially dangerous?"

I nod. "Yes, but not if there's a decoy," I observe Ellis for any further reaction but he doesn't give me any or even look my way. I feel embarrassed for kissing his cheek last night. Maybe that pushed him even further away.

He speaks finally. "A decoy is the wisest thing we can do in this situation. While the mages have historically been dearly loved by the people, people fear power they don't understand."

I reply, but Sourina chews on her lower lip. I've had a target on my back ever since I got these powers, but being an outcast in an orphanage has prepared me for this life in a way.

"I see your training session is done." King Addard appears beside us with no warning.

"Yes, Your Majesty." I curtsey clumsily and the others follow suit. "We're just wrapping up before Sourina and I move into studying."

He gives me a brief nod but looks at Sourina. "We will venture beyond the wall today into the southern city square for the announcement. Sourina, you will stay back with Finnon."

She nods at his instruction; the curls bouncing on her forehead.

"A formal king's proclamation is being done now," his gloved hands clasp together. "So the people will come to the southern city square to listen. A maid has been selected to be the decoy for this afternoon. Lylah, you will be dressed as a guard riding behind the decoy and Ellis on the other side."

I've seen several female guards in the king's service, so I should blend right in. The thought of a maid possibly getting hurt because of me is almost crushing. While most of them were mean to me, it doesn't mean they deserve to be harmed in my place.

A thought strikes me. "What if they ask for proof?"

"They don't get to ask for anything," he grits out with a rigid expression. "Be ready and meet us at four o'clock by the stables. Lylah, your maids have the uniform." He turns and walks up the stone stairs into the western entrance while we're left looking at each other.

"My daggers?" Ellis gestures to my waist, and I hand over all but one.

He raises an eyebrow. "All of them."

"I'd like to keep one just in case." A shadow passes across his eyes, but he nods before walking away as well.

"If you're ever in danger, your intuition should tell you something is wrong. Listen to it, just like we practiced." Sourina wraps her cloak tighter around her grandmother's book. "According to the book, your fire will spark up if it senses danger."

I wish I could read Maureen's book for myself, but Sourina always dodges the question when I ask. I simply nod and swallow the lump in my throat.

I'm dressed in a uniform that seems like it belongs to a woman of my stature. The blues of the uniforms contrast nicely with my blonde hair, red streak, and blue eyes, but the fabric clings to me in all the wrong places. My hair is braided tightly and put into a guard's cap.

Guards and horses have all gathered around the cobbled center space in the east garden. I push my way toward the front until I spot the king. He's impossible to overlook and spared no grandeur to look the part of the Narvidian king. This is his first time being out among the people in years, according to what he said last night. I'm sure he's as nervous as I am, if not more.

"Where is Lylah?" King Addard's voice booms over us as every head snaps to attention.

I lift my hand over the tall figures pressing in. "Here."

He doesn't look happy when the guards step aside, allowing me more than enough space to get by. Their intense gazes sear into my back.

King Addard motions for me to mount a horse that's ready for me. I'm surprised to notice it's the same one I rode from Arliea. I pat the mare's neck and she bobs her head.

Ellis appears on my other side and helps me get my boots into the stirrups. Once I'm positioned comfortably with the reins situated in my hands, Ellis mounts his horse and King Addard does the same.

A glance from Ellis blooms uneasiness in me as his eyes dart across the large group of people. The unpredictability of what we're about to do must have him on edge. I give him a nod and a smile, but he doesn't react.

I stare ahead, disappointed.

A female figure walks out of the eastern palace doors in one of my simpler dresses and a beautifully crafted leather vest wrapped tight around her torso. It blends flawlessly with the full blue skirt, as if it was always meant to be worn together. Her curled brunette hair drapes down her back. A black veil is turned upward over her hair, revealing her face.

I gasp loudly, and my stomach churns at the familiar face.

Jesimie turns to glare at me before mounting the horse behind the king. I hold my stomach as I take my time glaring back at her. Heat rises to my fingertips along with an overwhelming urge to release the anger building up inside me. Images from that night flash in my mind, the way her bony fingers clasped my jaw to force me to look at her. The pure hatred and evil in her eyes.

Ellis' eyes now bore into me as his horse steps beside mine. I ignore him and allow my eyes to watch her more intently. She can't hurt me here, especially not with the training I've worked hard to master. Her skin has mostly healed from the burn, but the front of her face is rippled with red markings all the way into her hairline. It doesn't take me long to notice that her eyebrows have no hair on them, as well as her eyelashes. Her nose is slimmer than I remember as it protrudes slightly upwards.

"Ready?" The guard captain shouts over us. Ellis scans my face one last time before calling back to the captain. I wonder if he knew but he's difficult to read as always.

I fixate on anything but that horrendous girl who's supposed to portray me on this outing. Resorting to counting the buttons on the blue uniform Ellis wears, I steady my racing heartbeat. The deeper hue of blue looks dashing on him with his auburn hair peeking out from his cap. The gold embroidery on his coat stands out against his tanned skin.

Jesimie lowers the veil over her face and adjusts herself in the saddle. We set out in a slow pace following the king, making our way to the ancient oak tree. People turn to watch as we pass by. Their eyes go round as they gawk at the sight of the king and his swarm of guards trotting through the city streets. A few girls giggle behind their hands at one another and I swallow hard.

"Make way for the king!" The guard captain shouts while riding ahead of us as people flock to the square in waves. Others arrive from the harbor and wagons slow to a halt to see the commotion. The massive branches over us sway in the wind as my eyes wander around the square. The barely visible mage's statues have been cleaned off with fresh flowers laid at their feet. It seems right to make this announcement here.

The guards restlessly shift behind us as hooves clack on the cobblestones. Jesimie remains rigid in her saddle as she turns her head towards the king, who gets off his horse with every pair of eyes trained intensely on him. Several guards follow him. Ellis remains beside me, his hand resting casually on his sword, but I know there's nothing casual about it.

"People of Rinmor. Citizens of Narvidium." The king holds his left hand to his heart as he scans the crowd. "My father, King Medrin, and all the kings and queens that came before served this kingdom well. We have done many great things together, you and me. We survived a war."

Heads nod and a few sniffles ripple through the crowd as he continues, "We survived near annihilation. We became the most profitable seaport in the world as a result."

Clapping erupts from the crowd, and a few men whistle loudly. "Your hard work is never far from my mind. Your sacrifice of loved ones who gave their lives for this kingdom will forever be remembered."

More cheering ensues and some guards join in this time.

"Our luck has changed." His voice echoes off the nearby buildings. Silence falls as they hangs on his every word.

"Movak was a great Fire Mage. His dedication to this world is legendary but it has been two hundred years since the mages of old passed on to our songs and poems." King Addard scans over the crowd as they press in closer.

"A Fire Mage has emerged again and stands before you." I hold my breath as if time has stopped. This is the moment the news is finally released to Narvidium.

Chaos explodes as people start shouting at each other and the king. The guards grip their swords in trained anticipation, but the crowd doesn't spring to violence, only shock.

A man cries out. "How can that be?"

"It was always written that another Fire Mage will rise again." The confidence laced in his answer is unmatched to how I feel. Every emotion washes over the people.

Jesimie is helped down from her horse by the guard captain and escorted to the king's side. King Addard extends his hand to her which she takes elegantly, the veil still hiding her face.

"This is your new Fire Mage." He smiles at Jesimie, clearly forgetting the snake that tried to hurt me is under there. I should be there with him instead of her. If I'm too afraid to face the people, what kind of a Fire Mage am I? Would Movak have stood there proudly, regardless of the dangers, or would he have hidden like me?

King Addard raises his hand to silence the voices. "In the next three days, the world will arrive in our city to witness this miracle and meet our Fire Mage. We will show them power."

Cheering follows as Jesimie remains on the king's arm, the crowd chanting praises. Once we are all back behind the safety of the palace walls, the singing of the mage's songs can be heard all through the evening and into the night.

Chapter 35
Lylah

The palace has never been more chaotic.

It's the day before the demonstrations and servants run past me with stacks of linens, towels, flowers, and various other things that royalty and the social elite might need in their rooms. The tension in the palace is unlike anything I've witnessed so far.

In the blink of an eye, my body slams sideways into the hallway's stone cold wall. I gasp at the impact before barely keeping myself from falling backwards. A hand reaches out to help me to my feet. I dust off my skirts and control my rising irritation.

"I am so sorry." A pair of dark brown eyes holds my gaze but I shrug off his hand. The man's red hair falls briefly over his eyes as he pulls his hand away, something blue clutched in them. His height towers over me several inches but I don't feel threatened.

"Watch where you're going next time," I snap but take a few deep breaths as heat stirs in my veins.

I turn to leave but catch a glimpse of his clothing. A green jacket with silver threading webs across his chest in the shape of wheat stocks. His jacket is accompanied by black pants with matching designs only worn by nobility, according to my books anyways. He's around my age and too young to be the king himself but perhaps a noble's son.

His voice is laced with amusement when he says, "My deepest apologies. This place is like a maze. I simply wasn't looking where I was going."

"It's alright. Good day, sir."

I turn to go, but he calls after me. "Tonight will be a night to remember, don't you agree? I think black is a particularly stunning color."

I narrow my eyes. "Yes, it will be." I'm not sure what to think about his random commentary.

His eyes soften as if studying me.

"Is there somewhere I can help you find?" I ask more firmly. Ellis will be upset if I'm late.

Tilting his head, he replies, "No. You could say I'm exploring." A wider smile crosses his lips.

"Very well but the west wing is off-limits to guests, so don't explore too far that way." What a strange man. I shake my head and quicken my steps to get outside.

"So glad you could grace us with your presence." Ellis's voice is mocking, but I barely notice it.

"Someone wasn't looking where they were going and slammed into me." I rub my shoulder, noticing the throbbing for the first time.

"Are you okay?" He narrows his eyes.

I nod. "Yeah."

"Alright, let's begin." He tosses the sword at me, and I catch it effortlessly by the grip. I'm grateful for the distraction of training during this last session. The anxiety of it all creeps in no matter how much I try to shake it off.

Ellis excuses himself after we finish going through the various movements and my jaw clenches. I feel him distancing himself more and more with each passing day.

Sourina is more stressed than normal as she takes the next few hours to go over advanced movements with me from her book. We examine the hand-drawn illustrations that would essentially allow me to release powerful flames but conserve my energy and control my body temperature.

"Just like that," she nods as she stands behind me while jets of fire shoot out from my outstretched hands. The plumes of flames reach far beyond the height of my head and are as wide as several wagons in front of each other. "Now, remove yourself from your connection to the flames. Like taking a step back, but not physically taking a step back."

I try what she instructs. I visualize myself mentally stepping away from the fire coming out of my hands and immediately notice a difference in how my energy doesn't burn through as fast. I'm not breathing as heavily either.

"Keep going," Sourina encourages as she looks up from the ancient pages. "Your mage energy has magnified tremendously from what I've seen so far and what's described here." There's excitement in her voice for the first time in weeks.

After four minutes or so, my energy starts to waver and my knees nearly buckle in.

She rests her hand on my shoulder. "That's enough."

My chest heaves as I double over, putting my torso to my knees in exhaustion. I know it's not a ladylike pose, but it's the only thing that helps control my wheezed breathing.

"That was the longest I've ever gone." I grin sideways at her. After finally catching my breath, I straighten.

"You ought to be proud of yourself. You're progressing nicely for the short amount of time we've been training." Sourina smiles back, her eyes brighting again.

I stretch for a little bit before turning to go inside. The maids must be waiting to dress me in time to meet our guests for the first night of festivities. But tonight is not just about the festivities. It's the first time I meet the other mages.

"I have something for you." Sourina's soft voice stops me before she reaches into her pocket. "My grandmother placed this in my hands moments before she died." Her voice cracks as she holds up a gold chain with the most beautiful bluish green stone dangling from it.

I take it gently. "This is absolutely stunning." I rub the stone between my fingers and marvel at how light illuminates it in my hand.

"My grandmother said it will help you." Sourina smiles sadly and shakes her head. "And no, she didn't tell me how and nothing in the book speaks of it, but she was confident you would figure it out." Tears form in her eyes as I clasp it on. The stone rests just below my neck, and I tuck it into the safety of my cloak.

"Thank you." I embrace her and rub her back gently. "I'll treasure it always."

She inhales sharply and wipes at her cheek. "When do we see the performances of the potential mages?"

The idea of meeting them is twisting my stomach more than I care to admit. Every eye will be on me, expecting every answer from me and pressing in close.

"We'll meet them tonight before the introductory dinner. The king has requested the performances to be done in the throne room. Only invited guests will be there, so that's something to be thankful for. More security that way too."

She squeezes my arm. "Don't be nervous."

I give her a forced smile. "Everyone will be watching us closely for the next few days. I can't help feeling anything but nausea." My feet stop mid-step. "Are you ready to feel their energies?"

Sourina holds her book tighter. "I feel your energy the strongest when I'm near you and that hasn't changed. I can only guess it'll feel similar to the first time we met."

My brows furrow as I turn to her. "I'm sorry for pulling you into this. It was the only legitimate way that I could think of to verify their claims of powers."

"I've studied this book cover to cover multiple times," she pats it gently. "I think I'm ready. There's a tea that's mentioned to heighten my senses. I'll go see if Finnon has the ingredients to make it."

"I'm glad you'll be by my side," I say as I pat her shoulder.

We part ways as I venture to my rooms to find a hot bath waiting. For the first time, I notice my hair has grown quite a bit as the maid rubs oils from exotic flowers into the strands. This maid has helped me several times over the last few weeks. My eyes scan over the few brunette strands that have fallen around her face.

With the room consumed by the swirling smell of florals, I lean my head back against the tub as my eyes flicker shut. The hot water licks at my powers, but I ignore the urge to make the water temperature rise. She combs my hair while I use the sponge to scrub the thin layer of sweat off my skin.

"Your hair is looking so healthy and voluminous," she says gently as her fingers glide between the strands and begin massaging my scalp. The sensation is so unexpected and relaxing that my eyes roll to the back of my head.

"It's all thanks to you," is all I manage, and those words are true.

It's because of the care the maids have given me that my skin glows the way it does and my hair glistens in the sun.

"Please don't thank me." Her voice is barely a whisper, which causes my eyes to flip open.

"Why?" I ask as I resume lathering my arms before moving to my chest.

"We were not kind to you when you were a maid. We called you names and said unkind things behind your back. This is the least we can do to repay you for some of our wrongdoings." She sets the comb down before twisting my hair up on top of my head and placing an ivory comb through it to keep it in place.

I fidget with the necklace Sourina gave me, refusing to take it off for any reason. I use the brief pause to wash away the soap still bubbling on my body and gather my thoughts.

"That's all in the past. You weren't one of the maids that attacked me in the library. They are the only ones I refuse to forgive." My voice is soft but firm in its meaning.

She nods before coming back with a towel and helps me out of the tub. The towel is warm, as if it had been hanging by the fire that's now blazing in the bedroom.

"Thank you, Thymine." Some of my anxiety slides off my shoulders when I spot her dimpled smile. "For everything."

The power presentations are going to start in a few hours, which I spend getting ready. Draped across my bed is another expertly crafted black dress with flames climbing up from the middle of the skirt and across the bodice. The silky shine of the cloth gives the illusion that flames are burning through the dress, fascinating me as my fingers skim over the fabric. A pair of long blue gloves lay on top.

Thymine takes down my hair which has now mostly dried into stunning waves. She twirls several ropes of hair back from my face and braids the rest loosely down my back. A few small radiant red garden roses are tucked into the braid secured with pins. Smudges of charcoal outline my lashes after red powder is dusted across my cheeks.

"Crushed pearl dust to accentuate the curves of your face." She smiles as she uses her warm fingers to apply it slightly on the bridge of my nose and cheekbones. Next, a rich deep red paste is painted onto my lips with a soft brush. After slipping on my gloves, she steps back with her hands over her beaming grin.

I glimpse in the mirror and blink a few times to make sure I'm looking at myself. The reflection is that of a grown woman with a mature flush to her sculpted face. The girl who looked at this mirror months ago is nothing like the woman who looks back at me now.

"One more thing." Thymine lifts a velvet box from a drawer in the mirror stand and opens it gently. "The king instructed us to place this on your head."

I peer into the box. "Why?"

"I'm not sure," Thymine hands me a card from inside. "It did come with this."

The curved golden writing across smooth ivory paper reads:

> To honor your service to Narvidium. May you always know

> your home is here.

The small crescent-shaped crown is placed on my head as Thymine adjusts it. The blue sapphire stones nearly matches the necklace that hangs on my neck. I touch the it briefly. I've never owned or worn anything so expensive and delicate.

"The king called it a tiara." She smiles at me for the last time before curtsying and closing the bedroom door behind her.

The tiara is truly what brings this look together. The weight is noticeable but not unmanageable.

I look at the small clock that sits on the hearth mantle and take a deep breath. I allow a flame to flicker off one finger as I stare at it in the mirror. I can do this. I'm stronger than I've ever been. I'll ignore their stares and hold my head high. Mostly because I'm scared this tiara will slide off my head if I don't.

A guard escorts me to the throne room and my breath hitches at the sight of Ellis awaiting me by the grand doors which are now open on both sides. He glances around and makes careful motions to smooths out his already perfect uniform.

He doesn't see me yet so I take my time admiring him with his slicked back auburn hair and blue uniform, a sword clasped at his waist, and daggers I'm sure hidden in every fold. Our eyes meet and the world stops for just for us. In a span of a second, his eyes harden and he waits for me to go through the open doors.

I try not to be hurt as I step past him. My chest tightens the farther I step into the throne room. I'm not sure what I was hoping would happen in those slowed moments, but my heart aches nonetheless.

The king is positioned in his rightful place on the marble and gold throne, with a blue furred robe pooling around him. Clusters of people are gathered around the room who blur briefly when the king meets my gaze. He dips his head to me with his crown unmoved on his head. My tiara has shifted slightly from the time I left the room but he was born to wear a crown while I was not.

I take a deep breath for courage before following the swirling blue and gold patterns of the carpet that lead to the foot of the dais. I see each head turn one by one and before long, the entire room has their eyes on me. The discomfort I feel in this moment is unlike anything I've ever felt, but I focus on counting the four steps to the throne and the king that sits on it. I hear Ellis follow behind me only by the soft clanging of his sword against his uniform pants.

Several councilmen and advisors I recognize from the dinners nod in my direction. A green jacket catches my attention to my right as I glance sideways. Deep brown eyes glance back at me and red hair dips down when I pass. It's the same man I saw in the hallway who almost knocked me over.

Once at the foot of the throne, I curtsy as deep as my dress will allow and lift my eyes. The king gestures to a seat that has been set to my right and I sit with as little friction as I can possibly manage.

Ellis positions himself a few steps behind me while I take the chance to look out around the room. I avoid their eyes but count the colors in the room instead, observing every detail of the dresses and ornate dinner jackets. A few notable outfits and uniforms stand out to me among the rest. Kings and queens alike sit in plush chairs, while the rest of the onlookers in their parties are forced to stand.

Sourina bows to the king and appears a few seconds later at my side with a beautiful red dress that clings to her natural curves and a skirt that folds elegantly to the floor. The red is a perfect shade to complement her kingdom color as well as her glowing rich skin. Her skirt is not as long as mine which I envy briefly, but I admit she looks stunning. A gold hairpin holds back the river of wildly beautiful curls on the right side of her head.

Her warm brown eyes scan the room as mine just had. She takes a deep breath before tightly clasping her hands. The Arliean king sits to our left in the front and I feel myself tense as well.

I give her a small smile, which she returns with a tightness in her cheeks. Our conversation from earlier flashes in my mind and my hand touches my necklace.

King Addard stands and every conversation fades to silence.

"We welcome you, our esteemed guests, to our kingdom. You have traveled far to witness the miracle of the last two centuries. The journey you have all taken to be here today will go down in the history books for future generations to sing about." King Addard pauses as everyone applauds in synchronized motion, including myself.

He gestures to the far left. "We are humbled to have our neighbors to the west, Murvoe. King Frandor has been a faithful trading partner for a century of sheep and wheat." Our king bows his head in respectful acknowledgment. King Frandor returns the gesture.

"Queen Polsta in Korrim is our equal in the seas and provide us with luxury goods." The queen dips her head as I admire her beaded silver gown that flows like water.

A deadly silence falls over the room as King Addard turns to the Arliean king. King Meadon wears his own crown with a decadent jacket radiant in Arliean red. He stands out in the red, yellow, blue, and green hues of the room, but his glare doesn't falter from our king. Tension rises as stare each other down while every pair of eyes shifts between the two most powerful figures. Decades of hurt on each side and the blood of thousands between them.

I gently clear my throat, despite the deafening silence. King Addard's gaze shifts to me and his shoulders relax. "Our Arliean neighbors are most welcome in my court, and I'm grateful to have them join our festivities this evening."

If I didn't know better, I would have believed those words, but King Meadon sits stiffer in his seat. The child he let live has grown up to look down at him from his throne. The child he lost will never be able to be by his side. The wounds in this room struggle not to tip the delicate balance of war that looms.

King Addard takes a few steps down from his throne and stretches his hand out to me. I follow to stand beside him with careful attention to how I hold my head high.

"We have been honored to see a Fire Mage reborn in our lifetime. Lylah Farrion is Narvidium's Fire Mage who manifested her powers two months ago." He pauses as every person turns to their neighbor to exclaim. A few women use their fans to disguise their whispers. I observe the disbelief settle on the faces in front of me. As if to sense my thoughts, the king steps back from me and nods.

I slip off my gloves and place them on my seat. Clearing my mind, I unleash a fraction of the heat that has been building inside me. I restrain my emotions while allowing the flames to lick gently at the crowd. A wave of loud gasps and exclamations crash over me. I pull my fingers in as the flames retract.

"How can this be?" King Meadon glances at me with a mixture of shock and obvious anger. The emotions raging behind his eyes makes me step back to the king's side.

"Great job." The king whispers to me and I feel my cheeks warm slightly. Turning back to the crowd, his voice teetering on the edge of annoyance. "Movak manifested his powers through an emotional event, as did Lylah. I assure you, this is not a trick."

Everyone bursts into conversation before King Addard escorts me back to my seat and climbs to sit on his throne. I slip my gloves back on, the soft fabric oddly comforting.

The room goes still at the lift of his hand.

"As history has it, four other mages will emerge to stand alongside the Fire Mage. As stated in your invitations, we will see those demonstrations now and judge if they are true."

And so it begins.

Chapter 36
Lylah

A glass chalice is brought to the king, and another one is offered. I shouldn't drink too much wine at such an important event, but I take the smallest of sip anyway. Maybe it will help ease my nerves and stop my hands from shaking.

Maggis steps forward and bows low. For a small man, his voice finds considerable volume as he announces the first demonstration from a scroll.

"Your Majesty, our next demonstrator is nineteen-year-old Verick Yowan from Arliea." King Medron nods his head in approval.

"He states to have the ability to create something called a protective shield, but asks for a guard with a sword to test his demonstration."

King Addard nods to Ellis, who moves out from behind me and toward Verick.

"Proceed." The king commands.

Verick takes a step back with his right leg and swirls his hands in a circular motion above him. The lantern above which burns nearly a thousand candles dims and light fall to his outstretched hands. With several more motions, the light spreads in front of him in the shape of a half-sphere. I'm immediately mesmerized by the colors that dance across the surface of the dome with its opaque purples and brilliant blues.

Verick signals to Ellis, who draws his sword and strikes the light dome with decent momentum. Sparks fly in all directions except towards Verick. The crowd gasps and claps at the unexpected display.

Sourina simply nods when I turn to her, the brown of her eyes reflecting the illuminating light. Verick uses another hand gesture that gathers the light from the dome and redistribute it back to the candles above.

King Addard claps. "Well done, sir Verick Yowan. We welcome you to the Mages Circle. If you would please join us at the front with the Fire Mage." He gestures towards the four empty seats on the other side of the throne.

When Verick approaches, he doesn't stand much taller than me with long black hair that's twisted into a tight bun. The bright red tunic rises and falls with each labored breath as he takes a seat closest to me. Out of the corner of her my eye, I see the narrowed shape of his eyes briefly glances sideways at me. I don't return his glance, forcing my attention towards the guests. His use of that much power must have consumed a lot of energy. I know the feeling of having all the energy sucked out of your bones. Especially if he isn't trained to breathe properly through the strain.

Maggis reappears with wide eyes like this isn't the type of day he thought he would be having, before introducing the next one on his list. "Derlin Raklev, a nineteen-year-old man from Korrim." From my reading, Korrim is the country across the Balgorn Sea, providing us with spices, salt, silk, and marble. They're said to have a thriving port city similar to ours but much smaller.

A man move out from the crowd. He's tall and slim with a yellow dinner jacket the color of summer sunflowers that complimentes his deep umber skin. Black hair lays in tight curls at the top of his head while his light green eyes don't leave mine. All of these formalities are starting to wear on me. I take another sip of wine to calm the building headache that begins to throb behind my eyes.

Maggis' voice turns every head in the room. "He claims to have the power to move objects without touching them."

How interesting, the same power as Bella from Narvidium. Sourina let me read that section of her story from her grandmother's book. Bella was precise with her powers and could wield several swords without ever holding them.

Derlin holds out his hand and his brows scrunch together. His eyes focused on the cup in my hand. The wine swishes slightly side to side but I loosen my grip on it. I hold my breath as the glass slides gently from my fingers and levitates inches away. As if hesitant, it travels slowly to Derlin, who grabs it when it gets within reach.

An older man next to Queen Polsta pulls Derlin into his arms. My chalice gleams in his hand as he hugs the man back.

Sourina nods before the king quiets the room. "Well done, sir Derlin Raklev. You are welcome among the mages."

Derlin's eyes brighten as he walks confidently to the front of the room. I hold his gaze as he hands me the chalice.

"My lady." Darkened freckles become more pronounced as I take the cup. He finds his seat next to Verick and my stomach knots painfully at the daunting thought of being their leader. I have no experience or skill in leading groups of people, much less men who are older than me.

"I introduce, your Majesty, nineteen-year-old -"

"Navia." Ellis' voice is barely a whisper only I manage to hear.

Maggis continues, "Navia Orseka of Arliea."

A girl steps out from the crowd with dark brunette hair falling across her shoulders in waves. A simple red dress hangs on her slender frame. A delicate gold chain with a pearl rests around her neck and small dangling pearl earrings to match.

"You've got to be kidding me," Ellis mutters under his breath and my heart hitches. Do they know each other?

"Navia has requested a subject to which she can use for her demonstration." Maggis announces. "She states her power will speak for itself."

The king nods to Ellis, who grumbles but walks towards her. I watch as Navia's face contorts into a smirk.

"Interesting to see you here." Her voice is silky as she stares him down.

Ellis shifts on his feet as he stands several feet from her. Through gritted teeth, he says, "Let's just get this over with."

Navia laughs and lifts her hand, fingers reaching towards him.

The room is quiet as they lean closer to observe. I find myself moving to the edge of my seat.

Ellis clasps his chest and groans loudly, as if trying to find air to fill his lungs. His knee buckles onto the blue carpet but catches himself with an outstretched hand.

"Stop!" I exclaim as I stand. Seeing him in pain like that almost snaps something dangerous in me. She drops her hand to her side and Ellis gasps for air.

Navia shifts her dark brown eyes to me and I can feel the coldness in them. I hesitantly look at Sourina who nods. A tiny tremor ripples across her clasped hands them in front of her.

"You can inflict pain." King Addard says and I feel heat rising to my fingertips. I grip my chalice harder and steam rises from it.

The coldness vanishes as Navia curtsies to the king with her eyelashes fluttering up at him. I don't look at her again when she takes the next open seat next to Derlin who starts up a conversation with her almost immediately. While her powers will be useful in future battles, it doesn't mean they aren't dangerous. My eyes don't leave Ellis as he shakily ventures to his feet. Everything inside me screams to help him but I chain myself to my seat.

Gripping his chest, he attempts a straight line to where he was stationed before. I grip my cup harder while keeping my other in my lap. Navia snickers loudly and I take controlled breaths as the fire rests at the edge of my fingertips.

"Your Majesty, our next demonstrator has an unusual request." Maggis looks up at the king, his footing hesitant. "He requests to speak to the Fire Mage alone."

Chapter 37
Ellis

The man in question leans down to whisper in the Murvoan king's ear before stepping forward. He adjusts his shoulders slightly as a smile spreads across his face. The sudden shift in his demeanor unsettles me and my hand goes on the hilt of my sword.

The king steps down from his throne and talks softly with Lylah which I can barely make out.

"Are you comfortable with this?" He asks, and she gives him a small nod.

King Addard turns to me. "Please use the council room through that door and be alert for any threats."

I ignore his words of caution. If I wasn't able to see a threat, Lylah could roast him alive with a lift of her finger. But as instructed, I escort Lylah and Sourina through the door on the side of the throne. The man follows behind us as I place myself between them. He just gives me a polite smile.

Once the door is closed, he wastes no time. "My name is Astian and my ability won't make sense unless I show you, but I have a request." He smiles at Lylah. "May I have one of your gloves?"

My back goes rigid.

"One of my gloves?" Lylah blinks.

He nods as if it's the most normal request in the world and she slips one of the blue gloves off of her slender hands.

"Thank you. You will believe me more this way." He takes it gently and straightens his shoulders while inhaling deeply. The glove is clasped tightly in one hand as his fingertips come together in front of him. I get closer to Lylah, ready to use my body as a shield if necessary for whatever he's planning to do.

With eyes closed, he says, "I will explain when I come back."

"What do you mean when you come ba–" Lylah begins to say when a bright red light radiates from his chest. Within a blink of an eye, he disappears.

Lylah gasps loudly and looks around. "Where did he go?"

My mind can't process what just happened. I blink a few times just to make sure because one moment he's there and the next he's gone. I walk over to where he just stood and the air feels warmer.

Sourina's mouth is wide open. "Did he just vanish into... thin air?"

"I think so." I step back to Lylah's side.

We pace in the room, waiting. Ten minutes later, he reappears with the same bright light. He adjusts his green jacket and grins. It's a different grin than he had earlier, a cocky grin instead of a nervous one.

His eyes land on Lylah. "I'm sorry I didn't get the chance to introduce myself earlier when we met." His tone is different as well. More certain.

"What just happened?" She asks shakily.

"I know none of this makes sense, but I promise I will explain," he replies and rubs his neck. "I arrived with my father this morning and have been in my room most of the day until the demonstrations."

He raises his eyebrows at her and waits.

"How did I meet you this morning then?" She asks. My eyes narrow at her question. When did she meet him? Earlier this morning, she said someone bumped into her.

Astian shifts on his feet. "No, you met me just now."

It'd make more sense if he stopped speaking in riddles.

A second passes. "I'm a time traveler. I can jump back in time only a few hours or half a day like I did just now. This morning, you didn't meet the me who was in my room but the me from just minute before."

She shakes her head. "I'm confused." I'm also confused. An uneasiness creeps up my spine.

"I traveled back to approximately where I was this morning, hoping to land in an empty room. But I am not familiar with this palace." He smiles as if he didn't just say something completely impossible.

"You nearly knocked me over." Her voice doesn't return his humor.

"Not intentionally, I assure you." Astian dips his head.

She lets out a huff. "It was a large hallway. You had plenty of space."

Astian's red hair pushes back as he runs his fingers through it. "That's the thing. I can't control it sometimes. Just now, I nearly landed on top of you when I meant to land a floor above. I can only see brief flashes of my surroundings before I arrive."

There's a long pause. My mind is still spinning from the information.

He breaks the silence first with a chuckle and lifts his hand to her with the glove in it. "I did tell you it was going to be an eventful night and black is an excellent color on you. Oh, and I hope you saw your glove."

Lylah takes her glove from him. "I did see it in your hand this morning."

Sourina speaks up, her forehead scrunched. "Your energy is different from the others. Your energy spirals around you in wild veins. Not centered at your core like the others."

Astian turns his attention to the left for the first time. His eyes scan her as if she'd spoken a foreign language. I admit, the Arliean accent tends to catch people off guard.

Lylah looks at Sourina thoughtfully before turning back to Astian. "Welcome to the team," she says before frowning. "Why didn't you want to say all of this out there in front of everyone?"

Astian shifts again. "A time traveling ability is dangerous. What will stop Arliea or any of the other countries from using me to change the past? I don't know the limits of my powers yet. Only my father and mother know the truth about them. And now you all."

"That's true." A worried look spreads across Lylah's face. "Your power is more valuable than any of ours. Can you travel to the future?"

He shakes his head. "I think I'll be able to but I haven't tried it yet. Honestly, I'm hesitant to even attempt it. I can go back to places I have been before but since I don't know where I'm going to be in the future, it is hard to navigate. I could land in the middle of the ocean or a fireplace."

Sourina nods at his logic and all of it makes sense whether I want to admit it or not.

He smiles and offers his arm to Lylah. "We better get out there before they start to make up rumors."

She hesitates slightly before taking it. They head for the door and venture out towards the pressing crowd just past the dias. Sourina and I follow close behind as silence enfolds the throne room. King Addard looks to Lylah who nods back, wordless communication between them.

Our king turns towards the crowd. "Prince Astian of Murvoe has demonstrated the powers of a mage and will join the Mages Circle."

Prince? Lylah's eyes go wide and my jaw clenches. He's a prince? Of course he is.

Maggis declares dinner will be served in the dining hall before going through the schedule for the remainder of the week. The guests listen intently and eagerly chatter at the announcement of the ball that'll take place tomorrow evening back here in the throne room. Those who were not privy to the demonstrations today will be invited tomorrow.

It's a different setup in the main dining hall tonight. When I station myself behind Lylah and the King, the head table is positioned at the front of the room which seats the guests of honor, including the mages and their royals. Two long rows of tables are set a short distance away for the other guests who are now streaming in through two sets of doors. A soft disjointed choir of voices echo in the vast hall before a band of musicals begin plucking a melody.

I carefully watch the rest of the guests take their seats. Almost immediately, the tension at the head table is palpable. King Medron gulps the fine wine as if drinking water while glaring at King Addard. The guests whisper to each other and glance around almost nervously. Servants begin moving in a dance to serve the decadent displays of multiple roasted pigs, oysters, seared squid, and vegetables sauteed in what looks like browned butter. The extravagant smells swirling around the room make my stomach clench.

I force my mind to continue to observe the rest of the royals thoroughly. The Marvoan king takes careful bites, as if to keep up his refined appearance. Korrim's queen dabs her face with her napkin, the silver crown nestled in her graying curls. She takes minuscule bites of food at a time while discreetly looking sideways at her table mates.

Eventually, each person settles into polite conversation and I feel like I don't belong among or behind them. At least I'm not the only one standing guard. Other royal guards stand by their kings and queens, their eyes surveying the room with trained precision.

My shoulders relax the further into dinner we progress. The cluster of musicians continue plucking their stringed instruments, which seems to ease the tension in the room to only a simmer. Lylah sits beside Prince Astian with King Addard on her other side. They talk about the various political figures in the room while Prince Astian cracks a few jokes that make Lylah erupt in a genuine laugh or giggle.

"I'm glad you are having a good time." King Addard takes a bite of frosted lemon cake and dabs his face with the satin napkin.

"The wine helps," Lylah says as she smiles brightly. She already has had four glasses of wine and the effect has been evident with her outgoing conversations. The tiara glistens in the bright candlelight of the room and her braided hair trails down her back in a messy but beautiful way. Red small roses on the braid adding to the floral scent that encircles her.

Earlier, when she appeared in the hallway, it was as if all the words were stolen out of my body. The way her hips swayed with the folds of the dress made me forget how to breathe. Her eyes searched mine so deeply that it created an ache in my chest that has yet to disappear.

King Addard leans closer and lifts a glass to his lips. "Prince Astian, what power does he possess?"

"Time travel," she whispers.

The king's eyes go wide and shift to Prince Astian. "He can time travel?"

Lylah nods. "Two of their powers differ from what has manifested before. Navia's power and his are very unique."

"Quite so."

Out of nowhere, the Arliean king stands while clanking a silver knife against the glass chalice in his hand.

"Might I propose a toast?" His voice carries and talking dies in the next breath.

King Addard's eyebrow twitches and I swallow hard. I want to drive my sword through the Arliean king for the bloodshed he caused. A man responsible for so much loss and grief. Regardless of what I think about our king, the calmness he exhibits at this moment is masterful.

"May prosperity and long life be before the Fire Mage and the mages of this century." He raises his cup. Lylah lifts hers in unison with the guests before they all take sips.

King Addard stands as well. It takes only a few seconds for King Medron to slowly sit, his face contorting like he tastes something rancid.

"Some people believed the mages never existed. Others believed the mages would never happen twice. But we are here to witness history," he bellows and gestures around him. "This means we must align ourselves towards a goal of peace more than ever before." King Addard's words settle as everyone looks up at him, most nodding in agreement.

His voice turns solemn. "I vow before you to become the best king I can be to provide safety to the mages. Our kingdom, with the sea at our back, provides the largest harbor and trading center of the Balgorn Sea. The mage's home will be among our people and every freedom to travel to build alliances amongst our neighboring kingdoms."

Lylah taps lightly on her cup.

"Today is a great start in shaping the future of this world." Clapping erupts before King Addard silences them with a lift of his hand. "We welcome you to explore the city. The weather is chilly outside, but the gardens are still lovely with beautiful views of the sea. The Solstice Ball tomorrow night will be an evening to remember. For further questions, please seek out Maggis, my head of household."

He bows his head slightly before sitting back down and conversations eventually resume again. The words still resounding in my chest, words of power but also humility.

Navia has avoided looking at me during dinner, but glances back several times before turning away. The searing pain she inflicted earlier mirrored the pain I felt when she walked away from me. She doesn't deserve even a fraction of my attention. I close my eyes and force the memories down.

This is going to be the longest week of my life.

Chapter 38
Lylah

In the morning, after I had breakfast in my rooms, a sealed envelope arrives. Inscribed in gold ink is the king's invitation to meet the other mages in the library.

Thymine dresses me in a simple yet elegant dress that fits the occasion. I pat the folds of the blue velvet dress and adjust the necklace Sourina gave me so the pendant is visible. It has quickly become a prized possession and it's a part of me.

Ellis is waiting outside in his more casual blue uniform with shoulders tense as he barely meets my gaze.

"Good morning," he says stiffly.

"Good morning," I say back with a knot in my stomach, not only from his cold demeanor but the fact that I'll be seeing the mages again. Their expectant eyes threaten to cripple me. Like I can give them all the answers to questions I don't even know to ask yet.

Morning sun pools on the wooden shelves as we enter the library I used before we went to Arliea through the open double doors. Just the sight of familiar book spines soothes my racing heart.

King Addard is already there, talking with Prince Astian. Off to the side, Derlin and Verick also talk amongst themselves. Navia stands alone as she examines her nails in the morning light. Sourina smiles up from behind a huge pile of scrolls.

"I apologize if I'm a little bit late," I say as I take a step into a circle they seem to have formed.

King Addard shakes his head. "You are just on time." His eyes shift to Ellis. "Can you close the doors?"

The doors close with a creaking sound that echoes.

"I wanted to have this meeting to allow you all a private time to interact before the ball tonight." The king smiles and his eyes brighten as he meets each one of their gazes. "To get to know each other better. No elite team is ever formed overnight."

Prince Astian bows his head. "Thank you for hosting us."

"Prince Astian, it is a pleasure to have you among us and to meet you at last," King Addard states and my chest tightens at his title.

Prince Astian glances briefly to me, but strangely enough, my eyes shift to Navia. Her arms across over her chest and meets my gaze with disinterest. A red tunic fits around her torso before I spot a pair of pants, which makes my eyes go wide. Women don't usually wear pants.

Their eyes all gradually turn to me and I'm forced to take a deep breath. How am I supposed to lead such a group of powerful strangers? I have nothing to offer them besides what some old history books have declared.

Swallowing the lump in my throat, I start with the most obvious truths. "My name is Lylah Farrion. I manifested my powers over a month ago by nearly burning a girl alive by accident."

Navia snickers, but I ignore her. Why does she have to act like that?

"I know we're all a little scared and unsure of what all of this means, but we we'll figure it out together." I pause and clasp my hands in front of me. "Maybe to start, it would be helpful if you could introduce yourselves and how you manifested your powers." I look at the first person to my right. "Prince Astian, if you wouldn't mind starting first."

"Just Astian is fine," he says with a boyish grin and I nod politely.

"I'm Astian Brisset. It is true, my father is King of Murvoe and I'm next in line to the throne." The room is silent as we listen intently. "I have the power of time travel." The other three mages gasp, and even Navia stands straighter. I'm instantly grateful for the thick walls and doors of this library. The opportunities his power could open to greedy kings or queens would wreak havoc on the peace we're destined to protect. We must keep his power a secret for as long as possible.

He continues, "I manifested my powers three weeks ago when I nearly died while taking a cold plunge in a river after a hard day's ride. A riptide pulled me under and I remember panicking. In the next second, I was on the shore looking at myself before I got in the river." He grits his teeth before a pleasant smile slides onto his face. "I told my mother that something strange happened, and she advised me to tell my father. The letter arrived shortly after, and my father responded with our acceptance to be here."

King Addard interjects while rubbing his chin. "It is most crucial that this conversation does not leave this room. Especially Prince Astian's powers. His power is dangerous not just to him, but to all of you. You are all now a team and you must move as one."

His words create a new level of tension in the room. As if we need any more of that.

"Derlin, would you go next please?" I motion to him and he shifts nervously in his yellow shirt and a black vest.

"My name is Derlin Raklev." He looks only at me as he talks, the intensity of his gaze making me slightly uncomfortable. "My father is a nobleman in Korrim. As demonstrated, I have the power of telekinesis, the ability to move objects without touching them. I first manifested my powers during a sparring match with some of our guards when a knock to the head made me lose consciousness briefly. While I was unconscious, they told me all the objects in the garden began to float, including the guard."

I nearly laugh at the last part as I picture the scene. It's interesting to learn that our inciting events were so vastly different.

Derlin breaks eye contact with me and finally looks at the others. "An odd thing happened when I fell though. I cut my head and was bleeding over the stones of the walkway. Our healer recalled binding the wound and when he went to change the bandage the next day, the wound had completely healed."

A few of the others look wide-eyed, but I respond first. "During my incident, I was cut with a knife down my arm." I instinctively rub it, even though I know nothing is there. "According to a few texts, the mages all had rapid healing abilities. They all fought in wars during their time and as protectors, injury is assumed."

Derlin nods. "It makes sense."

I let a few moments pass. "Navia, your turn."

Ellis' sword clanks behind me. I don't let the frown show on my face for too long. What's their history and why does she keep looking at him?

Navia leans casually against a bookshelf, almost like we're all boring her and she has better things to do with her time. She keeps her arms crossed as she says, "You all really want to hear my life story?"

Astian counters before I have a chance to open my mouth. "Not your life story. Just your name and how you manifested your powers. That's all Lady Lylah asked for." The title is unexpected and makes me feel incredibly out of place.

"Fine." A long irritated sigh escapes her angled lips. "I'm Navia. I was born in Arliea but have been all over the world on merchant ships." Her eyes fall briefly to Ellis before moving onto the others but skipping over me. "I manifested my powers several weeks ago when I was attacked in an alleyway during one of our stops. I couldn't get to my dagger when he came up behind me..."

She swallows hard, and I recognize that fear of being helpless. I felt that same way the night Ellis stepped in to protect me.

"Within a few minutes of us struggling, he started screaming at the top of his lungs before collapsing to the ground. I ran away, but it happened again to another shipmate when I simply touched him on the shoulder."

Verick speaks up softly. "I'm sorry you were attacked."

She nods in his direction but picks at the lint on her tunic.

I decide to show her compassion and move the attention to our last mage. "Verick, it's your turn."

Verick clears his throat. "As you heard yesterday, I'm Verick from Arliea. I have the power to create fields using light and other sources of energy. It's not only light, but I can use wind and fire as well."

King Addards raises his eyebrows as he leans against a table next to Sourina.

"My incident happened when I was trying to stop a thief who tried to rob my parent's store. The thief managed to take loaves of bread and when I went to stop him, his knife almost stabbed my abdomen. I moved out of the way quickly when the candles in the room all went out at the same time. He couldn't get the knife through the barrier I somehow created around myself."

He shakes his head. "He tried and tried, but finally gave up before running off. I answered the king's request for potential mages. The king didn't believe me until I demonstrated my powers to him."

Verick doesn't say anything more but briefly glances at Navia. Both of them being from Arliea creates uneasiness in me because my entire life I've been taught they are our enemy.

"Thank you for sharing." A small smile appears on my face. "We have a variety of powers, experiences, and stories in this room. There's a lot to learn from one another as we step into this new phase of our lives."

They all murmur under their breaths and I can't help but share their reaction. I don't know what we're doing or why we're here. We're protectors of peace, but what does that even mean?

"Lastly, I would like to introduce Sourina Loumon from Arliea," I motion to Sourina. "Her ancestors were there at the time of the first mages. They trained and fought beside them. She was able to sense all of your energies last night to show us who were truly mages. I've been learning from her the last few weeks and I recommend getting to know her as well."

It doesn't take long for Derlin and Verick to approach her first. She answers their questions the best she can, but I can tell she's uncomfortable by the sudden attention. I step back to lean against the desk that still has one of my maps spread across it.

King Addard steps next to me. "This was a success. The first step in building trust."

I fidget with my fingers and look at the odd group of people before saying, "I hope so."

Maggis announces us as we enter the quieted throne room later that night. All eyes trail our every movement as King Addard escorts us toward the middle with Ellis close behind on my heels. The other mages follows in groups of two a short distance behind him. Guests step out of our way like rippling water while staring in awe.

A servant comes by with trays of wine glasses and I happily accept one. The other mages take one as well while I gulp the strong liquid to calm my nerves. Astian gives me a lopsided grin before moving his eyes onto the other ladies, who bat their eyelashes at him over their fluttering fans. I force down the urge to roll my eyes.

Talking slowly continues and the same group of musicians from last night pluck their stringed instruments in the background. With each passing second, I can feel Ellis's eyes on the back of my neck. I didn't anticipate it being this way, him truly becoming my shadow. We're so close, but yet, it feels like we're worlds apart.

"The guests look like they're enjoying themselves," I say as I tap on the king's arm and he nods, but almost absentmindedly. I wish I could know what's going on in his mind when his eyes look so conflicted, like they do now. To others, his eyes may look thoughtful, but during the time I've spent with him, I understand some of his subtle mannerisms.

A distant thought comes crashing in. How could I be so stupid?

I squeeze his arm, forcing him to look at me. "It's the anniversary of their deaths, isn't it?"

Emotion rages even more behind those golden eyes and his jaw clenches. I want to lighten the grief he's carrying by squeezing his hand covered in rings, but I remain as I am. I don't want anyone to have the wrong idea about us beyond what they must already whisper.

"That's why you pushed so hard to have the announcement on this day," I whisper as the realization sits between us. With only the crown glistening under the candlelight of the chandelier above in the absence of words.

His voice is hoarse when he finally answers me. "They should have been here. I was never meant to be king." He blinks a few times fast and says through gritted teeth, "My brother was."

I squeeze his arm again before he suddenly lifts my glass out of my hands and hands it to a servant passing by. It only takes a few seconds to understand as he twirls me out away from him and uses the momentum to bring me back into his arms. Our eyes connect and I can't help but search them for an anchor in the storm brewing there.

The crowd claps and cheers. Fans flutter even more. He dips me down to the intoxicating notes of the instruments. Every person turns to watch us, their conversations fading. I want to disappear from their gazes, but King Addard keeps me firmly in his arms. When he brings me back to a standing position, he twirls me around, but this time around him.

Taking a deep breath, I concentrate on my steps and listen to the beat of the music to help me know when to step. If only to avoid stepping on his feel and looking like a fool. His unyielding arms force me to submit to his lead. With one hand taking his, I place my gloved hand on the fur of his robe and we begin moving around the room in dizzying circles as blurred figures step further from the middle.

I smile as the faces and lights disappear into a stream of colors and shapes. The corners of his mouth lift in a smile, the first one I've seen in weeks, before slowing us down when the music begins to fade.

I curtsy as he bows before we look up at the same time.

Clapping erupts and for one freeing moment, I feel happy.

Chapter 39

Ellis

The room feels overly crowded as I survey for any sudden movements. People press in to get a better look at Lylah and the mages, as well as the king. Nervousness radiates through me. There are too many unpredictable factors.

The throne room is beautifully decorated with unique flower arrangements and torches casting long shadows on the marble pillars they rest on. There are long tables in the back of the room with every kind of food imaginable for guests to enjoy. Servants carry trays of exquisitely crafted appetizers on gold platers and I'm almost tempted to take one.

My mind keeps drifting to earlier this morning. In the library, Lylah was a natural leader, using tactful prompting to get strangers to talk about themselves, leaving room for them to pick what they wanted to say.

What I didn't foresee was Navia admitting to being attacked in the streets. Weakness is her rival, a foe she fought every day when we were together. I know admitting to being weak at that moment was very difficult for her.

There are years of unspoken words in glances she gives me even now. Back then, I told her of my plan to get out of the mercenary shipping business. She promised me she wanted to as well. The morning after our last night together, she was gone. Deep down, I understood why she left. It took years to try to come to terms with it. Life at sea is what she loved most, and I couldn't fault her for that.

I hadn't seen her since, until the moment she stepped forward to demonstrate her powers. Now, Navia stands with the mages and glares at all the people staring at her. I remember she gets nervous in large crowds, but being at the center of attention must be even worse. A bright red dress with puffed sleeves clings to her slender frame. I can't help not smiling. This is only the third time now I've seen her in a dress.

My uniform begins to itch at the collar of my neck and I fight the urge to scratch the tender spot forming. This entire evening is outside of my comfort level. The dancing and royal decadence are far from what I know. Thankfully, I won't be dancing, and that's a mercy in itself.

I glance at the one person I should be focusing on. My eyes roam over Lylah, who has now taken the king's arm. The way she looks up at him with tenderness turns my stomach. It always has.

Will this be the rest of my life? Watching her be with someone else? I want nothing more than to stand beside her. I want her to be on my arm instead, looking up at me with those same eyes. But that's not my place, and the king was clear about that.

Looking away quickly, I scan the crowd in their hushed conversations, whispering to one another. I wonder what they're saying, but some of it isn't hard to guess. Most of the women point and smile at Lylah's voluminous light blue dress, specks of silver scattered on her skirt. Another tiara sits in her curled blonde hair that is delicately pinned at her neck. Another gift from the king, I assume.

Movement pulls my eyes again when the king leads Lylah to the dance floor others have been avoiding. My stomach tightens and I clench the hilt of my sword. Even though I can't stomach the way she looks in his arms, I can't force myself to look away either.

The music flows around them as each second is seared into my memory. His arm slides around her waist and dips her down, his face drawing near before bringing her back up.

My jaw clenches at the sickening demonstration. Continuing to move gracefully around the room, his robe and her gown intermingle as they glide across the smooth white floor. The crowd watches with awe-filled eyes. The way they fit perfectly together as they dance is enough to nearly send me over the edge.

I need to focus on something else. Sourina clasps her hands and looks as uncertain as I feel. The mages watch from the end of the dance floor when Prince Astian comments something to Navia, causing her to smirk. I size him up while paying close attention to the confidence he expertly wears. His request to have a private audience with the Fire Mage yesterday stirred quite the chatter among the guests. That confidence slipped only once. He was nervous to demonstrate his power to Lylah, but appeared relieved when reappearing back in that room.

Clapping erupts and my attention snaps back to Lylah. She has the brightest smile on her face, one that I've never seen. I feel a heaviness in my chest at the sight. They make their way back to where they stood before and other couples fill the dance floor with the next upbeat song.

"That was lovely! The spinning made me a little dizzy though." Lylah laughs as she looks up with flushed cheeks.

King Addard smiles in return. "I haven't danced like that in a long time. You are an excellent partner."

"You're too kind." She dips her head. "I was just trying not to stumble over my feet. This dress certainly didn't make it easy."

He shakes his head. "You did wonderfully."

"Well, thank you." Silence rests between them as I stand several feet behind, feeling invisible.

A guard approaches and bows before the king before whispering something in his ear.

King Addard turns back to Lylah. "If you will excuse me. This should only take a few moments."

Lylah nods politely as he steps away to talk quietly with the man. I can't make out their words, but whatever is being said feels unsettling. Prince Astian makes his way to Lylah's side. This time, I can't stop my eyes from rolling slightly. What an annoying prick.

"Would I be able to take the next dance?" He looks at her in a way that makes me want to grab him by the collar and drag him back to where he was. She smiles and nods, hands elegantly folded in front of her.

Movement out of the corner of my eye makes my head snap to look. In an instant, my hand goes to my sword and the other hand rests above my uniform belt, where I've hidden three of my throwing daggers.

The man's darkening eyes are only on Lylah, but I step around to place myself in front of her which slows down his steps.

"How about you stop right here." My voice is deep and threatening.

The scar on his neck is more pronounced in this light as his smirk grows. "Now, that isn't how you treat old friends."

"We're hardly friends." I spit out. The images of the blade against Lylah's skin will haunt me forever.

Taramin smirks again before leaning in closer. "If I knew who she was, I would've never let her out of my sight."

Anger simmers hotter within me, but I hold my ground. I motion to one of the guards on the outskirts of the room. Several of them make their way through the dense crowd. I take in his appearance as we stand there in the suspended moment. His black hair is tousled, but he wears an embroidered jacket like the ones nobility wear.

"Oslan," the king's voice sounds behind me. "What are you doing here?"

I don't move. Oslan? Do they know each other? I never told the king about the incident at the castle and I have a feeling Lylah didn't either.

"Addard, my boy, how are you?" Taramin smiles and the roughness of his expression melts away too easily.

"It is Your Majesty." The king's voice is unexpectedly firm as the other guards join us. The commotion has caused the guests and mages to glance in our direction.

"Your Majesty," I say as I pivot to the king. "Might I suggest we move this conversation into the hallway? Away from prying eyes?"

He nods and the guards escort Taramin into the hallway. Lylah follows behind me, but I motion for the rest of the mages to stay where they are. I catch Sourina's startled gaze and try to give her a reassuring nod.

Another guard moves closer to them while continuing to survey the room for any more uninvited guests.

Once through the massive double doors, the king stops. "I haven't seen you in years, uncle." My eyes go wide. Uncle? As in his uncle?

"Uncle?" Lylah is quicker to respond. "This is your uncle?"

"Yes." King Addard frowns. "Have you met before?"

Our eyes meet before I briefly nod. "When we headed back from Arliea with Sourina, his band of mercenaries captured us at the old royal castle by the sea." I turn to Taramin. "He put a knife to Lylah's throat and drew blood."

The king's eyes go cold as turns to Taramin. "Is this true?"

Taramin nods. "It's true, but in my defense, I didn't know who she was."

"That is no excuse." King Addard retorts firmly, fists clenching. "And mercenaries, really?"

"After the deaths of your parents and the children, I took you under my wing and raised you to be the king you are today. I had to leave when you turned eighteen to secure our future. I knew I couldn't do it under the banner of the crown." Taramin stuffs his hands into his pockets. Something about his demeanor doesn't feel right, but perhaps I don't know him well enough to assume that.

King Addard doesn't say anything but dismisses the guards with a wave of his hand. After the guards are out of hearing distance, he responds. "You left me to the councilmen and advisors to figure out how to rule on my own." He raises his voice. "At only eighteen!"

Taramin smirks and straightens his dinner jacket. "And look how well you are doing on your own. You are a competent ruler with the respect of the people and a thriving port once more."

King Addard keeps his hands at his side as he takes a deep breath. "What have you been doing the last six years?"

Taramin chuckles like the answer is obvious. "Building an army of loyal men behind me."

"An army loyal only to you? Why do you need an army?" King Addard doesn't take his eyes off Taramin. Anger clearly sparks in his eyes.

"An army that we can use to protect our borders and hold up our trading," Taramin states in a matter-of-fact tone.

"Narvidium already has an army." The king squints his eyes. "But I'm sure using yours has a cost."

"Your army is tied up north at the border." He raises his hands. "We are family. There is no cost to you. I'm only wanting to uphold my late brother's memory of a prosperous and powerful kingdom." Taramin doesn't take his eyes off the king. It's like they have completely forgotten about we're still standing here.

King Addard matches the intensity of his gaze. "We will talk about this later in my office. Tonight," he clasps his uncle on his arm, "We celebrate your return."

My blood simmers again. He threatened Lylah's life and held us hostage. He just admitted to building an army behind the king's back. And that's it? A celebration and all is forgiven?

They turn to head back into the ballroom, recalling old memories and chuckling at childhood stories. The tension between them washes away in a matter of seconds.

Lylah turns and clutches her stomach. "I need some fresh air."

I swallow hard. "Good idea."

Chapter 40
Ellis

The music can still be heard out in the garden, but it's muffled. Lylah walks in front of me with her gown swaying side to side. She's radiant tonight, and that same ache is back.

Another couple finishes their stroll and steps back inside, leaving us alone in the western gardens. Snow covers the ground in certain places, but it has been cleared from the stone walkways. She rubs her arms quickly. A small flame appears in her palm before she stops at the half wall that overlooks the city. The same place she cried into my chest. The same place where I nearly kissed her the first time.

"Here," I say as I begin unbuttoning my jacket and unbuckling the belt. I have only a dress shirt underneath but I don't mind the cold.

Lylah shakes her hand. "No, then you'll be cold. Plus, I have my fire."

I ignore her and place my jacket across her shoulders anyway. It's enormous on her, the squared shoulders looking odd on her curvier frame than when I first met her. The consistent access to healthy food has helped fill in her previously hollowed cheeks. The small flame burns out and she clenches the jacket closer.

Her deep blue eyes meet mine for a brief moment. Her lips part slightly as she scans my face. The light from a nearby torch lands ever so delicately across her nose, lips, and eyelashes. I rest my hand on the hilt of my sword before I lean my back against the wall to look towards the palace. Her face falls ever so faintly.

"Can you believe Taramin is the king's uncle?" Her voice cuts through the cold air.

"No, I'm having a hard time wrapping my mind around that. Why wasn't he ever mentioned?"

"I'm not sure." She frowns, as if recalling every conversation she ever had with the king.

Long minutes of silence pass.

She speaks again, this time barely audible. "What do you think will happen to us?"

I turn my head to her. "What do you mean?"

A tiny breeze sweeps loose the red strands across her face.

"What do you think will happen when history is done with us?" She squints her eyes, lost in thoughts that seem to worry her. "Will this be our lives until death, or do we get to live out the rest of our older years away from all of this?"

The history books and the songs don't describe the mages' lives past the Great Wars. I always assumed they got to live out their days however they wanted.

"I think they died of old age but you're the one that has read all of the books about them." I scan our surroundings out of habit.

Lylah nods, but still doesn't look at me. "Do you think they had families?"

"I don't know."

She smiles softly. "I like to think they did. I think they found their true loves and settled down in little cottages."

"They certainly deserved a life like that," I say gently.

"I want that life. I've never had a true family, but I hope I can find someone to love. Someone to have a family with." Her voice is so hopeful. A lump rests in my throat, keeping me from responding. I want that life for her too. To wash away the hurts of this world and show her that there can be beauty in trust and love.

The moment lingers, but there's nothing else to say. I want to wipe away the fear and uncertainty from her mind, but what hope can I possibly offer her?

"Lylah!" a voice sounds behind us and a hand waves. I straighten as Prince Astian approaches.

She looks back and smiles. "Prince Astian."

"Just Astian," he corrects her. "We never got to dance. We can hear the music out here if you will still dance with me." His boyish grin causes her to erupt in a genuine smile.

She dips her head. "I apologize. I needed some fresh air."

"It seemed tense in there when that man showed up." He tilts his head, "Who is he?"

I tense but it's like I'm not even here. A normality today and probably for the unforeseen future.

She looks out at the city. "Someone we met and didn't know was the king's uncle."

"That guy is King Addard's uncle?" He exclaims loudly and Lylah shushes him.

"It's not common knowledge, so can you keep it down, please?"

Astian looks around quickly. "Sorry."

A guard approaches us and bows to Lylah before turning to me. "Ellis, the king needs a word with you."

I examine the new soldier. I haven't met him before, but the king did end up bringing more guards in for this event.

"My assignment is to protect the Fire Mage. I can't leave her unattended." My voice sounds sharp and I feel irritation bloom in my chest.

"I'm sorry. He said it was urgent." The guard looks uncertain and adjusts himself.

Prince Astian pats my shoulder. "She's fine with me."

I fight the urge to laugh in his face. Time travel can't win a fight against swords.

Lylah nods at me. "It's fine, Ellis." A flame dances between her fingers in glowing red and orange hues. "I can take care of myself."

It has become easy for me to forget that she has almost cooked me alive with her flames and there isn't much more I can teach her. But my urge to protect her runs deep to my core.

I clench my hands over the hilt again but nod to the guard who guides me to where the king is. I look back and Lylah is chatting away with Prince Astian, who uses his hands to tell an engaging story.

Back through the doors, the music is vibrant and I can almost distinguish each string that's being plucked. Blissful dance partners bounce in an upbeat dance on the dance floor while clapping occasionally to a part of the song.

We make our way around the outside of the dance floor. The other mages chat amongst themselves except for Derlin, who has a young girl in his arms for a dance.

The guard leads me through the side door and out into the hallway, away from the throne room. I bet the king wants me to recall more of our time with Taramin, or perhaps to ask why I kept something so crucial from him. The relationship between them appeared tense and I couldn't read them entirely while they were talking.

He turns the corner to another hallway that leads to the main library. The king hasn't frequented that particular library since Lylah's accident, or that's what the servants have always gossiped about.

Something isn't right, but I can't tell what it is. A heaviness forms in my stomach. I slowly slide my fingers towards my belt. They are met with my white dress shirt. I close my eyes in a moment of realization. My jacket with my daggers is currently around Lylah in the garden.

Boots thump behind me and I turn ever so slightly to see two men dressed as guards with something dark in their hands. My heart races as I think through my options. The sword at my hip is more decorative than functional, but it's sharp enough to do some damage when used with extra force.

We turn at the entrance of the library when several hands grab me from behind. I attempt to twist out of their grasp, but they've somehow already clasped iron chains around my hands. I struggle regardless and one of the guards rips my shirt in the process. The other guard in front holds a knife to my throat.

I freeze.

It would only take one wrong move to cause this knife to slice open my throat. I don't care about what happens to me in this moment of staring death in the face. But my mind is consumed by only Lylah. Her life is in extreme danger if they're taking me out first. I struggle against my chains and stare furiously into the guard's eyes.

Who are they and what do they want? The mages would be my best guess, but this was thoroughly planned out with our security on high alert. How did they get in? The night's festivities and extra security had lowered my guard.

"Ellis Hartley. You're one tough man to outsmart." The guard smiles deviously. Like he just won a prize by cheating.

"What do you want?" I say firmly. The two behind me hold down my arms with ease. One of them punches me square to the left of my spine, right above my hips. I groan loudly at the impact, my vision darkening for a few seconds.

"Not so tough anymore, are you?" One of them says behind me.

A laugh escapes. "You had to chain me with two men to make this a fair fight." I continue laughing while the guard's face turns red. This earns me a fist to my stomach. I groan again. My torso is on fire, but I concentrate on my anger as blood pumps rapidly through my veins.

"The Fire Mage and her whole crew were quite impressive yesterday." He smirks with a smile that radiates dark intentions. "I think we'll take them for ourselves."

I need to get to her. I need to warn her. I struggle again, but this time I'm met with hard metal to the forehead. The guard turns his sizable knife back around and points at me.

"Struggling is pointless."

I barely hear him over the pounding in my ears and the blood that's dripping into my right eye. I shut my eyes to keep the liquid from clouding my vision, but it's not slowing down.

I spit at him. "You'll never get to her."

His shadowed eyes stare down at me. "I'm afraid we already have."

Chapter 41
Lylah

"So, this is where the fun is." A voice sounds from across the garden. Navia smirks as she moves her eyes between Astian and me. The other mages and Sourina follow close behind her.

I hold Ellis's coat closer to me. "It's where the peace and quiet is."

Her eyes furrow as soon as she spots the blue jacket and looks around. "Where's Ellis?"

She says his name so casually. Like it has come across her lips a thousand times before.

Motioning towards the palace where the music seems to get

louder, I say, "The king needed to see him, so he went with a guard."

She looks away, disappointment clearly written across her golden skin.

I decide to bravely ask the obvious question. "How do you two know each other anyway?"

Her eyes narrow. "We used to date if you really want to know."

Date? I've been assuming childhood friends, but them dating never even crossed my mind. My throat tightens slightly but I don't let any emotions cloud my face, even though I suddenly want to be alone.

I lean back against the wall as Ellis had done. Deep aches in my feet and my heart make me wish this night was over.

"Did you all need some fresh air as well?" I ask. I don't blame them. It was getting stuffy in that room with the protocols and formalities. The staring and whispering were just as exhausting to continue ignoring. Not to mention Taramin being there and how uncomfortable he makes me.

Derlin's voice projects from the left. "That guard," he points to the guard who has already started walking back, "Said you needed us to meet you out here."

Astian and I exchange a look as I push myself from the wall.

"I didn't," I say quietly. "How odd."

Sourina steps to my side and I can't help but admire her red form-fitting dress. Its silky fabric hanging down across her shoulders, the full-length skirt barely touching the ground. I haven't had the opportunity to talk with her before the ball or even during so this is a nice moment.

Another patrol marches from the left in their routine structured group of four. With their swords signaling their movements, they turn to go around us.

"What do you mean you didn't?" Navia says with her arms wrapped across her chest. The lacey red fabric of her dress sleeves doesn't do anything against the cold. "That's why we all came out here in the freezing cold."

I feel my fire rise up in response, but I push it down. A simple misunderstanding.

The group of guards stops as one of them approaches.

"Are you all okay? It's freezing out here." The guard asks, concern lacing his voice. His bushy eyebrows furrow as he looks at our attire.

I smile and nod. "Yes, we are, thank you."

"Where is your guard?" He shifts on his feet. "Ellis should be with you."

Wrapping his jacket closer to me, I say, "The king asked to speak with him, but he should be back any moment now."

His face appears to relax.

"Good," he says. I turn to Navia to respond when one of the other guards appears behind her. With one swift motion, he hits the back of her head with his sword. She gasps and crumbles to the ground.

"What are you doing!" I exclaim and rush to her, but the guard points his sword at me. I halt as the silver tip gleams in the torchlight.

Astian pushes me behind him. "Hey, stand down."

"Wrong country," the guard lunges and spits out, "Prince. You don't command anything here."

He swings his weapon toward him, but Astian holds me against his back as we dodge together.

Derlin lifts his hand out. The sword flies out of the guard's hand and onto the ground at his feet.

Ellis's coat drops onto the cold stone pathway. Ignoring the skirt the best I can, I adjust my stance like Ellis taught me. My fire rushes to my fingertips as if in relief. As if my fire knew we were in danger.

"Astian, step back." In seconds, he runs left before I release a fraction of my control. Brilliant colors of yellow and orange dance through the air, engulfing one of the furthest guards. Screams only last a minute before he collapses into a burning heap. The other three guards look wide-eyed at me but lift up their hands like they can shield themselves.

In the chaos, more men appear from the shadows of the garden, overpowering us in a matter of mere seconds. Before, I thought we had a fighting chance. But now, there are too many of them.

Sourina slides down to the ground and grabs the fallen sword at Derlin's feet. She swings it around expertly and lunges towards a guard who's almost on top of her. Their swords clash several times before she drives the sword into the man's shoulder, just between the crack in his armor.

"I didn't know you could fight!" I exclaim.

"I was trained to carry on my family's legacy," she says, her chest rising and falling. The pain she just inflicted doesn't seem to register.

Another man rushes towards me. In a panic, I release my fire but he dodges it. He nearly grabs my hand when Sourina slashes her sword across his back. A deafening cry slices the air before he drops onto the grass.

To the far right, two men dressed in all black slash Astian's side. He grunts and grips his side before being forced to the ground. He struggles before he's met with a kick to the head. I hesitate, even though my fingers glow red hot. I don't want to hurt Astian by accident.

Out of the corner of my eye, Derlin puts up a decent fight for a noble's son but a knife goes into his left shoulder. All I can do is watch, helplessness eating away at my focus. In a flash, several men hold a cloth over Derlin's face. His limp body thuds to the ground.

Sourina adjusts the sword in her hands as she eyes the black figures closing in. My hands shake as I struggle to control my anger. The fire is itching to be released but I can't. I have to fight the overwhelming need to let go.

Figures separate Verick from me; his eyes wide with fear and desperation. He lifts his hands as I shoot a short burst of fire at the leftmost guard, who's far enough away from the scattered unconscious bodies of the mages. His shirt and pants catch on fire while letting out a short-lived shriek that rings in my ear. He drops and begins rolling in a small patch of snow. One of the other guards drives a sword through him and the shrieking stops.

Verick funnels my flames from the burning man into a shield

in front of him. We share an unspoken nod. A united will to keep going.

The death I just witnessed doesn't even register when I shoot a fireball towards the second guard. It barely misses him and he snarls. Two men grab Verick from behind and shove his face into the cloth. He goes down in seconds. The fire shield he created disintegrated. They tie his hands and feet with a thick rope as he lays helplessly on the cold ground.

Hopelessness bubbles in my chest. I try to shove it away. I can still save them with Sourina's help.

One of them speaks as every head turns to me. "You can try to fight all of us or you can surrender now to save them."

He lifts Astian's unconscious body, standing him up in front of me. I feel tears threatening to fall, but I push them back. His red curls fall untamed across his forehead and his head sags on his shoulder. The silver gleam of a knife hovering over his chest. A determination that isn't afraid to finish the task rages in his soulless eyes.

"Stop!" I drop my hands. The fire revolts inside me. My body breaks out in a sweat as I fight to suppress my emotions. The strain feels like my body is getting ripped in two. I grunt loudly as pain swells.

"You promise to not harm them if I go with you peacefully?" I ask shakily. I thought I was ready. I thought I could fight a real enemy and win.

The guard lowers his knife and slyly smiles. "Yes."

"Lylah, don't give up," Sourina's desperate voice stirs my fire.

"You can roast them all just by focusing more."

A tear falls as I turn to her. "No. I have to think of the mages. I can't risk them getting hurt because of me."

My hands drop at my sides and several of the shadowed figures push me down, causing me to fall to my knees. I don't struggle as they bind my hands tightly behind my back. If there's a chance the others won't be harmed, I have to try.

"Do we take this one with us as well?" A gruff voice says as he points to Sourina. Sourina drops her sword and gets on her knees. Her hands raise in surrender.

A large figure strolls out from the darkness with a dark object flung over his shoulder. They come closer into the torchlight. I immediately struggle against my ties.

"No!" I exclaim as he throws Ellis down on the ground with a loud thud. "Don't touch him!"

"Lylah!" Ellis' voice yells out as he struggles to sit up. He looks at me through blood dripping from his forehead and nose. What did they do to him?

A man beside me holds a long curved knife to my throat. My body stills, but my fire simmers below my skin.

The large man looks to someone behind him. "Do you want to take him with us?"

"Load the others." Another voice instructs. "Kill him. He is no use to me anymore."

My mind halts as Taramin steps out into the light. I want nothing more than to lunge at him. I knew that him being here would only lead to trouble.

"No!" I scream and struggle to get to Ellis, but the knife cuts into my skin. My focus tunnels only to his beautiful eyes as they search mine.

I'm being pulled to my feet. I don't care about what happens to me. I need to know he'll be okay. Taramin can't kill him. Ellis will find a way to escape.

"Lylah!" He yells out as our eyes meet again for a brief moment. "I'll search the whole world if I have to. I'll always find you. No matter where you are."

Hot tears stream down my face, matching his own. My chest heaves at his words. "Ellis, I-"

My words are cut off by a flicker of Taramin's sword slicing through Ellis' back. I scream as the fire pounds to get out. Taramin wipes the blood on his pant leg and my vision is shadowed in red.

"What a waste." He ticks his tongue before walking past me and back into the shadows. "Grab them and let's go."

A cloth closes in over my nose and mouth.

My eyes flutter shut and I'm pulled into the awaiting darkness.

Acknowledgements

Oh man, we made it here. I can't begin to express my gratitude to God for giving me the creativity and need to tell the beautiful stories that live in my head. His hand on my life brought the pieces together so I could have the privilege to write books.

I want to thank my husband for being supportive and letting me go write when I needed to. Or holding me when I was exhausted from working full time and writing on top of that. You are the reason I could focus on finishing this book.

My warmest thanks goes to the many beta readers that have shaped this book into what it is today. I won't have been able to finish this without their hard critiques, encouragements and genuine reactions. Thank you especially to Hope Charlesworth for being my first critique partner and without whom I wouldn't have just thought my story was worth continuing. She encouraged me to keep going and that means the world to me. A special thank you to my

ARC team for receiving an early copy of my book and reviewing it. You all are a crucial part of our process and I can't be more grateful.

And I can't forget my readers. As an indie author, readers who take a chance on a small author who they have never heard of are incredibly brave. Thank you for taking a chance and I hope you stick around for the rest of the series. Lots of secrets and twists still to uncover!

Lastly, you may be asking about my dedication in the beginning of the book. I was an orphan from Russia who was adopted into a loving family, something Lylah never got to experience. Her character is an echo of my childhood self. Mirroring moments that I felt so alone and so unlovable, just like Lylah did. Writing a book centered around an orphan was a personal choice because I want every orphan to know I see and love them. And that they are NEVER alone.

And with that, I hope to see you soon!

Meet the Author

V. A. Sanchez is a debut indie author who has been writing and imagining unique worlds since childhood. When she's not writing or daydreaming, she's working full time in healthcare and living in Flagstaff, Arizona with her husband and chiweenie dog named Colby.

Find V. A. Sanchez on social media where her username will always be @authorvasanchez for updates about the next books in the series.

www.ingramcontent.com/pod-product-compliance
Lightning Source LLC
LaVergne TN
LVHW091657070526
838199LV00050B/2191